Whatever You Need

ALSO BY BARBARA LONGLEY

Love from the Heartland series, set in Perfect, Indiana

Far from Perfect
The Difference a Day Makes
A Change of Heart
The Twisted Road to You

The Novels of Loch Moigh

True to the Highlander
The Highlander's Bargain
The Highlander's Folly
The Highlander's Vow

The Haneys Series

What You Do to Me

To all the craftsmen and craftswomen who build and fix things

Chapter One

Wyatt sat at his drawing table and worked on a panel for his latest comic book series. Elec Tric, his super hero, had been hit by an otherworldly bolt of lightning one sunny day. Twice. Since then, he'd been able to generate his own electricity. Even stranger, an unseen world of demons and super beings had become visible to him from that day forward. Tric had been forced to make a choice: join the forces of evil who intended to reign supreme over the innocent inhabitants of earth, or join the forces of good who kept the evil at bay.

"Join me, Tric, or I will destroy you," commanded Delilah Diabolical, the demon queen.

"Never!"

"One demon down; three to go." Tric pivoted to shoot a bolt of deadly electricity at his archenemy. He couldn't destroy her, but he managed to send Delilah reeling, which bought him enough time to obliterate her remaining minions. *ZAP! SIZZLE! ZAP-ZAP! Gone.*

Wyatt finished inking in the bolts of lightning shooting from Tric's hands and eyes to where the superhero had reduced another pesky lower-level demon to a pile of glowing embers and ash. Then he moved on to the next panel, and a new challenge for his superhero.

"Help!" a pretty blonde cried, as two of DD's minor demons attempted to drag her off to the underworld. *"Somebody, please help me!"*

Elec Tric once again rushed to rescue the Mysterious Ms. M, which gave the superhero pause. Why did fate keep throwing the pretty blue-eyed blonde in harm's way? In *his* way. Was she another distraction sent by the evildoers to keep him from finding out what they were really up to? If not, what did the demon realm want with Ms. M?

Cue dramatic foreshadowing music. *Da-da-duhhh.*

Wyatt grinned. Sometimes his stories played through his mind like cheesy movies, and when that happened, he was in the zone. Nothing made him happier than working on his comic books while in the zone.

Noise at the back door leading to the parking lot pulled him out of his imaginary world. He rose from his stool and moved to glance out the window. There *she* was, the blonde who lived in the apartment above his—the pretty neighbor who'd been his inspiration for the Mysterious Ms. M. Her little boy carried a jug of laundry detergent, while K. Malone—he'd read her name on the mailbox more than once—lugged two large plastic tubs full of laundry, one stacked on top of the other.

K. Malone did her laundry every Saturday morning. Wyatt knew this because he took the opportunity to observe her as she left. And every Saturday morning he wondered the same thing: How would she react if he ran downstairs and out the back door to help her with her heavy load? Would she turn her thousand-watt smile his way, introduce herself and ask if he'd like to get together with her soon? He wished. Oh, how he wished.

Longing stole his breath, and he moved back from the window—as if K. Malone might be able to see him watching her from his apartment. "Curse this wretched shyness," he muttered in his best cartoon character voice.

He wanted so badly to talk to her, to introduce himself and maybe ask her out. He'd even tried a few times, but the words stuck in his dry mouth, his face turned to flame, and his lungs refused to do their job. He was a hopeless mess when it came to women. Hell, he was a hopeless mess when it came to people in general.

He peered out the window until mother and son drove off to the laundromat. Letting loose a heavy sigh, he returned to his drawing table and immersed himself in his made-up world of alter ego, heroic deeds and feats of superhuman strength. It sure beat losing himself in his usual diatribe of self-castigation.

A couple of hours later, Wyatt got up to stretch. He'd finished the panel he'd been working on, and his stomach had been grumbling "feed me" for the past fifteen minutes. He walked to the kitchen to make a turkey sandwich, when he smelled . . . smoke? A second later, the fire alarm went off in the kitchen above his.

"Cripes." K. Malone's apartment was on fire. Wyatt took his cell phone from his pocket and dialed 911. As he gave the dispatcher all of the pertinent information, he grabbed the fire extinguisher from under his kitchen sink. Snatching his keys from the table on the fly, he dashed out into the hall and down the stairs to the caretaker's apartment.

He pounded on the door and listened for signs of life from inside. No movement. Not a sound. He tried once more just to be sure. "Floyd!" he shouted, getting no response. "Shit." There were three floors with four apartments each. Wyatt took the stairs three at a time, racing to the top floor. "Fire. Get out!" he pounded on the doors of each apartment. "Fire!"

"What the hell, man?" The old hippie guy who wore his long hair in a ponytail, even though he was bald on top, walked out into the third-floor hall in his shorts, no shirt and barefooted.

"There's a fire on the second floor. Get out. As old as this building is, it's going to spread fast." Extinguisher still in hand, Wyatt dashed down the stairs and did the same on each floor. Then he ran back up to the third floor and herded his neighbors along until he was sure every last person in their twelve-unit building was out the door.

The blare of sirens reached their quiet street, and by the time he made it to the sidewalk, the engines were close. Two trucks with red lights flashing pulled up to the curb next to the hydrant on the corner. Wyatt stepped forward to meet the firefighter who appeared to be directing the crew. "The fire is in the apartment on the southeast corner of the second floor."

"Your place?" the fireman asked, as the rest of the crew scrambled with gear and attached a hose to the hydrant on the corner.

"No, my neighbor's. She's not home and neither is the caretaker. Otherwise I would've tried to put it out myself." He lifted his extinguisher. "I'll open the security door." Wyatt ran to unlock the dead bolt. He held the door wide as two firefighters rushed in, dragging the hose with them. "It might be electrical," he called after them.

"Got it covered," one of the two firefighters following the first pair told him. They had canisters strapped to their backs and axes and crowbars in their hands.

"Stay out of the building until we give the all clear," the firefighter in charge yelled.

Wyatt cringed at the sound of K. Malone's door being hacked open, but what choice did the firefighters have? Floyd had the master keys, and he was nowhere to be found. As usual. The guy was so lame. He did a piss-poor job of keeping the place up, and Wyatt often smelled pot smoke coming from the caretaker's basement apartment. He'd turned Floyd into a sluglike demon in his comic books. Might be time for Elec Tric to turn that particular demon into a pile of ash.

Wyatt had complained to Floyd about the wiring in the building several times, and each time he'd asked him to contact the owners about the danger. He'd noticed right off the building didn't come close to meeting code. When his requests failed to produce the necessary updates, Wyatt had resorted to sending letters to the city. When that proved to be unproductive as well, he'd done some research through city tax records and sent letters to the holding company in Chicago that owned the building. That got him nowhere either.

If his suspicions were correct, and the fire started because of the faulty electrical wiring, something had to be done. What if a fire broke out in the middle of the night when everyone was sleeping? He couldn't count on all the ancient battery-operated smoke detectors to work. His hand went to the scars on his neck, ear and jaw. Burns were excruciatingly painful, and things happened so fast. He didn't wish that kind of misery on anyone.

"Hey," one of his neighbors said, coming to stand beside him. "You're the hero of the day. I'm Mariah Estrada," she said. "Thanks for pounding on my door."

Hero of the day? He hadn't really done anything heroic. No people, puppies or kittens had been pulled to safety from a building engulfed in flames. Still, the words trickled through him in a pleasant rush. "No biggie."

"I've seen you around. You live in the apartment beneath Kayla's. I guess you heard her alarm go off, huh?"

Wyatt nodded. *Kayla. Kayla Malone.* He liked the way the syllables rolled around in his head. The Mysterious Ms. M had a name to go with his fantasies, a name that would lend itself well to a heroine in his comic books. Maybe he'd give her superpowers in the next story.

"You gonna introduce yourself? I know you only as Hoodie Guy, because you always have that hood up even when it's hot out. Like today."

Heat crept up his neck, and he tugged said hood forward. Did the rest of the residents know him as Hoodie Guy too? Great. His neighbors probably thought he had a few loose wires. He couldn't help himself. The hoods were a habit he couldn't break. That's all. Glancing at her, he expected to find derision. Instead, her espresso eyes held only a teasing sparkle. "Wyatt Haney," he told her.

"I'm a nurse at Fairview Riverside Hospital," Mariah continued.

Not knowing how to respond to that, he nodded again, and other neighbors drifted over, thanking him for alerting them to the fire. The two silver-haired ladies who lived on his floor even patted his shoulders. Face flaming, he nodded, mumbled and edged away as best he could. He even pulled out his phone, pretending he had important texts to read, so they'd leave him alone. What he wanted right now was to go into the apartment above his to see where the fire had been and to discover the cause.

Of course he couldn't do that, not without Kayla's permission. His heart thumped. Dammit, he'd find a way to ask her, because if he was right about what caused the fire, Wyatt intended to raise a ruckus. Something had to be done about the substandard wiring in their building.

All he had to do was find out which insurance company to contact, and he'd mention the many letters he'd sent to the owners. He'd even provide copies and pictures. Then he'd have his family's company, Haney & Sons Construction and Handyman Service, bid on the job. The outlets weren't even grounded, for cripes sake.

His heart thumped again. Harder this time. If he got the job, he'd be spending time in his pretty neighbor's apartment. If he had any luck at all, she might be there some of the time, and maybe . . . just maybe . . . he could muster up the courage to ask her out.

Kayla unlocked the back door to the apartment building and propped it open with one of the tubs of clean, folded laundry. She returned to her car to help Brady out of his booster seat before grabbing the second tub. "Let's get these things put away, and then we can go to the playground at the park."

"What's that smell, Mommy?" Brady asked once they were inside their building.

She sniffed. "Hmm. Smells like somebody had a fire earlier." Could it have been in her apartment? *No, don't borrow trouble.* There were twelve units in the complex, not counting the caretaker's. Since she hadn't cooked anything that morning, used her curling iron or burned any candles, the odds were in her favor the fire had *not* been in her apartment.

"Let's go, buddy." She climbed the back stairs, struggling to prop the tubs against the wall so she could open the door to the first-floor landing. She nearly toppled when it swung in on its own. There stood her downstairs neighbor, holding the door open for her and Brady.

"Thanks." She smiled. Though she'd been curious about her hooded but good-looking neighbor, smiling and the occasional "hi" were as far as they ever got. Most of the folks in their building were really friendly, but this guy kept to himself. Just as well. She had goals, and for the next few years, those goals did *not* include dating. She didn't need a man getting in her way. Besides, between school and single parenthood, she had no time for anything else. She was far too busy to pay heed to the occasional bouts of loneliness that came out of nowhere to sit on her chest.

"There's been a fire," he said, his face turning red. "In your apartment."

Dammit! So much for the odds. Of course the fire had been in her apartment. That's just how her life unfolded. The minute she believed things were going great for a change and—*BAM*—an accidental pregnancy her senior year, with her high school boyfriend. A few years later and *BAM* again—she's a war widow at the ripe old age of twenty-two.

Obviously life saw her as its own personal soccer ball to kick around, because not long after losing her husband, the only factory in her small town had downsized, and she'd lost her job. *BAM.* Now there'd been a fire in her apartment. At least the building hadn't burned to the ground. She still had a home. Didn't she?

Why couldn't fate or Mother Nature or whatever go pick on somebody else for a while? She tried to dislodge the lump of self-pity clogging her throat. Everybody went through rough patches, but her patches always seemed to turn into acres.

"What on earth could've started a fire in my place?" Her neighbor took the tubs of laundry from her. She was too stunned to react for a second. "How bad *was* this fire?"

"I don't know. I'm Wyatt Haney, by the way. I called the fire department when I heard your alarm." He nodded toward the stairs. "I was hoping you might let me take a look inside."

Her eyes narrowed. "How'd you know I wasn't home to call the fire department myself?"

"Your apartment is right over mine. I heard you and your son leaving earlier this morning."

"Oh." Kayla frowned, and her son grabbed her hand. "Why do you want to look at the damage?"

Wyatt took a long breath, and his face turned a deeper shade of crimson. He pulled the front of his hoodie over his forehead. Was he painfully shy? Did he have some kind of anxiety disorder, or was she just really that scary? Maybe she gave off warning pheromones: *stay away, because if you're in my proximity, shit* will *happen.*

"I've written more than one letter to the owners about this building not meeting electrical code," he told her. "The wiring is really old, still the original cotton braid with rubber coating. Our building still has the original knob and tube-type electrical system from 1911, and that's not good. The outer covering is definitely showing its age. The rubber is cracked, and the cotton loom is fraying."

"Oh." She had no idea what he was talking about. Knob and tube?

"If this was an electrical fire, I want to know, so I can see that something is done about the entire building before things get worse." He shifted the tubs and propped them on the banister. "I'm an electrician."

"Good to know." She nodded. "Sure, you can take a look if you want. I'm Kayla Malone," she said, glancing down at her son. "And this is Brady."

Wyatt smiled and held out his fist for Brady to bump. "Hey, little dude."

Brady smiled back and bumped Wyatt's fist before moving closer to press himself against her legs. Her five-year-old had always been shy with people he didn't know. "Thanks for calling the fire department . . . and for carrying my laundry."

"No problem."

Wyatt really was a handsome man, especially when he smiled. She liked the striking combination of tawny blond hair and dark brown eyes, not to mention his angular face and fine straight nose. Plus, he was tall. She was five foot nine herself, and she appreciated a man she could look up to. Though he was on the slender side, Wyatt's shoulders were broad. Very broad, and he was well proportioned, nicely put together in fact, and . . . *Stop. It.*

She started up the stairs, acutely aware of Wyatt's masculine presence behind her. What shape had she left her apartment in? She did a mental inventory: dishes in the sink, toys strewn all over the living room floor. What kind of mess had the firefighters made? *Argh.* Wyatt was willing to carry her tubs of laundry upstairs, and that made letting him take a look worth it, no matter how messy her place might be.

"You don't use the machines in the basement to do your laundry?"

His deep voice caused a tummy flutter. "No. The washing machines here are really old and kind of funky, and so is the basement in general." She shuddered. "Millipedes and spiders live down there. Besides, if I go to a laundromat, I can do all my loads at once," she said, turning to glance at him. Was he ogling her backside? Another batch of butterflies launched into flight in her midsection. "Saves time, and I don't have to run up and down these stairs all day."

A section of the ceiling outside her apartment had been torn down, and scorch marks spread out like fingers against the exposed wood beneath. White residue covered the blackened areas, the carpet and the debris below. The scent of burnt wood and a chemical she couldn't identify assaulted her senses. Her door had obviously been attacked by an ax, but someone had reinstalled her dead bolt above the wrecked part. The caretaker? Doubtful. She stuck her key in the lock. "My legs just aren't long enough," she muttered.

"I beg your pardon?"

Kayla shrugged and cast him a rueful look. "Don't you ever feel like you're running through life, trying to stay a few strides ahead of trouble?" She arched an eyebrow. "No? Well, I do, and my legs just aren't long enough to run that fast."

"Ah." One side of his mouth turned up as he set the tubs of laundry on the floor. "I reinstalled the dead bolt for you. You'll need a new door, but at least you can still use the lock until the insurance company settles, and you get a new one installed."

"*You* called the fire department *and* moved the lock for me? Where was Floyd while all this happened?" Their caretaker was pretty much useless, and this only proved the point.

"No clue."

"You ought to send an invoice to the landlord." Kayla steeled herself for what she might find and walked inside, Brady's hand in hers. Wyatt followed, sliding her laundry tubs inside with his foot.

"Yuck. Stinks in here," Brady said, pinching his nose.

"Yeah, it does." Kayla opened the windows in the living room wider before joining Wyatt to survey the damage. The ceiling in the dining area was now a gaping hole, and her table and chairs were covered in chunks of plaster and more of that white residue. "I've had nothing but trouble with the light fixture in here. Bulbs make this weird *zzzzt* noise and blow out, like, every few days. Another one went out this morning. I told Floyd about it months ago, but of course nothing was done."

"Mmm. The circuit was left open." Wyatt pointed to the light switch she'd left in the on position after the bulb had burned out. "Exposed electrical wires arcing started the fire," Wyatt muttered, walking around the table with his eyes on the blackened ceiling.

"So, if I'd flipped the switch off, the fire wouldn't have happened?"

"Not today, but eventually."

"At least it's not dripping wet in here. What a mess that would've made, what with the plaster and soot. Would've ruined the wonderful oak floor."

Wyatt took his phone out of his back pocket. "Water and foam are dangerous in an electrical fire. They're conduits."

"Oh." She ran a finger through the residue on her table and rubbed it between her thumb and pointer. The stuff felt like talcum powder between her fingers, only smoother. "So, what *do* firemen use to put out fires like this?"

"Dry chemicals, like PKP, or they use carbon dioxide." He glanced sideways at her. "My guess is it's going to take several weeks, maybe months before things get settled with the insurance company." He took a picture of the ceiling. "Do you have somewhere else to stay in the meantime?"

"No." Kayla's chest tightened. She had enough to deal with as it was. Having to look for a new apartment, packing and moving would definitely be more than she could handle right now. She'd already been through that nightmare once during her two-year program. The rent at her last place had gone up so high, she'd been forced to move. She leaned against the built-in oak buffet. "Why can't I stay here?"

Wyatt shrugged. "The circuit has been isolated, and the fire didn't involve plastics. If you don't mind the smell and the destruction, you could probably stay. But the fire marshal will have the final say once he investigates. No family nearby?"

Why did that question cause him to blush again? Was he fishing for personal details about her life? He went back to his picture taking, studying the screen on his phone before taking another.

"Nope. All of my family is in Iowa. I moved to the Twin Cities to go to school." She could've gone to school in Iowa and saved herself some money by living with her folks. But the truth was, she'd been eager to get away, especially from her judgmental, controlling in-laws, and she'd always wanted to live in a big city. Besides, after all the *BAMs* she'd suffered in the past few years, she'd really needed a change in scenery.

"I have less than six months to go before I graduate as a dental hygienist. My life will be more manageable if I stay here despite the smell and the hole in the ceiling." Now that she got a good look, this mess didn't really qualify as a *BAM*—more like a *bam*. The landlord's insurance would take care of the damage, and she could live with a torn-up ceiling for a while. She'd be done with her program in December. Then she'd look for a really good job. Dental hygienists were in demand, and she'd done well in the program, which would earn her great references from her instructors.

Besides, she liked living in this building with all its Old World charm. She loved that she had a friend living right across the hall who was willing to watch Brady. In fact, all of her neighbors were great. Her apartment was close to a nice playground, the river parkway with walking and biking paths, and good schools. A good school was important because her baby would be starting kindergarten next fall.

She studied the chunks of ceiling all over her floor, but then her gaze snagged on Wyatt's long legs and traveled up his tall form as he took pictures from every angle. All serious like this, a man on a mission, he looked way too studly, entirely too appealingly masculine. He studied the ceiling, a determined set to his angled jaw. She studied him. Sexy. Definitely sexy. How nice would it be to wrap herself around him, and . . . *Down, hormones. Sit. Stay.*

He tucked his phone back into his pocket. "All right if I see where you still have power and where you don't? Since you want to stay, we might have to rig a few things so you can use your kitchen."

We? He didn't know her at all, and she didn't know him. Should she be worried about having him roam around her apartment? What motivated him to help a perfect stranger? Well, not perfect by a long shot, but she *was* a stranger. He seemed nice, and he *had* put her dead bolt back on her door, which showed genuine concern. During the months she'd lived here, no police officers had ever come looking for him. Her gut told her he was safe. Surely the fact that he kept to himself had more to do with shyness than felonious tendencies.

"Be my guest." She followed him as he checked the fridge and flipped switches.

"Kitchen power's out. Do you have any extension cords?"

"I think so. Two maybe." Wyatt continued to check the rest of her place. Thank heavens she'd changed the sheets and made the beds this morning. She didn't want him to know what a total slob she was when it came to that stuff, but making their beds every day had never made sense to her. Why bother when you were just going to unmake them again that night? The only time she made the beds was when she changed the sheets or when she was expecting company.

Someone knocked on her door, and she left Wyatt to the task of turning lights on and off. Maybe their caretaker finally decided to make an appearance.

Brady got to the door before she did. "Who's there?" he called like she'd taught him.

"It's Mariah, and I brought pizza."

Kayla opened the door. "You are the best neighbor ever." She and Mariah were both single moms, and they'd become friends from the first day she and Brady had moved in. "Thanks for bringing pizza. I don't have any power in my kitchen. I guess I missed all the excitement this afternoon, huh?" She moved the tubs of laundry out of Mariah's way, stacking them by the wall.

"You're welcome, and yes. You missed the thrilling evacuation of our building and the sight of hunky firemen in action." Mariah set the pizza on the living room coffee table. "I also brought beer. I figured you might want one after coming home to find a mess," she said, lifting the six-pack.

"Where's Rosie?" Brady asked. "Can she play with me?"

"Rosie is with her daddy on the weekends." Mariah tousled Brady's mop of blond hair. "Remember? She'll be home tomorrow afternoon, though, and the two of you can play then."

Brady nodded and went back to his superhero action figures, his favorite toys.

"You have electricity everywhere except in the kitchen and bathroom." Wyatt strolled into the living room. "Where do you keep the extension cords?"

"Oh. Look who's here—our hooded hero." Mariah grinned. "Join us for pizza and beer?"

"Uh . . ." He glanced at the door leading to the hallway, looking as if he might bolt.

"Please stay, Wyatt. I'll get the extension cords." Kayla headed for the walk-in closet by the front door. The huge closet was another reason she loved her apartment, that and the elegant woodwork and the great neighborhood. She rummaged through a cardboard box of stuff and pulled out her two extension cords.

"Pizza and a beer sound great," Wyatt said from the closet door. He glanced at the cords in her hands. "Those aren't going to work. Too short, but they'll be good to use for your toaster and coffee maker. I have something you can use until you can get a cord of your own. I'll be right back."

"Thanks." He was out the door before she even finished speaking.

"Can I have pop with my pizza, Mommy?" Brady had his Superman and Spiderman action figures clutched to his chest.

"You can have milk."

He shrugged, his expression one of abject disappointment. "Chocolate milk," she compromised, and Brady graced her with a cherubic smile.

"It took a fire to bring Hoodie Guy out of his shell." Mariah grabbed a pile of napkins from the kitchen counter. "After he called

911, he herded us all out of the building. He had a fire extinguisher in his hands, and *he* was the last one out the door."

"Oh?" Kayla found paper plates in the back of a cabinet. She pulled them out, along with a plastic cup, and set them on the counter. She grabbed milk and chocolate syrup from the fridge. "I wouldn't say he's out of his shell. The poor guy turns scarlet if you even look at him." She mixed Brady's chocolate milk and put the ingredients back in the dark interior of her fridge. "I'm grateful he was home to call the fire department. He also moved my dead bolt."

"I know," Mariah said. "I helped by handing him tools and offering an extra set of hands while he worked. I tried to chat him up, but he hardly spoke three or four words. That one's not much of a talker, but he sure is hot."

Her husband had been a good-looking guy too, and built. Her gaze touched upon the shadow box on the living room wall, the one holding the folded flag from her husband's casket, along with his formal military picture with name and rank underneath. Regret and sadness gripped her. They'd been so young, still in their teens, and neither of them had wanted to marry. They'd been way too immature to raise a child together. *BAM.*

Hot or not, she'd never felt drawn to shy silent types. "Yeah, Wyatt's definitely hot."

"I'm hot too," Brady piped in. "Can we turn on the window air?"

Kayla shared a grin with Mariah, mentally thanking her little boy for once again turning her away from her dark thoughts. "Not now. Only when it's eighty-five or above."

The window air conditioner blew fuses if any other electrical appliances were on, even the vacuum cleaner. Wyatt was right. This place was an electrical disaster. Even she knew there should be circuit breakers instead of fuse boxes. She'd spent a fortune keeping herself in fuses and lightbulbs. Thanks to her downstairs neighbor, only the dining area had burned today. Things could have been a whole lot worse.

"It's obvious Wyatt is painfully shy, and it's clear he's self-conscious about the burn scars on his neck," Kayla said. Had he been in the military too, like her husband? Maybe he'd been close to an exploding IED, and that's how he got the scars. She and Mariah carried everything to the living room and set it on the coffee table.

"You should flirt with Wyatt," Mariah said, taking a seat. "If I weren't already seeing someone, I'd be after our hot neighbor myself."

"What's *flirt* mean?" Brady asked.

"It means being friendly with someone," Kayla said, sharing another grin with Mariah.

She set a place for Brady and lifted him onto the couch. "We don't know that Wyatt isn't already involved, and I'm not interested. Being a single parent and trying to get through school are enough." Not to mention she'd missed so much by getting married at eighteen and becoming a mother by nineteen. She needed time to figure out what she wanted in a relationship before seeking one.

"It's been two years since you lost your husband, Kayla. Going out on a date now and then would do you a world of good. I'll even . . ."

Wyatt walked back into her apartment before Mariah could finish. He had a long coil of bright orange industrial-sized extension cord looped over his shoulder. Mariah had stopped midsentence. Even Brady had stilled. All eyes turned to the hot guy in the hoodie. Had he heard any part of their conversation?

"What?" he muttered, his face once again turning crimson.

"Pizza and beer, that's what. We've been waiting for you. My fridge can wait a few minutes. Let's eat while the food is still hot." Kayla scooted over to make room for him.

Maybe if she made an effort to be his friend, she could help him get over his shyness a little bit. *Stop.* She didn't know anything about him, and he wasn't her pet project. Who did she think she was, anyway?

Mariah nudged her with her elbow and whispered, "I'd even babysit for free."

"Like either of us would ever charge the other," she whispered back, shaking her head slightly. "Not going to happen," she mouthed. Nope. She had her hands full. She had a plan, and no matter how hot Wyatt might be, she was not interested in dating or fixing him. Didn't mean she couldn't be friendly, though, and she owed him. Kayla smiled and patted the spot beside her on her ratty old, smoke-scented couch. "Join us."

Chapter Two

Judging by the way Kayla and Mariah went silent the instant Wyatt walked through the door, *and* by the way they were communicating with nudges, pointed looks and whispers, they'd been talking about him. *Yay.* Pits and palms sweating, mouth dry and his heart flopping around like a fish out of water, he seriously considered fleeing the scene.

He imagined what they'd been saying. *He's got to know the hood doesn't hide the scars, right?* Yep. He knew. He had mirrors. *He's kind of a loner and a social misfit.* No kidding. But then Kayla smiled at him, and the jolt nearly knocked him off his feet. Whatever they'd been saying about him no longer mattered.

Today would go down in history. He'd talked to the Mysterious Ms. M—about exposed electrical wires and the fire, anyway. Nothing personal other than she was from Iowa. Kayla patted the spot beside her, inviting him to sit. Could he do it? Could he walk right over there, take that seat next to her and eat pizza as if his internal organs weren't in total chaos?

He glanced at the door to the hallway. He wanted so badly to stay, but he needed a minute, or thirty, to pull himself together. "Go ahead and start without me," he mumbled. "This will only take a minute."

He reached into his pocket for the socket adapter he'd brought with him and plugged the extension cord into the nearest living room outlet.

Sucking in a long calming breath, he uncoiled the cord on his way to the kitchen. Focusing on the task before him might help him pull himself together. The avocado-green appliances in this building had to be thirty-five years old. Not efficient at all, but hey, they still worked. He slid the fridge away from the wall far enough that he could reach the cord and the outlet.

"Need help?" Kayla came into the tiny kitchen, two beers in hand.

And . . . there went his heart and his ability to breathe again, just when he'd begun to bring himself under control too. "Nah. I got it." He plugged in the fridge, a whirring sound starting up immediately, and then he pushed the appliance back into place. "All set. You have refrigeration at least, and another outlet to use." He pointed to the end outlet of the extension cord where it sat on the counter. "If you have a lamp, you could set it on the counter. That would give you enough light to use your kitchen."

"I'll figure the kitchen out later, and I'm not even thinking about cleaning up this mess right now either. Beer?" she asked, handing him a bottle.

"Thanks." Their fingers touched as he took it from her hand. His breath caught, and yeah—heat surged up his neck to fill his face. Again. *Damn.* Turning away, he tugged his hood forward and studied the kitchen. He'd had years of practice talking to clients about their jobs. At least he could communicate about impersonal practical stuff. "You can still use the stove, but you'll have to light the burners with a match. The ignition is electric."

"I've *always* had to light the burners with a match." Kayla snorted. "The oven too, and yes, I informed the caretaker months ago. Come have pizza, Wyatt."

"OK." Times like this, he wished he *were* Elec Tric, the alter-ego superhero of his imagination. If he were, he'd be able to talk to Kayla, ask her important personal questions about her life. Like, where was Brady's dad? Was she seeing anyone? If not, would she like to go out with him? Job stuff was about all he could handle, the same way he did with clients. Even then he had to force himself. He *would* sit beside her, dammit. He followed her to the couch, mouth dust-dry and pulse racing.

She wore denim shorts, which gave him a nice view of her long shapely legs. Taller than average, Kayla had curves. Real curves. He'd never been attracted to skinny model types. He preferred a woman with flesh on her bones, someone with plenty of snuggle potential—not that he'd ever come close to having the opportunity.

Just as he'd managed the superhero feat of sitting down beside the woman of his dreams, his phone rang. Wyatt reached into his back pocket and pulled out his cell to check the ID. His brother. "Hey, Sam."

"Hey yourself. Where are you?" Sam asked. "You're supposed to be here for a wedding planning session and dinner."

"Cripes. Sorry." He shot up from the couch. "Totally slipped my mind. We had a fire at my apartment building this afternoon, and I—"

"Is everyone all right? How bad was it?"

"No injuries. The fire department got here before the fire had a chance to spread much." Wyatt edged his way past Kayla. Their knees touched as he slid by. Hers were bare; his were covered in denim. Still, his lungs seized. "I'm on my way. I'll tell you about it when I get there." Wyatt ended the call and stuffed his phone back into his pocket. "Sorry. I have to go. I totally forgot I'm supposed to be at a wedding-planning thing right now."

Kayla's blue eyes widened. "Oh."

"I'll bet you look great in a tux," Mariah purred.

"I'm late. Gotta go," he muttered.

"Wyatt," Kayla called just as he opened her door.

"Yeah?" Amazing how much he liked the sound of his name coming from her mouth.

"Thanks for everything. I owe you. Rain check on the beer and pizza?"

"Sure." She wanted a rain check with weird, scarred Hoodie Guy. Grinning, he took the stairs to the back door, to the lot where he'd parked his truck. He climbed in, cranked the engine and set out for his grandparents' house. They lived in a grand old two-story saltbox near Macalester College, the Mac-Groveland area. After his parents died, he and his siblings had lived there too, and he loved the big old house. Living close to Grandpa Joe and Grandma Maggie was a priority for him. They were already in their early seventies, and if either of them ever needed him, or if something happened, he could get to their place quickly.

Wyatt parked his truck and hurried inside. He passed through the front of the house to the kitchen, where a patio door led to their private fenced yard. Gramps was grilling burgers and brats. Wyatt's mouth watered at the scent of the grilling meat, and his stomach gurgled in agreement. He'd never gotten around to making that sandwich for lunch, opting to reinstall Kayla's dead bolt instead. "Sorry I'm late."

"We heard you had a fire at your apartment," Grandma Maggie said, coming toward him. "Are you all right? Was there much damage?" She wrapped her arms around his waist. The top of her head didn't even reach his chin.

"I'm fine." He hugged her back. "The fire wasn't in my apartment, Gram." Nothing beat one of his grandmother's warm, pillowy hugs. She always smelled like cookies and love.

"Tell us what happened?" Haley called from her place in one of the patio chairs.

"Let me get settled first." His sister handed him a beer. "Thanks, Josey," he said, twisting off the cap. His soon to be sister-in-law's two best friends were also there. Felicia, Kathy and his sister would be Haley's attendants, while he, their cousin Jerry, and Haley's brother Frank would stand up for Sam. "What have I missed?"

Sam came through the patio doors just then. "Well, we settled on where we're having the groom's dinner, and since you weren't here, we all voted. You get to pick up the tab."

"Ha-ha. Not very funny." Wyatt gave the BBQ grill a wide berth and wended his way to an empty chair. Ever since the stupid accident he'd had when he was a kid—the source of his ugly scars—he'd avoided charcoal grills altogether.

"So, tell us about the fire," Sam said, taking his place beside Haley.

"The apartment above mine had an electrical fire in the dining area. The woman who lives there wasn't home. When I heard the alarm go off, I called the fire department and got everyone out of the building."

Sam's brow rose. "The blonde with the little boy?"

Wyatt nodded. "Her name is Kayla, and her son's name is Brady. The building doesn't even come close to meeting electrical code. Once the fire marshal investigates, there *will* be a citation."

Would the fire marshal allow Kayla and her son to stay in her damaged apartment after the investigation? He hoped so. Otherwise, she'd move and he'd lose his chance to get to know her.

He twisted around to face his grandfather. "Grandpa Joe, I want to bid on the rewiring job. The entire building needs a complete rewire, grounding and circuit boxes. The electrical there is an ancient mess. I've never done an estimate for a commercial job this big before. Will you help?"

If he got a jump on the bid, getting it ready so they could submit it as soon as the building was cited, he'd increase their chances of getting the job. After all, citations came with time frames for compliance.

"Of course." Gramps transferred burgers and brats onto a platter of waiting buns. "Let's do a walk-through Monday morning. Do you know which insurance company the owners use? If we're lucky, it'll be a company we've worked with on claims in the past."

"Not yet. I'll get that information ASAP. I do have contact information for the owners, though. There's other work to bid on besides the wiring. The firemen tore down parts of the ceiling in Kayla's apartment and in the hallway, and some of the ceiling joists will need to be replaced. The apartment above hers is vacant right now, which will make everything a lot easier." A good thing, since the fire compromised the floor in that apartment.

Wyatt sipped his beer, thoughts of Kayla dancing around in his mind. She'd offered him a rain check on beer and pizza. The prospect both thrilled and frightened him. He was six foot two and twenty-five years old, yet he blushed like a little girl over just about everything. Worse, he mostly clammed up or mumbled when anyone he didn't know spoke to him. It sucked to be him.

He'd done the "shy brain" research and understood the physiological effects. Shy brains reacted differently to stimuli than most people's. His amygdala viewed strangers, authority figures, and for him, the opposite sex—*especially* those of the opposite sex he found attractive—as though they were threats and a cause for fear. That reaction translated into humiliating blushes, heart palpitations, dry mouth and sweating. Understanding gave him no control over it, though, nor did it make socializing any easier. Too bad there were no anti-shyness pills.

"I don't get why you don't just move," Sam said. "You've done your part, sent all those letters and gotten nowhere. Why not buy a condo or a townhouse? Start earning equity."

"Well, aren't you all domesticated and mature all of the sudden," Wyatt teased. "Moving has no bearing on whether or not we bid on the job. Besides, I don't *want* to move. I'm close to Gram and Gramps. I can walk to several nearby restaurants, and the river parkway is only two blocks away." The Mississippi River offered spectacular views in every season, and he loved to bike the trails along the bluffs. "I'm surrounded by historical sites and grand old houses and buildings." He shrugged. "I like where I live."

"OK." Sam flashed him a wry grin. "So, we'll bid, but that's no guarantee we'll get the job."

"I know, but it's worth a try." He didn't mention he intended to persuade the insurance company and owners to grant them the job by sending copies of his letters and the date-stamped pictures he'd taken over the years of the many electrical code violations. He wouldn't say it outright, but hiring Haney & Sons could be perceived as a way for them to avert a lawsuit for negligence.

"I like that elegant old building, Wyatt," Grandma Maggie said with a nostalgic smile. She brought a large crockery bowl of her famous baked beans to the table. "Reminds me of my youth."

Josey frowned. "Gram, his apartment complex was built in 1911, which was way before your time."

"But not before my parents' time, and that building was there when I was a girl. Perhaps my folks knew people who lived there." She sighed. "I've always loved old things."

"Why, thank you, sweetheart," Grandpa Joe said, kissing her cheek. "I love you too."

"We aren't quite antiques yet." Gram chuckled and swatted his shoulder. "Dinner is ready. Come and eat, everyone."

Wyatt moved to the table. Starving now, he loaded his plate as each dish was passed his way, taking a burger and a brat. Haley, her friends and his sister sat clustered together at one end, chatting happily about the upcoming wedding. She and Sam had chosen New Year's Eve for their wedding date, and they'd already booked a ten-day Caribbean cruise for their honeymoon.

Wyatt was jealous of his brother's domestic bliss, but in a good way. He'd worried about what would become of his older brother. Sam had shut his heart off from any possibility of happily-ever-after after their parents died. And then there had been that unfortunate promiscuous phase Sam had gone through. Good thing all that stopped when he met Haley.

He glanced at his soon to be sister-in-law, and his heart warmed. She'd saved his brother from a sad, empty life, and Wyatt loved her for that. As an added perk, she was fun to tease, another thing he appreciated about her. "Haley, you don't want your last name to be only one letter different than your first name, do you?" Wyatt called down the table. "Have you decided what to do about that yet?"

"I have." Haley put down her burger and nodded, her expression solemn. "I've given it a lot of thought, and I've decided Sam will have to take my last name instead. We'll be the Coopers, like my mom and dad." A triumphant grin lit her face.

"Oh, you're good," Wyatt chuckled.

"What?" Sam's brow creased. "I don't remember having that discussion."

"Taking Haley's name *would* rid you of that pesky rep you have from the *Loaded Question* radio show, Sam," Josey offered. "Nobody would know you were once Sam Haney, the handsiest handyman in the Twin Cities."

"Good point," Felicia, one of Haley's bridesmaids, agreed. "Besides, this is the twenty-first century. No reason for a woman to take a man's name anymore, and there's no reason why a man can't take his wife's name."

Kathy, Haley's maid of honor, nodded. "I know quite a few women who've kept their last names when they married. It's fairly common now."

The debate about who should take whose name continued on through the rest of the meal and dessert. Once the table had been cleared, the wedding books and magazines came out, and bridesmaids' dresses were scrutinized at Haley's end of the table.

"How would you two feel about buying matching suits for the wedding instead of renting tuxes?" Haley asked, glancing at him and Frank. "We're thinking you could all wear gray suits, matching shirts, vests and ties. That way, you'll own something nice to wear for other dressy occasions."

"I'm cool with that," Haley's brother Frank said. "I need to buy a suit for job interviews anyway."

"I'm fine with whatever you two want," Wyatt agreed.

"No hoods." Sam glanced at Wyatt. "You OK with that?"

"Well, duh." He'd have to be fine with it. Even he knew hooded sweatshirts weren't appropriate wedding attire. Although . . . he imagined what his wedding would be like if he ever got that lucky. He'd do it up comic book–style. He and his groomsmen would all wear hooded sweatshirts with their favorite Marvel or DC Comics superheroes silk-screened on the front and back. They'd also wear jeans. What would his bride wear? Probably a Wonder Woman costume, because it would be a wonder he'd managed to get a woman to the altar in the first place.

A pang of loneliness gripped him. Would he ever find someone who would see through the blushes and tied tongue to the man he was inside? He'd always wanted a family of his own, but to find a wife, he first had to date. And to date, he'd have to meet a woman with the patience to stick around long enough for him to get past his shyness to ask her out.

He wanted to ask Kayla out, but even thinking about it turned him into a tangled mess of nerves. Every time she looked at him, his face heated and he broke out in a sweat. Not attractive. She probably saw him as a weirdo—Hoodie Guy, the socially awkward loner in the building by day, superhero in his fantasies at night. *Oh, yeah. I am a comic book character.*

Thursday afternoon, Kayla walked into the day-care center, and Brady ran to her, wrapping his arms around her legs. She liked the center. They provided a preschool curriculum as well as day care, and all for one exorbitant, bank-account-breaking price. At least it was convenient, and even more important, Brady was happy there.

"Mommy," Brady said, grinning up at her.

"Did you have a good day, kiddo?" she asked, cradling his adorable face between her palms.

"Yeah. You wanna see the picture I drawed?" He took her hand and tugged her toward the bulletin board.

"Of course I want to see the picture you *drew*." Kayla waved at the director, whose office walls were windows facing the three different age-grouped rooms. The director smiled back and waved. Brady pointed to his work of art done in crayon. Round-bellied figures with sticks for arms and legs, but at least they had all the appropriate appendages now. "Do you want to tell me about your picture?"

"Uh-huh. This is Superman," he said, pointing to the figure scribbled with red and blue. "*This* is a bad guy." Brady touched each figure as he explained the plot. "The bad guy wants to steal all our snacks and toys, but Superman won't let him."

Well, that explained the various blobs of color surrounding the characters. Snacks and toys. "Cool, Brady. I like your drawing and your story." Kayla ran her fingers through his hair. "Ready to go home?" After spending the entire afternoon cleaning teeth, she was beat, and her shoulders ached. But at least she was at the point in her program now where she was able to do the job she'd been trained to do, albeit under careful supervision. Intense scrutiny actually.

The patients she saw didn't have dental insurance, so they took advantage of the low rates offered to have their teeth cleaned and checked by students. Some were real challenges. One lady she'd worked on today hadn't been to a dentist in ten years—ten years' worth of tartar buildup she'd had to scrape away. Kayla rolled her shoulders, attempting to loosen the tight muscles.

"Yep." Brady bounced around to emphasize his willingness to go home.

"Let's go, then." It had been five days since the fire, and the smell in her apartment had begun to fade a bit, thanks to gallons of Febreze.

She'd bought an extension cord like the one Wyatt had loaned her, but she hadn't seen him to give his back yet. Maybe he'd be around tonight. If so, she'd stop by and return his cord.

The fact that he'd left for a wedding-planning session had piqued her curiosity even more. Tall, good-looking and sexy, of course he was engaged, not that it mattered. They were just neighbors, and maybe they'd become casual acquaintances. Perhaps they'd even graduate to friends. She might even meet his fiancée, and they'd become friends too, and that would be a good thing.

Kayla signed her son out, and they walked through the front door and into the late July heat. Dare she use the window air conditioner in her living room today? What if having the AC running started a fire while she and Brady were sleeping, and it spread really fast? All the way home she obsessed about the tragic possibilities, about bigger and badder *BAMs*.

By the time she pulled into her parking spot behind the building, she'd stirred herself into a stew of worst-case scenarios. Brady, though, had fallen blissfully asleep. Her insides melted at the sight of her sweet, innocent little guy. She hoped like hell her son's rough patches in life would be just that—three-inch-square patches, and not acres.

As she eased her son out of his car seat, Wyatt pulled into the lot. Her heart flip-flopped. *What?* Was shyness contagious all of a sudden? She lifted her son's limp form out of the car. He was getting too big for her to carry, and right now he was sweaty from sleep. She straightened, pushed the car door closed with her hip and waited as Wyatt approached. "Hi. How are you?"

"I'm fine," Wyatt said, his face turning crimson. "I'll get the door."

"Thanks." What must it be like for him? It's not like he could control the blushing. "I bought an extension cord. Are you going to be around for a while? I'll bring your cord downstairs if you are."

"Yep. I'll be around." He opened the door.

Brady woke up then and held out his fist the way Wyatt had done to him the day of the fire. Kayla's heart did another double somersault.

"Hey, Brady." Wyatt grinned and fist-bumped her son. "Rough day at the office?"

Brady nodded, a huge smile on his face. "I can walk, Mommy," he said with a yawn.

"Good, because you're heavy." She set her son on his own two feet.

They entered through the back door, and she frowned. An official-looking yellow form had been taped to the inside of the glass. "What's this?"

"Looks like the fire marshal issued a citation. The building's electrical wiring doesn't meet code, and it's dangerous."

She whipped around to stare at him, dread lodging in her stomach. "Does this mean we're being evicted?"

Wyatt let the door swing shut, and then he read the form. "Nope." He pointed to a section of the citation. "It means the owners have six months to bring the electrical up to code, or our building might be condemned. If that happens, then we will have to move, but these things take months." He glanced at her. "My company has already sent in a bid to do the work."

"*Your* company? You have a company?" Even through his embarrassment, she glimpsed the pride shining in his eyes.

"Yes. It's a family business. Haney & Sons Construction and Handyman Service. We can do just about anything: general contracting, new construction, remodels, plumbing, electrical. You name it; we can do it." He grabbed Brady under his arms and swung him up the first three steps, climbed to the same step and swung him up again, this time to the landing. Brady giggled, and Wyatt flashed her a heart-melting smile.

Oh, man. She really liked his smiles and the way he treated her son. In fact, she'd even begun to find his blushing kind of sweet. *She*, Kayla Malone, ordinary nobody from a small town in Iowa, had the power to make this gorgeous man blush. *Gah! Stop it.* He was already taken, and she didn't want a man in her life. She needed time to be on her own, time to grow up, to get her life together and start her career. Then and only then would she be ready to enter into the world of dating.

"I'll be down in a few minutes." Taking Brady's hand, she climbed the rest of the steps to her apartment.

"I'm hungry," Brady announced once they were inside.

"Me too." Kayla let him go, and Brady made a beeline for his toy box. "Let me change my clothes, and then I'll figure something out for dinner."

Kayla changed out of her scrubs and into comfortable shorts and a T-shirt before going to the kitchen to see what might be scrounged from the fridge. Three beers remained from the night of the fire. Not much else filled the shelves. She'd have to go grocery shopping soon. Three beers. Pizza. She had offered Wyatt a rain check. "Brady," she called.

"Yeah?"

"Let's bring that cord back to Wyatt, and we can ask if he wants to have pizza with us tonight. If not, you and I will call for delivery anyway. Can you last that long?"

He joined her in the kitchen. "Can I have a snack?"

"Sure." She checked a cabinet. "You're in luck. I have one chewy granola bar left to tide you over." Yep, she really did need to get to the grocery store. She took the six-pack holding the three beers, and then she draped the coiled cord over her shoulder. Grabbing her wallet out of her purse, she stuffed it into her back pocket. "Come on, buddy. Let's go."

On the way downstairs, her stomach fluttered. How awkward would it be if he had plans with his whomever, or if he turned her down even if he didn't have plans? She shook that notion off. This was a friendly gesture to repay his kindness. *Rejection* had no place in the equation. Either he accepted or he didn't.

Brady beside her, she knocked on Wyatt's door. A few seconds passed, and she heard his approaching footsteps. He opened the door. A pleased expression suffused his features, along with a fresh rush of color. "Hey," she said, holding the three beers aloft. "Are you free for that beer and pizza I owe you?"

One side of his mouth turned up. "Sure. Come in." He held the door wide and took the cord from her shoulder as she passed.

Curious, she entered her shy neighbor's apartment and surveyed his living room. Wyatt Haney was a neat freak, and he liked tasteful, contemporary furniture. A sectional couch and a large square coffee table faced an entertainment center bracketed by matching bookshelves. A really nice area rug covered a large portion of the oak floor, and the colors in the rug accented the soft brown of the sectional. Two matching antique floor lamps stood at opposites sides of the seating arrangement. They shouldn't go with the modern furniture, but they did. Somehow the two lamps, with their heavy glass shades of cream swirled with browns and russets, pulled the room together.

Colorful framed pictures hanging on the wall caught her eye. She set the beer on the coffee table and moved closer to get a better look. Comic book superheroes in vivid ink filled each frame. None of the characters were familiar to her.

"Brady," she said, glancing at her son. "Come look at these." He ran to her side, and she hoisted him to her hip so he could get a closer look. She noticed a signature in the lower right corner of each of the illustrated pieces. "Wyatt R. Haney," she exclaimed. "Wow. These are yours?" He had a bold, angular style with heavy black lines used to add depth and shadowing. "Your work reminds me of the Adventure Comics produced in the late 1930s, early 1940s."

Wyatt came to stand behind her. "You know comic books?"

"Some. My dad and granddad are both collectors. It's kind of a bonding thing for them. My brother and I were always in trouble because we got into their comic books all the time. He and I loved

reading them, which caused my dad and granddad all kinds of grief. "
She grinned at him over her shoulder. "These illustrations are amazing."
Inordinately pleased by the blush her praise elicited, she couldn't tear
her eyes from him.

"Who's that one?" Brady asked, pointing to the largest of the
illustrations.

Kayla's attention returned to the piece her son asked about. In the
upper left corner of the drawing, a man in jeans and a hooded sweat-
shirt, all but his strong jaw hidden in the shadows of his hoodie, seemed
to walk right off the paper. The effect was practically 3-D. A man in
a dark blue superhero-type costume took center stage. The superhero
had a bolt of lightning emblazoned down the front of his chest. He
held his arms out, palms up, and bolts of lightning streaked across the
paper. She studied the figures. What did this particular illustration say
about the artist?

"That's Elec Tric, the main character in the comic book series I'm
writing." Wyatt pointed to an illustration in a different frame. This
one held a buxom female figure with long purple hair and black eyes.
Dressed in dark purple trimmed in black, this character projected a dark
vibe. She also had black-tipped purple horns growing out of her temples
and curving upward. "This is Tric's archenemy, Delilah Diabolical. DD
for short."

"You write comic books?" Appreciation for her shy neighbor grew
by leaps and bounds. "Are you published? Can I see them?"

"Um . . ." His expression turned to consternation, and his face
flushed with a fresh shade of red almost as vivid as the red ink in his
drawings. "How about you order pizza, and after we eat, I'll gather a few
finished panels for you to see. But first"—Wyatt tousled Brady's thick
hair—"wait until I show this guy what I have here for him to play with."

Her curiosity once again piqued, Kayla set Brady on the floor and
followed Wyatt with her gaze. He disappeared into his walk-in closet,
reemerging a few seconds later with a wooden treasure chest with thick

rope handles on either side—a really cool, realistic-looking pirate chest. Where could she get something like that for Brady?

"Wow." Brady dashed across the room to his side.

Setting the chest on the floor by the couch, Wyatt turned to Brady. "Do you like to play with superhero action figures? I noticed you have Superman and Spider-Man at your house."

Brady nodded, his eyes wide. Wyatt glanced at her. "The pizza takeout menus are in the drawer to the left of the fridge. Choose anything you know Brady will like. I'm not picky." He turned back to her son and opened the lid, and that's all it took. The two of them were lost to her. Boys and their toys.

"Oh. OK." *Don't include me.* She went to the drawer in his kitchen and sorted through the takeout menus. Dang, she wanted to see what was inside the really cool pirate chest too. Kayla chose the pizza place she was most familiar with, the place where they knew her by name, because she ordered pizza delivery so frequently. They ought to give her a frequent-buyer discount. Running her finger down the menu options, she opted for the large, thin-crust sausage pizza and made the call.

By the time she returned to the living room, Wyatt and Brady had taken out several action figures, and they were playing together on the floor rug.

"I got you, bad guy!" Brady said, his young voice forceful and determined. He pushed his Teenage Mutant Ninja Turtle into Wyatt's DC Comics Green Lantern figure.

"*Augh!*" Wyatt's figure fell to the ground backward. "Can't . . . beat . . . you, Donatello!"

"Well," she said, her insides turning to mush, "since you two children are playing so nicely, I'm going to have a beer." There was so much more to Wyatt than met the eye, so much he hid under those hoodies. He was creative, funny, sweet . . . If she got any closer, she'd be in trouble. Serious, distracting heart-at-risk kind of trouble, and she wasn't ready to set herself up for any chance of being hurt again. She hadn't gotten over her disastrous marriage yet. "Want a beer, Wyatt?" she asked, taking a bottle from the six-pack.

"Sure," he said, grinning up at her, his brown eyes warm and . . . sexy.

Gah. Kayla's insides quivered. She twisted off the top of the bottle and handed it to him. Their fingers touched, sending a current of electricity zapping through her all the way to her toes. *Elec Tric indeed.* She jerked her hand back and reached for a beer for herself.

"Mommy, do you want to play with us?"

"No, you two go ahead without me." She sat on the sectional and picked up a magazine from a basket on the floor, a *National Geographic.* Interesting. What did his choice of reading material say about him? That he had a natural curiosity and intelligence? Yep. Wyatt Haney was turning out to be way more complex than she'd suspected. She paged through the magazine and listened to Brady and Wyatt as they did battle and forged alliances with the plastic toys.

She snuck peeks when she could and studied the scars his hoodie failed to conceal. Once again she wondered how he'd gotten them. His profile, strong and exceptionally masculine with his slightly darker five-o'clock stubble, held her attention way more than the magazine in her lap ever could. As if he felt her eyes on him, Wyatt turned and caught her staring. Her turn to blush.

Kayla dropped the magazine on the couch, got up and wandered over to the bookshelves. Family photos grouped together on various levels begged for a closer look. One of the pictures was from a long-ago Christmas, a family portrait by a decorated tree, with Wyatt, an older brother and sister, and his parents, all bearing a strong family resemblance. Wyatt might have been about Brady's age in this photo. No scars back then. No hoodie either.

She moved on to another. This one held four figures: Wyatt, and the brother and sister all grown up, plus a petite, pretty brunette. The four had their arms around each other's waists, and all of them smiled broadly for the camera. The brunette stood between Wyatt and his brother. Her heart dropped. This *had* to be Wyatt's fiancée. She was about to ask him when the door buzzer went off.

"That'll be our pizza," she said, as Wyatt started to get up. "Stay where you are. I'll get it—my treat, remember?" She set her beer on a coaster on the coffee table and hurried out of Wyatt's apartment, a mix of disappointment and relief churning her insides. Probably a good thing he had a fiancée, because Wyatt Haney was far too distracting for her peace of mind. She didn't need or want to complicate her life right now, or for some time to come. After tonight she'd steer clear of the shy, sexy, creative, playful, intelligent, sexy—had she already mentioned sexy?—good-looking man with his bedroom brown eyes. *BAM.*

Chapter Three

Once Kayla left his apartment to get the pizza, Wyatt could finally draw a breath. The entire time he'd played with Brady, his senses had really been attuned to *her*. He'd noticed her studying him more than once. It had to have been the scars that drew her attention. What else? People were always curious about stuff like that.

"What's this?" Brady asked, pulling out Wyatt's red cape from the toy chest.

Wyatt took the superhero cape and fastened it around the little boy's neck. "*This* is my Superman cape. See the symbol on the back? My mom made it for me, and my dad made the toy chest." His dad had given him the pirate trunk on his tenth birthday, the last birthday he'd celebrated with his parents before the single-engine airplane accident that took them from him.

"Wow." Brady's eyes saucered as he fingered the red cloth. Then he lifted his skinny arms over his head and ran around the living room while making whooshing noises.

Wyatt chuckled, remembering all of the times he'd flown through the air in the very same way. He'd also jumped off couches, coffee tables and beds in his efforts to become airborne, much to his mother's aggravation. A soft knock on his door, and his heart rate surged. "That'll be your mom with pizza. Are you hungry, Superkid?"

"Yeah." Brady came to a stop by Wyatt's door. "Who's there?"

"It's me," Kayla's muffled voice came through the door.

Brady grinned at Wyatt, before calling back. "Me who?"

Laughing, Wyatt opened the door. The delicious scent of pizza wafted over him. "Do I smell Italian sausage?"

"You do. Awesome cape, kiddo." She nodded, her eyes on her son. "Do we want this in the dining area or on the coffee table?" she asked, lifting the large pizza.

Was she avoiding eye contact with him? "Let's eat at the kitchen table."

"OK." Her posture slightly stiffer than before, Kayla carried their meal to the kitchen.

Had something changed between the door buzzing and Kayla's reappearance in his apartment? Her vibe was different, and her expression had gone from open to reserved. His stomach knotted. What had he done to cause her to go from friendly to not so much? She wasn't angry, just . . . she'd withdrawn somehow.

Having a shy brain had given him his own kind of superpower—a super sensitivity when it came to reading body language and other people's moods, and Kayla's had definitely altered where he was concerned. Things had been going so well, and now? His mouth dried up and his tongue flat out refused to form words. He followed her and Brady, confused and hugely bummed. He'd been making progress with her. *Eh*. With her son, anyway. He'd never had a problem with children.

"Do you happen to have any juice or milk?" Kayla asked, setting the pizza at the center of the table. "If not, I can run upstairs to my place to get something for Brady to drink." She cast him a brief look.

Wyatt nodded and went for the carton of milk in his fridge, while she retrieved their beer bottles from the living room. Had the demons from his comic book world accosted her on the stairs, casting aspersions on his character or something? He poured Brady a glass of milk and set it on the table, then he took three plates down from a cabinet and placed them on the table next to the napkin holder.

"Do you mind if I help Brady wash his hands in your bathroom?" she asked, her tone awkwardly polite.

His face flamed. "Course not," he mumbled. Wyatt busied himself with washing his own hands at the kitchen sink, all the while trying to puzzle out what could have possibly gone wrong between the front door to their building and his apartment.

Kayla returned, and Brady flew circles around her, his arms in the air and the cape billowing. "So," she said, "when's the wedding?"

"Huh?" Wyatt frowned, once again knocked off balance.

"You had to leave the afternoon of the fire because of your wedding-planning thing. When's the happy day?"

"Oh. This coming New Year's Eve."

She smiled. "That'll make it easy to remember anniversaries."

Why did she want to know about his brother's wedding? "I guess, but—"

"Wyatt, can I keep this cape?" Brady flew into him, bumping against his legs.

"Whoa, Superkid." Wyatt hoisted him into the air and plopped him on the seat where he'd just placed a fat electrical supplies catalog as a booster. At least he could talk to children. "Hmm, afraid not, buddy. You can always play with the cape when you visit, but like I said earlier, my mom made it for me. I lost her when I was ten, and this cape is kind of special to me."

"Oh." Brady's face fell. "Your mommy died?"

"Yes, and my dad too. They were in an accident."

Brady's brow scrunched. "My daddy died in a accident too." He glanced at Kayla. "Right, Mommy?"

She placed a couple of pizza squares on Brady's plate and grabbed a few napkins for him. "That's right, sweetie." Another brief glance at him. "He was in the army, stationed at Bagram Airfield in Afghanistan." She sat down and took a plate for herself. "He died in a freak accident."

"How old are you?" The words left his mouth before he had a chance to think about how rude they sounded. The fact that they flew out of his mouth at all was a first for him. Kayla Malone seemed way too young to be a widow, or a mother for that matter.

Her chin raised a notch and she met his gaze dead on, a glint of defiance in her eyes. "I'm twenty-four. I had Brady when I was nineteen. OK?"

Heat flooded his face. Nodding, he helped himself to pizza.

"Did you get those scars from a accident too?" Brady asked around a mouthful.

"Not the same accident as my parents', but yeah, I did. Listen up, Superkid, and don't be stupid like I was. When I was a few years older than you are now, I decided to find out what would happen if I squirted lighter fluid onto hot coals in the barbeque grill, and—"

"What's lighter fluid?" Brady asked, curiosity lighting his features.

"It's a liquid people squirt onto charcoal to help it catch fire." His answer seemed to satisfy the little guy, so Wyatt continued. "Anyway, the stream of lighter fluid caught fire, the can exploded, and I got burned."

"Oh, Wyatt." Kayla's expression softened, and her pretty blue eyes went from defensive to sympathetic. "That must have been awful."

"It was. I have more scars along my left side where my clothes caught fire. It all happened so fast." He preferred her open friendliness to pity, but at least the distance between them had closed—for a few seconds anyway.

After the three of them had made a good dent in the large pizza, Wyatt reached into a kitchen cabinet for the package of Oreos he always kept on hand. "Is it all right if Brady has a couple of *c-o-o-k-i-e-s*," he spelled out.

"*S-u-r-e.*" She laughed. "You must spend a lot of time with children."

"I have loads of cousins who have children, and I've done my fair share of babysitting over the years, plus family gatherings for holidays and stuff. I love kids. They're so"—*nonthreatening*—"funny and honest."

"Can I see your comic books now?" Brady asked. "Will you read one to me?"

"Sure. I'll go get the first in the Elec Tric series while you eat your cookies." Wyatt handed Kayla the package of Oreos, taking one to stuff into his mouth on his way down the hall. How would she react if she saw the Mysterious Ms. M?

He didn't want to find out and gathered up the illustrations sitting on his drawing table to tuck into the cabinet. He pulled out one of the color copies of the first Elec Tric comic book he'd written. He never touched the originals and kept them stored between acid-free mat boards on the top shelf of the cabinet.

Wyatt returned to the kitchen to find Brady dunking half an Oreo into his milk. "That's the best way to eat a cookie. Right, bro?"

Brady popped the rest of his cookie into his mouth, and milk dribbled down his fingers. Nodding, he wiped his hand on the front of his shirt.

"Brady, I *did* give you napkins. It would be nice if you used them."

The kid shrugged and picked up his glass of milk, polishing off the contents in a few gulps. Kayla sighed, moved to his kitchen and tore a few paper towels from the dispenser. She dampened them at the kitchen sink, and then she headed for her son, a maternal expression of disapproval on her pretty face.

Wyatt grinned as the Mysterious Ms. M wiped her son down, including the front of his shirt, which held pizza stains along with cookie crumbs and milk. In typical little-boy fashion, Brady grimaced at the indignity of such motherly ministrations.

"We don't want any of this getting on Wyatt's comic book," she admonished, and Brady sent Wyatt a very disgruntled, put-upon-male look.

The comic book tucked under his arm, Wyatt lifted his shoulders and held out his hands palms up—the universal bro code for *nothing I can do about it, buddy.* His heart turned over. Such an ordinary scene—a scene he'd witnessed hundreds of times in his large extended family. But with Kayla, it did something to him. A powerful yearning overwhelmed him, once again tying his tongue and knotting his stomach. He headed into the living room and set the comic book on the coffee table. How was he supposed to read to Brady in this state?

Mother and son soon joined him. Kayla sat close enough that he could smell the flowery scent of the shampoo she used, along with her own unique sweet essence. Her body heat melded with his—adding blood rushing to his groin into the mix of internal mayhem. He forced himself to focus on the comic book, the story of how ordinary Rick Hart became the superhero Elec Tric. "*A Superhero Is Born,*" he read the title page.

Brady started out sitting on Kayla's lap, but once Wyatt started reading, he slid off and moved to stand between Wyatt's knees to study each and every illustration. Wyatt had to lean closer to peer around him so he could read. Brady's total absorption filled Wyatt with pride, and he took on the roles of his characters, changing his voice for each one.

"*Nooo! What's happening to me?*" Wyatt pointed to the dialogue bubble, as a second lightning bolt scorched through Rick, lifting him off the ground and suspending him in midair.

"*Get him!*" The strange, horned woman in purple shouted to her minions.

"*Who are you? What do you want with me?*" Wyatt's superhero held out his hands in front of him, and currents of electricity sizzled and arced from his palms. "Rick didn't know what to make of that," Wyatt commented.

"That was the day the poor guy saw the demons and the portals leading into their realm for the first time," he told his rapt audience of two. "And his life was forever changed." He turned the page to show Brady and Kayla how his poor, confused superhero escaped the demons in this first installment.

Magical. This brief moment in time, with Kayla beside him and Brady wrapped up in the story, planted itself in Wyatt's memory forever. Once he finished reading, he leaned back. So did Brady, placing his little hands on Wyatt's knees while propping himself on the edge of the couch. "So? What did you think, Superkid? Did you like my comic book?"

"Yeah." Brady grinned, his head bobbing. "Can we read another one?"

"Maybe another time. It's getting late." Kayla nudged Wyatt with her shoulder. "Great story. Even greater illustrations. Have you tried to get your comic books published?"

His pulse racing from the brief physical contact, Wyatt glanced sideways at her. "I've submitted them to several comic book publishers, and I've been rejected by every one of them."

"What about agents? I have an aunt who writes books for middle-grade children, and she never got anywhere either until she had an agent. She says submitting on her own put her books in huge slush piles seen only by interns, and like interns everywhere, they don't know anything. That's why they're interning. To learn." She rose from the couch. "Do some research and look for agents who represent your favorite comic book writers and illustrators. Start submitting to them."

"Maybe I will." Wyatt rose too. She'd gone back to her friendly, open self, and he really wanted to pull her into his arms and kiss her good night. Even thinking about acting on the impulse caused an internal whirligig spinning.

"This was fun," Kayla said, gracing him with a knee-weakening smile. "Do you want me to help clean up before we go?"

"No. I got it. Thanks for dinner." He stuffed his hands into his front pockets, wanting like hell to suggest they do this again soon, or maybe go out for dinner sometime. But the words got stuck somewhere between his lungs and his lips, and the suckers refused to budge past his pounding heart.

"You're entirely welcome. Thank you for all your help after the fire." She put her hands on Brady's shoulders just as the kid let loose a huge yawn. "Come on, Brady," she said, untying the Superman cape and handing it to Wyatt. "Time to get ready for bed, and thanks to Wyatt, you've already had your bedtime story."

Her eyes sparkling, she smiled again, rendering him even more incapable of speech. Wyatt followed them to the door. *Please stay a while longer.* How would she react if he said that out loud?

"See you around, Wyatt," she said, ushering her son into the hallway.

"See you," he mumbled, watching the two of them until they disappeared up the stairs. Finally he closed the door and walked to the kitchen to wash the dishes. He replayed the entire evening in his mind. Kayla truly was a mystery, all open and friendly one minute, and reserved the next, finally returning to friendly.

What had that been about, and why had she brought up his brother's wedding? Had she been flirting, hoping he'd ask her to be his date? His hopes soared, then sank just as quickly. Not likely, since New Year's Eve was months away, and they hardly knew each other.

One thing was certain. The Mysterious Ms. M confused and fascinated him all at the same time, and his attraction to her grew stronger each minute he spent in her company. She knew comic books. What were the odds he'd meet a woman familiar with his favorite hobby? That had to be a sign.

Unfortunately, the more attractive he found her, the stronger his damned fear response kicked in. Only time and familiarity could ease his shyness. Once he felt more comfortable around her, he'd ask her out. For now, all he could do was try to figure out ways to be with her more.

Hopefully he'd hear from the building owners and insurance company soon, and Haney & Sons would be awarded the bid. How perfect—and perfectly impossible—would that be? Too much to hope for, so he had to have a backup plan or two. What if some other company got the job, and some another electrician got to know her and beat him to the punch? *Arrrgh.*

He left the dirty dishes in the sink and strode down the hall to his studio. He needed to lose himself in his imaginary world, and he had a great idea for an illustration. The dishes could wait. His inspiration? Not so much.

By Sunday afternoon, Kayla had finally found time to stock up on groceries. Her shopping cart loaded, she pushed it through the lot to her car with Brady riding in the seat. "I'm going to need your help carrying this stuff upstairs, kiddo. We're going to the playground with Mariah and Rosie in"—she checked her phone for the time—"an hour and a half."

"OK. Can we get Happy Meals for supper?" he asked.

"Excellent idea." She hit speed dial.

"Hey," Mariah answered. "My ex dropped Rosie off a few minutes ago. Are you two going to be home soon? We're ready for some fun at the park."

"We're on our way from the grocery store right now. Do you want me to get McDonald's at the drive-through before we head to the park? We can have a picnic."

"Great idea. Tell you what, I'll go get the food now, and by the time Rosie and I return, you'll be here. It won't take you long to put your groceries away, will it?"

"Nope. We'll hurry." Kayla popped her trunk. "I'll pay you back when we get there." She told Mariah what to order for her and Brady, and then she tossed her bags into her car. "Come on," she said, helping her son out of the cart and into his booster seat. She buckled him in. "Mariah and Rosie are going to get our supper, so we have to hurry."

She pushed the speed limit all the way home and pulled into her spot in the back lot. Kayla helped Brady out of his seat, and the two of them circled around to the trunk of her car. "We should be able to get everything inside in two trips," she said, handing her son a couple of the lighter plastic bags. She gripped as many of the heavier sacks as she could handle, shut the trunk and headed for the back door.

They'd just made it to the first-floor landing when the front entrance buzzed and opened. The petite brunette from Wyatt's photo hurried up the steps, a folder in her hand. The fiancée. Guilt surged. *What?* It's not like she could help being attracted to Wyatt, and she'd never act on it in any way. After all, she knew firsthand what it felt like to be on the "cheated on" side of that equation. Her gut wrenched, but she did her best to force a smile. "Hi."

Wyatt's door opened, and he stepped into the hallway. His eyes lit up at the sight of the other woman, and Kayla's heart dropped to the region of her belly button. He noticed her and Brady, and color flooded his face. "Hey." He nodded. "Haley, this is my neighbor Kayla and her son Brady. This is Haley, she's my—"

"It's nice to meet you," Haley said, a warm smile making her even prettier. "Wyatt mentioned you had a fire in your dining room. Good thing his apartment is beneath yours, and he heard the alarm." The diamond ring on her left hand sparkled as she shifted the folder.

"Nice to meet you too." Kayla's smile faltered a bit. "Yes, we were lucky." She glanced at the folder Haley carried. No doubt wedding stuff to go over. "Congratulations on your upcoming wedding."

"Thanks." Haley's radiant expression said it all. They were in love.

"Well," she muttered, lifting her sacks of groceries, "we'd better get going. I have another load in the car."

"Do you need help?" Wyatt asked, taking a step toward her.

"No, no. We can manage, and you have company. Thanks for offering, though." Kayla hurried up the stairs without another glance, Brady trailing her. She should be happy for Wyatt and Haley, but no matter how hard she tried, she couldn't rise above the unsettling feeling that she very much wanted to stick her hand into someone else's cookie jar. *Oh, right.* Hence the guilt. *Avoid him.*

Once she and Brady were in her apartment, she put away the things that needed to be in the fridge and freezer and left the other stuff on the counter. "Brady, stay here. I'm going to get the rest of the groceries."

"OK." He wandered into the living room, grabbed a few toys and climbed onto the couch.

Kayla hurried down the stairs and came face-to-face with Wyatt. Her heart bounced back up to its rightful spot and tapped against her ribs. She couldn't meet his gaze.

"I'd like to help with your groceries," he said. "And I made something for you and Brady."

"You did?" She frowned. "What?" And why was he being so sweet?

"Groceries first."

"Where's Haley?" She started toward the back door, and Wyatt reached around to open it for her. More heat flooded her face.

"She only stopped by to give me information about where to buy my suit for the wedding."

"No tuxes?" How could a man smell so good, like the soap he used mixed with his own masculine yumminess? Should she feel guilty about stealing a whiff or two? Because she did.

"Nope. Haley's practical, and she figured we'd all get more use out of a nice suit."

"Oh." By the time they reached her car, her insides were a mess of remorse and desire for the man who was clearly off-limits. Every minute spent with him, she found him more attractive.

Kayla handed Wyatt half of the remaining bags of groceries and took the other half herself, and they carried them to her apartment. Her neighbor was so thoughtful. Her husband had never been the considerate type. In fact, he'd been mostly sullen and resentful toward her. She had to blink away the sting in her eyes as she opened her apartment door.

"Wyatt!" Brady hopped off the couch and ran across the living room.

"Whoa, slow down, Superkid," he said with a broad smile as Brady hugged his legs. "Let me put these bags down, and—"

"Hello," Mariah called, poking her head into the apartment. She and Rosie came in, holding a large tote bag and a cardboard tray of beverages. The scent of McDonald's wafted into the apartment. "Oh, hey, Wyatt. Are you coming to the park with us?"

"Yeah." Brady let go of his knees and started bouncing. "Come to the park with me and Rosie."

"Sure," Wyatt said. "Sounds like fun."

"I already bought burgers and fries, and we have plenty to share. Have you eaten?"

"I have, but thanks."

Kayla set her bags down on the kitchen counter and rolled her eyes. Great. More time with Mr. Tall-and-Tempting. "Let me just put away the perishables. The rest can wait until later," she called.

Wyatt walked into the kitchen and placed his bags next to hers. "Is it all right with you if I join you at the park?"

"Of course." *Not.* His arm brushed hers, causing a pleasurable tingle of sexual awareness.

He searched through her groceries, pulling out the items that needed to go in the fridge. "Oreos," he said with a deep chuckle, his tall frame leaning around her to place the package in the to-put-away-later pile. "My favorite."

Yikes. The tingle of awareness morphed into full-fledged ignition, and heat spiraled through her. Oh, man, her kitchen was tiny, and Wyatt filled the space with all his stupid masculine gorgeousness. Kayla's breathing went shallow, and her pulse skyrocketed. This was bad; this was *very* bad.

She leaned over and shoved a load of fresh vegetables into the crisper drawer, bumping right into him—groin level—as she backed out to straighten. He sucked in an audible breath, and she nearly jumped out of her skin. "BAM," she muttered under her breath.

"Bam?" He leaned around her and set the milk on a shelf.

"Yep. Bam. We're done." Was he doing this on purpose? Crowding her space, brushing against her . . . No. He was just being helpful. The man was way too shy for that kind of subtle seduction. Wasn't he? Besides, he was engaged. She glanced at her pile of stuff to make sure only nonperishables remained. "Too bad Haley couldn't join us. She seems really nice." There. Cold water dumped over hot body.

"She is nice, but—"

"Come *on*, Mommy." Brady raced around the corner. "Let's *go*."

Kayla snuck a peek at Wyatt. His brow was creased, and a look of confusion clouded his sexy brown eyes. "OK. Let's boogie," she said.

Rosie and Brady raced ahead once they reached the sidewalk, and Wyatt joined the two children, finally giving Kayla the chance to breathe.

"He's into you," Mariah whispered.

"No. He's not. He's engaged. I met his fiancée in the hallway about thirty minutes ago."

"You're kidding."

"Nope." She shook her head. "The wedding is on New Year's Eve." She raked her fingers through her hair. "I'm in trouble, Mariah."

"What kind of trouble?"

"I'm really attracted to him, and . . . Oh, God. He's so sweet, creative and fun to be around. He writes and illustrates comic books. Did you know that?"

Mariah blinked at her. "No, I didn't."

"He lost his parents when he was a kid, and he let Brady play with a Superman cape his mom made for him when he was little, and he has this really cool pirate chest full of toys, and he smells so good." She came up for air. "He's tall and hot and I—"

"You're in trouble, all right." Mariah laughed. "He's not married yet. All's fair in love and war."

"No. It really isn't." Never in a million years would she inflict that kind of hurt on another woman, especially after having been on the receiving end of that kind of humiliation herself. "There's nothing *fair* about war, and there's nothing *fair* about making a play for another woman's man."

Kayla raised her hand to shield her eyes from the late-afternoon sun and watched Wyatt. He'd lifted Brady over his head, so her son could fly through the air like Superman. Then he set him down and did the same for Rosie, who squealed with delight. "Why on earth did you invite him to the park with us?" she muttered.

"He was in your apartment with you. I figured you'd already included him. How was I supposed to know he was the kind of man who could make you speak in run-on sentences?" Mariah arched a brow. "If he's happily engaged, why did he accept?"

"Good question." Why had he helped her with her groceries right after his fiancée left, and hadn't he said he'd made something for her and Brady? Confusion stirred her thoughts as she replayed the time she'd spent with Wyatt. Had she misjudged him? He seemed really sweet and shy, but maybe he was a total player. Not that it mattered either way. She was not interested in dating. Period.

Brady's laughter drew her attention again. Obviously it was her son's turn to fly. Perhaps she'd misread all the signals where Wyatt was concerned. After all, he wrote comic books and played with plastic action figures. Could be he was just a big kid himself and liked an excuse to play at the park. She had noticed he didn't suffer any shyness with Brady, which was probably a nice break for the guy. The fact that he'd agreed to join them might not have anything to do with her. Oh, Lord. Was that creepy?

No. He didn't give off creepy vibes, more like big-kid vibes. Didn't she do the same thing sometimes? Like when she used her son as an excuse to go see children's animated movies? Still, she'd be vigilant. "Well . . ." she murmured.

"Well?" Mariah glanced askance at her.

"That's all. Just . . . well."

She didn't know what to think. Best to stick with the current plan. Avoid and curtail. She and Wyatt were just neighbors, and even that was temporary. Her attraction probably had more to do with the fact that she'd been without a man in her life for way too long. In fact, she'd never really had a man in her life, since Brad mostly chose not to be present in their marriage.

With Wyatt, she was experiencing a passing fancy with a hormone chaser on the side, that's all. Eventually she'd find someone else to obsess about, and then she'd forget all about Wyatt Haney and his sexy brown eyes, tall lanky frame, and his amazing smile.

They found an empty picnic table by the playground, and Mariah laid out their feast. Kayla cleaned Rosie and Brady's hands with wipes and helped them get settled on the benches. She took a seat next to Brady, and Wyatt slid into the spot beside her. *Great.*

She busied herself with tearing ketchup packets and squeezing the contents onto the paper wrapper from Brady's cheeseburger. Motion caught her eye, and she turned in time to catch Wyatt stealing a few of her fries. "Hey." She flashed him a mock scowl.

He grinned and shrugged as he scarfed them down, his eyes sparkling with a teasing glint.

Yet another adorable side to her already way-too-attractive neighbor. Grinning, she set her hand protectively on the side of her fries and focused on her meal. Wyatt chuckled, reached around her and stole another fry. His move brought him even closer, and that turned her on. She narrowed her eyes at him, which only made his grin grow wider.

"Kayla tells me you write comic books." Mariah shoved a straw into one of the kiddie drinks and set it in front of Brady.

"Yep." He nodded.

"That reminds me," Kayla said. "What does the *R* in your name stand for?"

"Richard. Wyatt Richard Haney." There went another one of her fries.

She moved them to the other side of her burger, farther out of his reach. "Oh." Her brow rose, and she studied him. "Rick for short, like Rick Hart in your story."

"Mmm-mm." He leaned close and reached around her again—it was almost like being in his arms—and stole three fries in one swoop.

"Grrr." She picked up the container of fries and set it in front of him. "There. Happy now?"

He nodded, his eyes filled with amusement. "I *might* share."

"You two get along, or I'll put you both in a time out." Mariah put a bunch of fries on the paper next to Kayla's burger.

"Yeah, Mommy," Brady said, handing her a few of his fries as well. "You should flirt to Wyatt."

Mariah choked on her soda and brought her napkin up to cover her nose. Kayla wanted to shrink to the size of an ant. She swallowed her mouthful before she too choked. "Brady heard that word and asked me what it meant," she muttered. "I told him flirting means being friendly."

"And *my* mommy said Kayla should flirt with *you*," Rosie added helpfully. "Right, Mommy?"

Mariah tried to muffle her laughter and ended up coughing. Kayla looked everywhere but at Wyatt. She saw a couple of familiar children and their mothers by the slide. "Oh, look, guys. The kids you two played with on the jungle gym last week are here again." She gestured toward the playground, sneaking a sideways glance at Wyatt. His expression had turned thoughtful, and he'd gone quiet. Well, even more quiet than usual. She should explain, put him at ease.

"Mariah teased me the afternoon of the fire, because you saved the day and all. You know how kids are. Little pitchers with big ears and even bigger mouths."

With a slight smile, he nodded and popped another fry into his mouth. Kayla expelled a breath. Of course he got it. Didn't he say he had tons of little cousins? Mariah's brow rose and her lips parted like she might say something. Kayla narrowed her eyes and shook her head ever so slightly, praying she'd let the subject drop.

"Mommy, can we go play now?" Rosie asked, around a mouthful of sliced apple from her Happy Meal.

"Sure." Mariah shifted around to straddle the bench, so she faced the playground. "Stay on this side where we can see you."

Rosie and Brady ran off, and the awkward moment passed. Kayla shrugged and flashed an apologetic look Wyatt's way. "When Mariah suggested I should flirt with you, she didn't know about . . . well, you know. Sorry," she said. "She didn't mean anything by it." He blushed, and heat coiled its way down to her center. When had a man's blush turned into something erotic?

She *could* keep her hands out of the cookie jar, dammit, and she would. Besides, she'd already done the relationship thing, and it had been a disaster. *Avoid. Curtail. Repeat.*

"Wow, can you believe it's the last week of July already?" she chirped. "Wonder how long it's going to be before something is done about my apartment?"

Chapter Four

Wyatt gripped the edge of the picnic bench, while Kayla's words reverberated inside his head. *When Mariah suggested I should flirt with you, she didn't know about . . . well, you know.* No, he didn't know. He frowned. What the hell was there to know about him? He was desperate to ask what she meant, what she knew that he didn't, but little Rosie's announcement about how Kayla was supposed to flirt with him had triggered the usual sweaty palms, dry mouth and frozen tongue.

I agree. You should flirt with me. That's what he should've said—what he still longed to say. Wyatt stared at the empty cardboard french-fry container in front of him, his insides churning. The moment for witty comebacks had sailed right past him. As usual. If he said anything now, he'd come across as being off. He swiped his damp palms down his jeans.

At least he'd managed to flirt and tease a little when he'd stolen Kayla's fries. That could be viewed as progress, unless she didn't get that he was flirting. What if she thought he was just an irritating guy who liked to steal food from other people's plates? No. How could she not realize he'd been coming on to her? He'd had his arms around her for a few glorious seconds. She had to have noticed. He certainly had.

His muddled thinking receded a bit, and it finally registered that Kayla had asked him a question. He *could* answer nonpersonal questions, dammit. Keeping his eyes on the table, he forced himself to focus on her question. "As far as your apartment is concerned, it might take weeks before things start moving. Has the insurance adjuster come by to look at the damage yet?"

"Not that I know of, but the caretaker might have let someone in without telling me."

"I'm pretty sure that's illegal," Mariah said. "You have to be notified in advance."

Wyatt shrugged. "Yeah, but this is Floyd we're talking about. If you catch him in the hall, ask. I'll do the same." He rose from the table, pretending casual ease when what he really wanted was a quick getaway, so he could pull himself together enough to think straight. He stretched for good measure. "I'm going to head back. I have a few things I need to do. Thanks for letting me tag along."

"Thanks for joining us." Keeping her gaze on her half-eaten burger, Kayla tore a little piece off the bun.

Rosie cried out from the playground, and Wyatt glanced over. She'd tripped and fallen but appeared to be more indignant than hurt. She was already on her feet again. No blood. No major injuries. Mariah hurried off to take care of her daughter. Wyatt opened his mouth to say more to Kayla, but her attention was on the children. He took the distraction as his chance to slip away. He needed to run things by his brother and sister. Maybe they'd be able to offer some kind of insight into this whole flirting business.

He jogged the four blocks home, needing to burn off some of the pent-up energy so he could relax. He unlocked the back door and entered the building, just as Floyd was hurrying up the basement stairs. Speak of the devil. They met on the landing by the back door.

"Say," Wyatt said, moving out of Floyd's way, "has the insurance adjuster been by to take a look at Ms. Malone's apartment yet?"

"Not that it's any of your business, but no . . . *asshole*," Floyd bit out before shoving his way past him and out the door.

"OK?" Wyatt's heart pounded loud enough that his ears rang. *Asshole?* He really did need a night out with his pack, because things here were turning to the weird side pretty quick. He let himself into his apartment, threw his keys on his dining room table and headed for his studio—his happy place. Taking a seat at his drawing table, Wyatt pulled his phone out of his back pocket.

His gift for Kayla still sat on the drawing board, and he studied the colored-pencil portrait he'd done for her—Supermom and Superkid, standing side by side against the world, their capes billowing out behind them, stances proud, with their arms crossed in front of them. He ought to frame it before he gave it to her. Grandpa Joe probably had remnant pieces of trim or casing he could use, and he could get a piece of glass cut at a frame store. Wyatt hit the number for his brother's speed dial.

"Hey," Sam answered. "What's up?"

"Are you and Haley doing anything this evening?"

"We're on our way out the door right now for Sunday dinner with Haley's folks. Why?"

Wyatt pushed his hoodie off and ran his hand across the back of his overheated neck. "I was hoping we could get together tonight, maybe head over to The Bulldog for a beer. How about after your dinner with the Coopers?"

"Nah. Not tonight. Haley and I put in a full day on our upstairs remodel project. We're both planning to veg out after dinner, watch some TV and go to bed early. How about tomorrow night?"

"Sure. That'll work." Wyatt had already done some rewiring on Haley's upstairs half-story, and he'd put in the new track lighting for them. She and Sam planned to put her house on the market once they were done with the updates. They wanted to buy something larger, a house to hold a family.

Another twist to the gut gripped him. It wouldn't be long before the happy couple started said family, and that would mean an end to their frequent and spontaneous meet-ups for beer, burgers or pool. Josey wanted to pair up too, and when she found someone, where would that leave him? What would he do to keep himself from turning into a total recluse? "Have fun with the Coopers."

Sam chuckled. "I'll do my best."

Wyatt tried his sister next but got no answer. He left a message about getting together Monday evening, and finally, he called his grandparents.

"Hello?" his grandmother answered.

"Hey, Gram. I was wondering if I could stop by for a visit."

"Of course. We'd love to see you. Have you eaten? We're just sitting down for supper."

Sweet. He'd lied to Kayla and Mariah when he'd told them he'd already eaten. He hadn't wanted them to feel awkward about eating in front of him. "I haven't. I'm on my way, but don't wait for me. I'll be there in a few minutes."

Wyatt shoved his phone into his back pocket and raced out of his apartment. He needed to be with people who loved him and in a place where his stupid brain didn't cause his tongue to cement itself to the roof of his mouth. A few minutes where he could think without the fog of confusion, and he'd be able to figure things out.

The minute he walked into his grandparents' house, the tension bunching his muscles eased. The delicious smell of his grandmother's rosemary chicken made his mouth water. "Hey," he said, entering the kitchen. "Smells amazing in here, Gram." She and Gramps were already seated at the kitchen table. Wyatt leaned down to kiss his grandmother's cheek.

"Wash up and join us." Grandma Maggie patted his face.

"How was your weekend?" Grandpa Joe asked, taking a big spoonful of mashed potatoes from the serving dish.

"Disturbing." Wyatt washed his hands at the sink and dried them on a dish towel. "I asked the caretaker if the insurance adjuster had been by to assess the damage from the fire, and he called me an asshole."

"Hmm." Grandpa Joe's brow lowered. "Any idea why?"

Sliding into the same chair he always sat in, Wyatt shrugged. "I've complained more than once about him to the owners. Maybe the flak has finally gotten back to him."

"Most likely." Grandpa Joe nodded. "Especially since the fire."

"That's not all." Loading his plate with chicken, mashed potatoes, and green beans, Wyatt considered how to broach the subject puzzling him the most. His grandparents had always encouraged open communication, and they'd stressed over and over that he could talk to them about anything. Still, he'd never talked to them about women, because he hadn't really dated much. No one had drawn him the way Kayla did. The times he had gone out, it had been through fix-ups by a friend or a cousin, and those instances had been disasters.

"There's this woman. I'm interested in her, and I . . . she's . . ." He blew out a breath and stabbed his fork into his chicken. "I'm so confused."

Grandpa Joe chuckled. "Well, that made perfect sense."

"I don't know what to think," he said, shaking his head. "She's friendly, and I think we're making progress, and then she . . . kind of . . . withdraws."

He told them about what had happened at the park, how she believed there was something about him that warranted a "you know." "I don't have any deep dark secrets, believe me, so I have no idea what that was all about. The shyness isn't helping." He glanced at his grandmother. "Is there any hope for me? Do all women do that?"

"Do what?" Gram asked, her eyes twinkling. "Vacillate when it comes to a particular man?"

"Exactly." He slumped in his chair.

"Depends. Where'd you meet her?" Grandpa Joe asked.

"She and her son live in the apartment above mine, the one where the fire happened."

"Well, there you go, sweetie." Grandma Maggie patted his arm. "She's a single mom, and single moms can be very hesitant when it comes to getting involved. Especially if their past relationship was unhappy. Be patient."

"I don't have a choice. I can hardly talk to her as it is. She's the one who needs patience, and I'm not sure she's even interested in me *that* way."

Grandma Maggie got up and hugged his shoulders. "How could she not be? You're a Haney." With a final squeeze, she crossed the kitchen to the fridge and took out a pitcher of iced tea.

"Gram." Wyatt rolled his eyes. "Being a Haney doesn't mean instant attraction." He cringed inwardly, remembering how it was for him when Sam admitted on the air how women threw themselves at him on the job. His idiot brother had told the radio show's entire listening audience their last name. Women assumed because Wyatt was a Haney too, and he worked at Haney & Sons, he must also be game for after-the-job *activities*. He'd been forced to fend off unwanted advances for weeks after *Loaded Question* had aired. Not something he handled well at all. "I'm not like Sam, you know."

"Sam isn't like Sam anymore either," Grandma Maggie laughed, taking her seat again. "Thank goodness."

"So, you think her being friendly one minute and withdrawing the next might have something to do with being a single mother?" he asked. "She's also a widow."

Gram slid the pitcher of iced tea toward him. "Her ambivalence makes even more sense if that's the case. Perhaps she's still grieving. How long has it been since her husband passed?"

"I have no idea, but it can't be too long ago. She's only twenty-four." Grief might be at the root of her mood swings toward him, but it didn't explain the "you know" part.

"Poor thing." Gram clucked. "So young, and didn't you say she has a son?"

"Yep. Brady. He's a great little guy. Funny. Cute as all get out."

"You have a good heart, Wyatt," Grandpa Joe said, peering at him from beneath his bushy eyebrows. "Always have. If she's someone you can see yourself with in the future, then be patient, and be there for her."

Be there for her? He could do that, especially if it didn't involve talking. He snorted. "I break out in a sweat, and my tongue ties itself into a knot whenever she looks at me. What chance do I have?"

"That'll pass," Grandma Maggie said, her eyes filling with sympathy. "Things will work out."

He hoped they were right. Wyatt dug into his supper. He still had the portrait he'd done for Kayla, which gave him an excuse to knock on her door at some point. He hoped she'd allow him to read more of his comic books to Brady too. If so, that would give him another chance to sit next to her. "Gramps, can I use your workshop to make a frame for an illustration I drew?"

"Of course. You know the rules. Clean up after yourself, and remember to lock up when you're done. Do you remember the combination for the electronic lock?"

"I do, and I will." Gramps had taught him how to use and care for power tools in that workroom. "Do you have any scraps of window casing, trim or quarter round out there I can use?" His grandfather, Wyatt's dad, and his uncles had added the workshop to the back of his grandparents' garage decades ago. In fact, that shop had been the birthplace of their family business. Now it was mostly his grandfather's man cave, and the space had everything a guy could want for tools and workspace.

"Sure. There are a few pieces stacked in the scrap barrel. Help yourself."

"Thanks. Great chicken, Gram," Wyatt said around a mouthful. Be patient. If that's what it took, he'd be a rock, silent and still. He'd be as patient as time itself. Whatever Kayla needed, he'd be there for her.

"Thanks for supper and for listening. I'll do the dishes tonight." Feeling much more settled than he had before talking things through, he now had a plan. Patience and persistence. The patient-as-stone part he already had down pat. He'd work on the persistence part.

Being an electrician wasn't nearly as glamorous as people might think. Wyatt brushed remnants of old particleboard from his shoulders on the way to his truck. He often worked in tight, nasty places where he had to deal with old insulation and years of accumulated dust. Like today. This had been one of *those* Mondays. He was itchy all over and covered in a fine grit.

At least he'd finished the job a little early, which meant he had time to hurry home for a shower before meeting his pack at The Bulldog. He gave himself a final shake and brush-off, put his tools away and climbed into his truck to set out for home.

Kayla's car was already in its spot when he pulled into the back. Wyatt's breath caught. Not that he'd see her or anything, but knowing she was there—one floor above his apartment—affected him that much. Wyatt looked at her second floor windows as he strode to the back door.

He met Floyd and a serious-looking guy carrying a metal clipboard and a camera coming down the stairs to Wyatt's floor. The insurance adjuster, no doubt. Floyd glared and mouthed the word *asshole* as he passed. Wyatt ignored him and took the stairs two at a time to Kayla's apartment. He knocked on her door and waited.

"Who's there?" Brady called from the other side.

The kid must see asking who was on the other side of their door as his life's work. "It's Wyatt," he said, grinning. The door swung open, and heat rushed up his neck to fill his face. Kayla stood with her hands on Brady's shoulders, a welcoming light filling her pretty blue eyes.

"Hi," she said, her voice slightly breathless.

"Hi back." Wyatt held out his fist for Brady, but Kayla bumped it first. Her teasing smile weakened his knees.

"Hey," Brady protested, scowling at his mom over his shoulder.

Kayla laughed and held the door open wider. "Come in."

Wyatt tousled the kid's hair as he entered. "Was that the insurance adjuster I saw leaving the building?"

"It was." She gave him a once over and frowned. "Wow. Where did you work today, in a crawl space under an old house? You're a mess."

"Close. In a nasty old attic. Did the insurance adjuster say anything?"

"Let's sit. It's been a long day, and I've been on my feet for most of it," she said, leading the way toward the dining room. "The adjuster didn't say anything, but I sure got an earful from Floyd before the insurance guy got here. He's pretty pissed at you."

"Yeah, I got that impression." He snorted. "Does it have anything to do with the many complaints I've sent about him to the owners?"

"Yep. Do you want anything? Bottled water or a soda?"

He pulled out a chair and sat. "No. I'm fine, thanks."

Kayla took a seat, and Brady climbed onto her lap. "Citing the many complaints they've received—you weren't the only one to send complaints, by the way—Floyd has been let go. The owners have hired a property management company to take care of our building, and Floyd has to start paying full rent for his crappy basement apartment or move out."

"Ah. At least I'm not the only one on the receiving end of his hostility." Wyatt shook his head.

"The insurance adjuster took pictures, measured, and wrote a bunch of stuff on an official looking form. Floyd had to take him to see the basement to check out the electrical down there as well. I hope this means something will be done soon."

"Me too." At least he knew for sure why Floyd had been such a jerk. "Did he mention the name of the property management company?"

"No, but I'm sure we'll hear soon enough. Someone will come by and leave contact information for us."

"Wyatt, will you read me one of your comic books tonight?" Brady slid from his mom's lap and came to stand before him. "Can he stay for supper, Mommy?"

"I'd love to, buddy, but I have plans tonight. Maybe another time." A fierce blush suffused his face, but he forced himself to glance at Kayla anyway. "My brother and sister, Haley and I are meeting at The Bulldog for burgers and beer in a little while. Have you ever been there? It's not too far from here."

"No." She arched an eyebrow and tipped her head in Brady's direction with a wry smile. "Other than school, a trip to McDonald's now and then, and the playground, I don't get out much."

"Maybe Mariah would be willing to watch Brady for a couple of hours." *Gulp.* "Would you like to join us?" He'd done it. His heart raced like he'd run a marathon, his mouth turned into a moisture-free zone, but he'd managed to get the words past his lips. He'd asked the Mysterious Ms. M out for burgers and beer, and he hadn't even planned to.

Holding his breath, he studied her, trying to gauge her reaction. Her mouth opened slightly, and her eyes widened. He'd surprised her, and it was clear the surprise hadn't been unpleasant. *Yes. Hurdle cleared.* He refrained from fist pumping the air.

"I'd love to, but . . . Mariah is working second shift today. She's already gone."

He rose, disappointment and relief chasing through him simultaneously. She'd said she'd love to . . . Oh, God, she'd said *yes.* He stood up and held out his fist for Brady to bump, which the kid did with enthusiasm.

"My turn for a rain check?" Wyatt asked. "Reading another comic book to Brady and burgers and beer out with the gang sometime soon?" *Go me!*

"Sure." Kayla got up and followed him to her door.

"I have a bunch of teenage cousins who babysit. They've all gone through the YMCA's babysitter-training classes. If you ever want their names and numbers . . ."

"I'm always looking for backup sitters. That would be great."

He nodded and floated into the hall on a fat, fluffy white cloud of euphoria.

She leaned against the doorframe and crossed her arms. "I'd love to get to know Haley better, your sister and brother too. Being an Iowa transplant, I'm always glad to make new friends in the area." She flashed him one of her heart-stopping smiles. "Let me know the next time you plan to meet them somewhere, and I'll ask Mariah to watch Brady."

"OK."

"G'night, Wyatt."

Wyatt nodded, and she closed her door. His fluffy white cloud of euphoria turned to a gray mist of confusion. Kayla had said yes because she wanted to get to know his soon-to-be sister-in-law better? So, did that mean she had no interest in him, or . . . what? What the hell did it mean? Shaking his head, he made his way to his apartment for a much-needed shower, not only to rid him of the grit covering him but to clear his head too.

An hour and a half later, he walked through The Bulldog's front doors and scanned the busy bar and grill. Josey waved at him from a table next to the large front windows. He waved back and made his way to her. "No sign of Sam and Haley yet?" He took a seat.

"They're right behind you." Josey jutted her chin toward the door and held up her hand to catch their attention.

Wyatt glanced over his shoulder as Sam and Haley approached. He'd already talked things through with his grandparents, and it had helped, but, man, did he appreciate the three people joining him at this table tonight. Once greetings and getting settled were out of the way, the server stopped by their table, and they all ordered beer, with the exception of Haley, who always had hard cider instead.

Wyatt waited until the server left, and then he leaned in. "I asked Kayla to join us tonight." Haley and Josey squealed and fussed over him, and he couldn't keep the grin off his face.

"So, where is she?" Sam leaned back in his chair and cocked an eyebrow.

"She said she'd love to join us, but she didn't have a babysitter for Brady. The next time we get together, I'm supposed to let her know, and she'll ask a friend who lives in our building to watch him." Wyatt glanced around the table. "I'm counting on you guys to help me out here. Can we schedule another night out soon?"

"So you managed to ask her out." Josey shoved his shoulder. "I'm happy for you, Wyatt."

"Thanks, but I'm not sure she sees me as anything but a potential friend. When I asked her to join us, she said she'd like to get to know Haley, you, and Sam. I have no idea if she's interested in me, or if she's just looking to expand her social circle." He shook his head. "Half the time I spend with her I have no idea what she means."

He launched into the short version of his interactions with Kayla and Brady, including her cryptic "you know" statement. "What do you think?" He looked to Haley and then to Josey. "She's a widow and a single mom, by the way."

Haley canted her head. "She's probably protecting herself, but I have no clue what she thinks there is to know about you."

"Me either. Are you holding out on us, bro?" Josey teased.

"No." He huffed out a laugh. "I'm not even a little bit complicated *or* secretive."

Their drinks came, and they put in their food orders. "How're things coming along with your upstairs remodeling?" he asked Sam and Haley. That started a conversation about the updates, then Josey shared her most recent dating fiascoes and finally they settled into talking about their lives in general.

Wyatt relaxed. Completely. These were his people, his pack. They had his back and he had theirs, and he thanked his lucky stars every day that he had his brother, sister and Haley in his life. But it wasn't enough.

He craved intimacy. He wanted the same kind of closeness Sam had with Haley, someone to call his own and who would see him as her own. How crazy wonderful would it be to go to bed every night with a woman he loved, to hold her in his arms while they slept, and wake up to greet her with a smile and a kiss each and every morning.

Man, he wanted that more than anything. Could Kayla be that someone? He didn't know, but he hoped. Patience no longer came so easily since he'd met Kayla—patience with himself or with the situation, because he'd wanted the same thing for so damned long. If it weren't for his shyness, he might have that life already.

His mom and dad had been great together and the best parents a kid could have. He was pretty sure his grandparents still had the hots for each other, even after all the years they'd been together. Wyatt didn't need fame or fortune. He didn't need to go down in history or make the news. All he wanted was to love and be loved in return. Give him a couple of kids, a house near his extended family, and he'd be a happy man. Yet what he wanted seemed to be the most difficult and elusive goal he'd ever set for himself.

"Anything going on with your comic books?" Sam asked.

"Huh?" His attention returned to the present. "Oh. No, not much. Kayla has an aunt who writes children's books. She says her aunt didn't get anywhere either until she had an agent. Kayla thinks I should look for an agent, but I haven't had any time lately. That'll be my next step."

Josey and Haley were deep into a conversation about wedding stuff, and his brother leaned closer. "So, you really like this girl?"

"Well, I'd really like to get to know her better." Wyatt picked at the label on his beer bottle. "I'm attracted to her."

"We'll help anyway we can. You know that, right?"

Affection and gratitude swelled in his chest, and he managed to nod. Their food arrived, and that stopped conversation for a while.

"Should we try for next Monday? If you tell her right away, that'll give Kayla a week to arrange for a babysitter," Josey said. "You can always call one of the second cousins to sit for her, you know."

"Or even Grandma Maggie and Grandpa Joe might be willing," Sam suggested.

"Sure. Let's plan on next Monday, and I'll call one or two of the cousins for backup in case Kayla's friend isn't available." Anticipation surged, and he grinned. He'd asked Kayla out, and she'd said yes. Maybe he could muster up the nerve to kiss her good night after their first date. That thought set off a whole host of erotic thoughts about her, his hands on her soft, generous curves. Kisses that led to touches, touches that led to—

"Pass the ketchup, Wyatt," Haley said.

Heat flooded his face. He passed her the ketchup and focused on his burger. Thank God thoughts and images didn't appear in bubbles above his head the way dialogue did in his comic books.

Chapter Five

Kayla stood in front of her stove, stirring the chicken noodle soup she'd made for supper. Someone knocked on her apartment door. She turned down the flame beneath the pot just as Brady went into his *who's there* doorman routine. Chuckling she hurried to join her son.

"It's Wyatt," Brady announced, his eye wide with excitement.

She opened her door. "Howdy, neighbor. What brings you to our door this fine Tuesday evening?" Hopefully he didn't notice the way she went breathless at the sight of him.

"You said to let you know the next time my brother and sister, Haley and I are planning to get together." Wyatt handed her a sheet of paper, his face tinged with the beginnings of a blush. "We're getting together next Monday at The Bulldog. Are you free?"

She gaped at him. "You were serious about my joining you?"

"Why wouldn't I be?" His Adam's apple bobbed.

"I thought you were being Minnesota nice." She stared at the sheet of paper. Names and telephone numbers? "You know, polite, because Brady put you on the spot by asking you to stay for supper and all."

"Nope. I meant it." Wyatt pointed to the list in her hand. "Those are a few of my cousins who said they'd be willing to watch Brady. They're all experienced, responsible babysitters."

"I'm not a baby," Brady protested.

"Did I say babysitters?" Wyatt grinned. "I meant Superkid sitters." He shifted his weight from one foot to the other. "If Mariah isn't available, I'll pick up whoever you choose from the list and drive them home afterward."

"Oh." Brilliant response, but her brain had seized up at *Nope. I meant it.* He'd even put together a list of sitters for her.

"So? Are you in? We'd love to have you join us." Wyatt stopped rocking and widened his stance.

Was he bracing himself for her reply? The "we'd love to have you join us" brought her back to reality. He wasn't asking her on a date. He was inviting her to join the group. *Duh. He's engaged to Haley.* "Sure. I'd love to."

Brady tugged at the hem of her T-shirt. She set her hand on his head and looked down at him. "What?"

"Can Wyatt eat supper with us *tonight*, and read a comic book to me?"

Her gaze swung to Wyatt. His eyes met hers, his expression inscrutable, but his face an interesting shade of cerise. "Would you like to stay for supper? We're having homemade chicken noodle soup and blueberry muffins." There went his Adam's apple again, and didn't that just send her pulse racing.

"I'd love to. Let me go downstairs for installment number *two*"— he held up his hands and spread his fingers—"in the ELEC-elec-elec TRIC-tric-tric SAGA-saga-saga," he said in comic book echo speak. He winked. "I'll be right back."

"Yeah!" Brady jumped up and down beside her.

Wyatt took off, clomping down the stairs in a noisy rush, probably skipping a couple steps in his haste. Baffled, Kayla stood frozen to the spot. He sure was making it hard for her to avoid him. Perhaps the two of them needed to have a frank discussion. She'd make it clear she wasn't interested in coming between him and his fiancée.

Having suffered through that particular brand of brokenheartedness herself, she definitely had an aversion to becoming the other woman—and for dating in general. Her poor heart still hadn't recovered from the injuries sustained from her sham of a marriage. She might not ever recover. The entire thing had been one colossal, stupid, painful mistake from the beginning to its catastrophic end.

Brady had been the only good thing to come out of the fiasco. She ran her fingers through her son's hair as the two of them waited at the door for Wyatt's return.

It could be Wyatt had asked her to join them in an effort to be nice to the new kid on the block. Haley had certainly been friendly when they'd met in the hall that day. Perhaps *she'd* been the one to encourage Wyatt to include her in their circle. His apartment door shut downstairs, and her tummy fluttered. There wasn't anything wrong with sharing a meal with a neighbor, was there? Especially when doing so involved another comic book reading.

Oh. Right. That made sense. Wyatt must love having an appreciative audience for his work. As shy as he was, she and Brady might be his only fans. Whatever the reason, the entire situation was driving her buggy.

She'd accepted the invitation because she wanted to meet Wyatt's siblings. Even more important, she was dying to see how he interacted with Haley—*his fiancée.* Were they openly affectionate with each other? Haley's face certainly had that "I'm in love" glow the day Kayla had met her.

Wyatt's rapid footsteps climbing the stairs back to her apartment sent her pulse racing again. He wasn't even winded from running up the stairs when he came through her door. She turned Brady toward the dining room and gave him a little push. "Go wash your hands, kiddo."

"I already did," Wyatt said, closing the door behind him.

"I meant the *other* kiddo," she quipped. Wyatt walked through her living room to set his comic book on the coffee table. For a tall man, his movements were easy, fluid, like he was comfortable in his skin, even though he wasn't comfortable with people. Lean, with nicely formed biceps, narrow hips and long legs, he reminded her of the runners she'd seen on TV during the Olympics. "Do you jog?"

His brow rose, and fresh color filled his cheeks. "I was in track and field in high school, and I've run a few half marathons locally, but not so much lately. Why?"

"You have a runner's body. Your legs are so long." Long enough to outrun trouble. Maybe she should warn him about her acres of emotional crap. Friends warned friends, didn't they? Brady returned and held up his clean hands for inspection. "You pass," she said. She took his hand, led him to the dining room and lifted him onto his seat.

The table had already been set for two, and Kayla went to the cupboard for another bowl and a bread plate. She turned to take them to the table and almost collided with Wyatt. He was right there, sleeveless hoodie and all that sex appeal way too up close and personal. Close enough that she could hear him breathing and feel his body heat. Mmm. He smelled good, too, like soap and clean man. He must've showered before coming to knock on her door.

"Do you ever go without a hood?" she blurted. Nerves. It had to be nerves. Was it her fault her eyes had a mind of their own and roamed all over his face? He had such a nice mouth. Wide. Generous. Kissable.

His brow rose even higher, and his oh-so-sexy brown eyes took on a teasing glint. "Occasionally I'll sleep without a hood on, but that's about it." He took the plate and bowl from her, his fingers sliding over hers.

"Is it because of the scars? Do they bother you, because they're not that bad, you know. You're a really nice-looking man."

"As to the first part, yes. The scars bother me. I used to get teased a lot when I was a kid, and people stare." He shrugged. "Being stared at is uncomfortable. I know the hoods don't hide them, but they're a habit. As to the second part, I'm glad you think I'm nice looking."

Again, a current of tingly goodness shot through her. She swallowed against the sudden dryness in her mouth and turned off the burner under the soup. Kayla took a spoon and knife from a drawer and brought them to the table. "Were you always shy, or is it something that happened after your accident, with the scars and the stares?" What was with her mouth today?

Wyatt chuckled. "Did you compile a things-to-ask-my-neighbor list this week or something?"

"No. I'm sorry. None of my business." Once she'd transferred the soup into a serving bowl and placed everything in the middle of her table, she took her place.

"I want lots of noodles, Mommy."

"Have you forgotten how to say *please*?"

"Lots of noodles, *please and thank you*." Brady shot her a disgruntled look.

"That's better." Kayla split a muffin for her son and filled his soup bowl with mostly noodles before serving herself.

"I don't mind your questions. I've always been shy," Wyatt said, touching her fingers again as he took the ladle from her. "My third-grade teacher wanted to have me tested for special education. That was long before my accident and before I lost my parents. Mrs. Wright thought I was mildly mentally impaired, because I never said a word in class, and I wasn't very social at recess or during free time." He shook some pepper into his soup. "She even accused me of having my brother or sister do my homework for me."

"Oh, man. What an awful thing to do to a little kid just because they're quiet," she said.

He nodded. "My mom and dad were livid. They told my teacher in no uncertain terms there was nothing *wrong* with me. I was just shy and introverted. My parents brought in some of the things I'd done at home, samples of my work to share during a meeting about me at my school."

Kayla's heart broke for Wyatt. Her own son was shy, and the thought of a teacher misinterpreting his silence for any kind of deficit brought on a rush of protectiveness for her little guy—and for Wyatt. "What kind of work?"

"I was already drawing comic books and writing stories by then." He flashed her a crooked smile. "Being a member of a family in the construction industry, I'd also learned what tape measures, T squares and levels were for about the same time I stopped wearing diapers."

"How old was that?" Brady piped in. "I was potty trained before I was two. Right, Mommy?"

Kayla chuckled. "That's right."

"Like I said." Wyatt winked at Brady. "You're Superkid. I would expect nothing less."

Brady basked in Wyatt's praise, and her insides warmed. "Go on with your story," she prompted.

"OK. Well, thanks to my dad and my granddad, I'd been figuring area and perimeter and designing fortresses and stuff for my superheroes since second grade. Mom and Dad brought in a pile of drawings and stories I'd written, things I'd built with scraps of wood."

He grunted. "I'll never forget that meeting, which included my teacher, the principal, the school psychologist and the special educa-tion team. My parents also brought all my glowing report cards from kindergarten on up to when I was placed in Mrs. Wright's third-grade classroom. They set her straight about who did my homework, and it was pretty obvious to everyone that Mrs. Wright was completely wrong. Instead of getting tested for special education, I was moved to a different classroom."

"Wow."

"Yep." He nodded and took a spoonful of her homemade soup. "Mmm."

"No, I mean *wow*. That's the most you've ever said to me at once," she teased.

Of course that caused his face to color up.

"I'll bet you can't tell a lie to save your life, can you?"

"Probably not, which is why I didn't even try to get away with anything as a teen." Wyatt reached for his muffin and peeled the paper from the sides. "Great soup. I know who to call when I'm sick with a cold. Did you make the muffins too?"

She did a little basking of her own. "They're store bought. I do bake, but not so much in the summer. It gets so hot in here when I use the oven, and I don't have the time during the weekdays anyway."

"Oh, right. You have school and all. How was your day?" he asked, breaking off a piece of muffin and popping it into his mouth.

He asked as if he really wanted to know, and another flood of warmth washed through her. When was the last time a man in her life cared enough to ask how her day had been? "It was good. I get to work on actual people now, which is a lot more interesting than being in classes all day."

"Did you always want to be a dental hygienist?"

Her gaze touched upon her son for a second, and the familiar mixture of unconditional love and regret tightened her chest. "Not really. I wanted a four-year degree, and I'd been accepted at Iowa State." Of course, her plans had fallen apart once she'd found out she was pregnant. A lot of dreams got squashed after that. Not just hers.

"After my husband passed, I got an insurance settlement, and I receive survivor benefits. I figured I'd use some of the insurance money to go to school and opted for a program I could finish in a couple of years. I need to come out with an employable skill, and dental hygienists are in demand right now. I've thought about becoming a maxillofacial surgical assistant. Maybe at some point I'll continue my education. We'll see."

"Smart." Wyatt's eyes filled with an appreciation as he regarded her. "You're a great mom, Kayla, and Brady is an amazing little boy."

Her eyes filled so fast she had no chance to shut off the tears before they leaked down her face. "Thanks," she whispered, grabbing a napkin to blot her cheeks. Hearing this funny, sweet, creative man say something so nice about her, seeing her son bask in the warmth of Wyatt's praise . . . He'd managed to get through a few cracks in the shell she wore around her heart. "Gah. Let's change the subject."

"Whoa, I didn't mean to—"

"Mommy, are you crying?" Brady's tone held a note of anxiety.

"I accidentally bit my tongue. That's all, kiddo. I'm fine." She straightened, drew in a breath and pulled herself together. She did a pretty good job too, but then Wyatt placed his hand on her shoulder, giving her a gentle squeeze, and she almost fell apart again.

"Guess what I have for dessert, you two?" she asked.

"What?" Brady asked, and both of them looked to her with identical expressions of avid interest.

"Oreo-cookie ice cream."

"All right!" Wyatt held out his palm to Brady, and they high-fived each other.

Kayla laughed. "You two are so easy to please." She sucked in a breath as the impact of her words registered. Nothing had been easy with Brady's dad. He'd turned everything into an argument and a struggle. Oh, she liked to fool herself into thinking she didn't want to date because of school and Brady, but her aversion to involvement ran way deeper.

By the time they'd all finished eating, the pot of soup, which was supposed to have lasted for a few more meals, had been reduced to just enough for her school lunch tomorrow. She probably shouldn't feel so pleased that Wyatt had eaten three helpings, but she was. Kayla started to clear the table. Wyatt helped, and then he wiped down the kitchen counters, brushing her arm and bumping into her at every turn. Again.

"This kitchen is too small for two people," she huffed, her poor nerves stretched to the point of snapping. "Let's go read your comic book. I'll do the dishes after Brady goes to bed."

"OK." Wyatt folded the dishcloth he was holding and draped it over the faucet. "If you want, I can stay and help clean up."

Oh, man. That was a shade of red she hadn't seen on his face before. Offering to stay must have been really difficult for him. She said nothing and gestured toward the living room. Brady was already there, turning the pages of Wyatt's comic book to look at the illustrations. "You shouldn't touch Wyatt's comic book without permission, buddy."

Brady's face fell, and he put his hands behind his back. "I was jus' *looking*. I wasn't touching."

"It's OK, Superkid. That's a copy." Wyatt placed his hand at the small of Kayla's back as they moved to the couch. "I keep the originals in a cabinet," he said, leaning close. "The copies are for show-and-tell, so I don't mind if Brady wants to page through the pictures on his own."

Her breath caught, and a tingle spread from the point of contact through her entire being. "You know what? I'm going to let you read to Brady, and I'm going to do the dishes." She stepped away from his alluring every-damn-thing-about-him self. "I can hear you reading from the kitchen anyway."

Peeking at him out of the corner of her eye, she couldn't help but catch the way his face fell, just like Brady's had when she'd told him not to touch the comic book. If Wyatt knew how he affected her, he'd understand, but she wasn't about to open that can of awkward. "I'll join you two when I'm finished. It won't take more than a few min-utes." Yeah, she'd stretch it out as long as she had to.

"All right." Wyatt joined Brady on the couch.

Kayla returned to the safety of her kitchen. Thou shalt not covet another woman's fiancé. She was pretty sure if the Ten Commandments were to be rewritten for modern times, that one would be on the list, number two or three at least. She filled the plastic tub in her sink with sudsy water, bowls and plates.

By the time the dishes were clean, Wyatt had finished reading his comic book. She'd heard everything, including Brady's endless questions. She'd been impressed with how patient Wyatt was with her son. He'd answered every one without a hint of exasperation. Kayla walked into her living room. Her insides melted again at the sight of Brady leaning against Wyatt, one of his hands placed trustingly on Wyatt's forearm.

"That was a great story. Lots of action, and I'm *so* glad Elec Tric chose to go with the good side." She grinned. "Have you done an agent search yet?"

"Nope. Not yet. Summer is the busy season for construction, and I haven't really had the chance to give it much thought." He gathered his comic book pages together into a neat pile and put the clip back on the upper corner. "I'll get to it this coming winter."

"Right. But then it'll be wedding stuff taking up all of your spare time."

"Other than the bachelor party, I don't really have a lot to do with the busy stuff." Wyatt tousled Brady's hair as he rose from his place beside her son.

"I suppose not. All you have to do is show up." Kayla's stomach clutched at the thought. "Thanks so much for sharing your comic books with us, Wyatt. They're really good."

"You're welcome. It's great to have someone to share them with. My work mostly sits on a shelf." Wyatt crossed the room to the door.

"Thanks for feeding me tonight. In case our paths don't cross before next Monday, I'll be by for you at six. Let me know before then if I need to pick up a cousin to sit with Brady."

"I will." When Wyatt finally disappeared down the stairs, she closed the door. "Are you ready for a bath?" She ran her fingers through her son's thick hair, so like hers.

"Can I have toys this time?" he asked, peering up at her.

"Sure. It's still early. After you wash, you can play in the tub until your skin turns all wrinkly." She tickled his ribs, reveling in the sound of his giggles. "And then it's bedtime."

"OK." He ran to his toy box for his favorite toys for the tub.

Was she making another colossal mistake by agreeing to join Wyatt at The Bulldog on Monday night? Probably, but maybe if she saw how sweet he and Haley were together, she could quash her annoying obsession with him and be happy for the couple. "Like that'll happen."

"What, Mommy?"

"Nothing, sweetie. Just thinking out loud." She followed her son into the bathroom to get his bath ready. After she put Brady to bed, she'd take a nice hot bath herself, and then do some studying in bed. Hopefully the hot water would calm her overstimulated nerves, and the studying would put her to sleep. *Not likely.*

Kayla let Brady knock on Mariah's door, and it swung open on the second rap. She smiled at Rosie. "Hey, look who I brought to play with you tonight." Mariah stood behind her daughter, and Kayla handed her the bag with Brady's jammies and toothbrush.

Rosie grabbed Brady's hand. "Come on. I got my toys in my room." She glanced at her mother. "Can we go play?"

"Sure. Go." Mariah waved them away, and the two of them ran off together down the hall.

"Am I doing the right thing here, Mariah? Is it weird that someone else's fiancé is picking me up *without* her? Shouldn't I be meeting them there?"

"You're overthinking this. Does it make much sense to take two cars when you're both starting out and returning to the same place? That would be fuelish."

"Fuelish? I guess you're right." She bit her lip. "But—"

"There you are." Wyatt crossed the hall. "Hi, Mariah. Thanks for watching Brady tonight."

"I'm always happy to have Brady hang out with us," she said. "He keeps Rosie busy, and I get to enjoy a few hours to myself. I might even read or watch an entire TV show without interruption."

"You ready to go?" Wyatt glanced at Kayla, his face going crimson.

"I just need to grab my purse." She pulled her keys from her back pocket. "We won't be too late, Mariah."

"Don't feel like you have to hurry home," she replied, waving them away like she had with the kids. "I'll have Brady in his jammies and his teeth brushed. He can nap on my couch until you pick him up."

"Thanks. Bye." Kayla crossed the hall to her door, her midriff a riot of flutters. She hadn't felt this stirred up since her first junior high school dance. "I'll be right back," she muttered as she unlocked her deadbolt and shot through the door. She hurried to her bathroom to check her makeup and brush her hair one last time. Grabbing her purse from the dining room table, she joined Wyatt in the hall and locked her door. "OK. Let's go."

He gestured toward the back stairs. "I hope you like The Bulldog. They have great food. It's one of our favorite places to hang out. Do you play pool?"

"No." She gripped the railing on her way down the stairs. "Why? Are we going to play pool there?"

"Uh . . . no. The Bulldog doesn't have tables."

She huffed out a nervous laugh and glanced at him. "Then why'd you ask?"

"Just . . . wondering." His face turned a darker red.

Why did this feel like a first date? Five people getting together for bar food and beer was no big deal. She wrestled her nerves into submission. "So, you're an electrician in your family's business. Are your brother and sister part of the company too?"

"Yep. Sam is a carpenter, and Josey is a licensed plumber, although she can do just about anything, including fixing cars." He opened the back door for her. "Sam is pretty versatile too, but other than helping with heavy lifting, I stick with electrical stuff." They crossed the lot to his truck, and he opened the passenger side door for her before striding around to the driver's side.

"Why do they do all kinds of stuff and you don't?" she asked once he was settled behind the wheel.

"Because we do a lot of handyman jobs besides construction." He started the engine and twisted around to watch over his shoulder as he backed out of his spot.

Kayla frowned and fastened her seat belt. "I don't get it. You stick with electrical stuff because of handyman jobs?"

"That's it exactly." He grinned. "Lots of people call a handyman rather than a plumber, because they think it's less expensive. Clogged toilets and drains make me gag. Have you ever seen what comes out of bathroom drains?" He shuddered. "I really don't understand why my sister chose that profession at all."

She laughed. "Well, now I get why you stick with electricity."

"I do have other skills, but I'm not interested in carpentry. I don't like slivers or sore thumbs."

"Did you always want to be an electrician?"

"No." He checked the street for oncoming traffic and turned onto the main road toward downtown. "I wanted to be Superman when I grew up, but I couldn't find a school offering superhero classes."

"At least you have the cape," she teased.

"Yeah, but it doesn't fit me anymore." He flashed her a crooked smile. "So, naturally, I became an electrician."

She canted her head, pretending to think about what he'd said. "I can see how one led to the other."

"You can?" He looked askance at her, his eyes wide.

"Sure. Wiring things to light up or perform a task with electricity is kind of a superpower. I couldn't do it."

"But you can clean teeth. I couldn't do that."

She snorted. "Because working in other people's mouths all day would make you gag?"

"Probably." He chuckled.

Smiling, she settled back, no longer nervous. Wyatt was her friend, and maybe Haley would be too. Having friends was a good thing, and eventually she'd get over her unfortunate attraction to him. "You're funny."

"Funny good, or funny odd?"

Their gazes met for a hot second, and he looked so vulnerable, she wanted to reach out and take his hand. He swallowed. Could it be his mouth had gone as dry as hers? "Definitely funny good," she said, twining her fingers together on her lap.

He nodded and focused on driving. Ten minutes later, they were parking at a metered spot next to Mears Park. "The Bulldog is right across the street." He pointed before climbing out of the pickup and coming around to her side to open the door.

"You don't have to do that, you know."

"Do what?"

"Open doors for me. I can manage."

"Does it offend you when I do?"

80

"No. Not at all, but—"

"Good, because Grandpa Joe raised me and my brother old-style, and it's a hard habit to break. I'd hear his voice scolding me inside my head if I didn't open doors for you. And if not his scolding voice, then Grandma Maggie's, which is worse."

Wyatt took care of entering his debit card into the meter, and she couldn't tear her eyes from him. What was it about this man that she found so fascinating? He wasn't available, and really, that was for the best, because neither was she.

She directed her attention toward the park. It had been nicely landscaped, with white birch trees growing along a man-made stream lined with boulders.

"All set," Wyatt said from beside her.

Kayla slung her purse strap over her shoulder. "Lead the way."

They crossed the street and approached the bar and restaurant, which was situated on the first floor of an old red-brick building. The front faced the park, and people took advantage of the sidewalk tables by the entrance. Wyatt held the door for her, and they had to push their way through the crowded entry and the bar area to search the interior. Wyatt waved, took her elbow and guided her across the floor where Haley and Wyatt's brother were already seated.

"Josey's not here yet?" Wyatt asked, pulling out a chair for her.

"She was held up at a job, but she's on her way." Haley smiled at Kayla. "Glad you could join us."

"Thanks." She took a seat, her stomach twisting with nervousness.

"You've already met Haley, and this is my brother, Sam." Wyatt slid into the chair between her and Haley. "Sam, this is Kayla Malone."

"Nice to finally meet you." Sam's smile was openly curious and friendly.

"Nice to meet you too." Oh, wait. Had Wyatt asked her to join them in an effort to fix her up with his brother? Why hadn't that occurred to her before? Though, looking at him, she couldn't imagine Sam needing anyone's help finding dates.

A server came by, set coasters down and asked if she and Wyatt wanted anything from the bar. Wyatt ordered a beer, and she told the server to bring her the same.

"Here comes Josey," Haley said, holding up her hand to wave.

Kayla studied Wyatt's sister. Good looks definitely ran in the Haney family. Josey's hair was more tawny blonde, thick and straight like Wyatt's, while Sam's was lighter and wavy. Josey wasn't very tall, but what she lacked in height, she made up for in fitness. She wore a denim skirt and a soft cotton top. The males at the bar definitely took notice as she walked by.

"Hey," Josey said, sliding into a seat. "Sorry I'm late. I ran into a sewer drain with stubborn tree roots growing through it, and it took a little longer to clear them out than I thought."

"No problem." Wyatt slung his arm around the back of Kayla's chair. "This is Kayla Malone. This is my sister, Josey."

"Glad you could make it tonight," Josey said with a welcoming grin. Then her attention swung to Haley. "You know what occurred to me about your name on the way here?"

Haley rolled her eyes. "I can hardly wait to hear."

"Me too." Wyatt barked out a laugh.

"Well," Josey's gaze turned solemn. "After you and Sam are married—"

What? Kayla blinked. *Wait. Haley is marrying Sam . . . not Wyatt? Oh, hell.*

"The first two letters of your first name are *H*, *A*, and the first two letters of your last name will be *H*, *A*. That makes you—"

"Ha-Ha," Haley muttered.

"Exactly." Josey laughed and high-fived Wyatt. "It's the perfect nickname."

"Very funny," Haley said, her tone flat. "Do you see now why you have to take my last name, Sam? These two clowns will never let up with their lame jokes. Last week, Wyatt told me the 4-H organization would be calling soon, because my initials will be too close to infringing on their trademark. If we don't go with Cooper, I'm going to have to deal with this crap for the next fifty years."

"I hope it's more than fifty years, Ha-Ha," Sam teased, putting his arm around Haley's shoulders and drawing her close for a hug.

Wyatt winked at Kayla. "We do tease her a lot, but it's only because we love her."

She nodded. Stunned, Kayla pressed back against her chair and ran through every time the wedding had come up. He'd never actually said *he* was getting married, and she'd never actually asked the direct question. Talk about monster game changers. *BAM.*

"Want to split an order of the fried pickles?" He slid a menu between them, leaning close so they could read it together. "The burgers here are really good. We could order two different burgers and share those too. You don't have to though. Get whatever you want."

A thrill, followed by a wave of panic, swamped her. Yep. This was a date. This sweet, shy, adorable man had mustered up the nerve to ask her out, and she'd accepted. She'd misled him, and now she had to find a way to explain to him that she wasn't ready to date.

"What's wrong?" Wyatt leaned forward to catch her eye.

"Nothing." Kayla stared at the menu. "Sure, let's share an order of the pickles and a couple of burgers." Why hadn't she noticed earlier he was wearing some kind of aftershave tonight? She took in a lungful of his tantalizing scent. There ought to be a law against a man smelling better than a woman.

"I like the 50/50 burger."

"Of course you do." She snorted. "It's half bacon. How about splitting the turkey avocado sandwich instead of another burger? We can pretend we're eating halfway healthy."

"All right. Tater tots or fries?"

"Tater tots." Honestly, she could hardly breathe, much less eat. His timing was way off. She needed a few years before she could even think of putting her heart on the line again. At the same time, she didn't want to cut him out of her life, which was totally selfish on her part. Could they be friends? Dazed, Kayla half listened to the banter going around the table while struggling to come up with a way to explain to Wyatt exactly why they couldn't be a couple.

Chapter Six

Wyatt had his arm slung across the back of Kayla's chair. They were going to share food. If she was willing to share half her sandwich, wouldn't she also be willing to share a kiss? He was hard-pressed not to test his theory right this minute. Amped up with an entirely different kind of *happy*, he smiled so hard his cheeks hurt, and it all had to do with the woman sitting beside him—the lovely and mysterious Ms. M.

She'd gone quiet once his sister showed up, but Josey had started out by teasing Haley right off the bat. Kayla might be feeling a little out of her element. "Kayla is going to school to become a dental hygienist," he tossed out, giving her shoulder a brief bolstering squeeze.

"Wow. Good for you," Haley said. "How long before you're done?"

"December, and then the big job search begins." Kayla wrapped her hands around her beer mug.

Josey peered at her over the top of her menu. "Don't you have a child?"

"Yes." Her chin lifted slightly. "I have a five-year-old son."

He'd seen the same defensive chin lift when he'd asked her how old she was. Defensiveness was the last thing he wanted her to feel around his family. "His name is Brady," Wyatt added. "He's a great little guy—cute and really bright."

"Thanks," she said, ducking her head. "I think he's pretty wonderful myself."

"It can't be easy managing single parenthood and going to school," Sam said. "How do you do it? Do you work too?"

"No, I don't have a job outside of school, which is more than enough. I have a small income because my husband died in the military. It's not a lot, but it's enough that I get by. Honestly, that's the only reason I can manage."

Heads nodded, and their server returned. "Are we set? Fried pickles, a burger, the turkey sandwich and tater tots?" Wyatt asked her.

"Sure."

He gave the waiter their order, a ridiculous pride swelling his chest. He'd mustered the courage to ask the Mysterious Ms. M out on a date, *and* he'd managed to put her at ease about her son. Once he handed the menu to the waiter, he slid his arm around the back of Kayla's chair again. He could get used to having his arm around her. He *wanted* to get used to having his arm around her.

Still grinning like a fool, he shared a look with his sister. She smiled back, her expression full of approval, and he reveled in a moment of pure bliss. The next date he took her on, it would be just the two of them. A movie, or he'd take her to a Twins game, and he'd hold her hand as they walked to the stadium. "Do you like baseball?"

"Hmm?" Her brow rose.

"Baseball. Do you enjoy watching sports?" He loved sitting so close to her and wanted like hell to be even closer.

"I do, but I've only watched high school sports." Kayla shrugged. "I grew up in a small town. There aren't any professional stadiums nearby."

"Where was that?" Haley asked.

"I was born and raised in Decorah, Iowa, population around eight thousand."

"What about hockey?" Sam asked. "Do you like hockey?"

"My brother coaches a peewee hockey team with one of our cousins," Wyatt explained. "Sam also played in high school."

"I guess I've led a sheltered life. I've never been to a professional game of any sort," Kayla said, her tone rueful. "That's one of the reasons I decided to move to the Twin Cities to go to school. There's so much going on here all the time. Once I finish school, and I'm making a decent living, I plan to take advantage."

"Hockey and baseball games?" Haley flashed her a questioning look.

"Not sports so much. I'm leaning more toward the old State Theatre, the Orpheum, Guthrie and the Ordway." One side of Kayla's mouth quirked up. "I've never been to a live play either, other than high school performances back home. I was even in a few of those dismal productions."

"You know what?" Josey leaned in. "I've been to lots of live concerts, but I've never gone to a play either, and I've lived here my whole life. We should plan a night out at the theater." She looked around the table. "If I do the research, are the rest of you interested?"

"I'm game." He loved that his sister was trying to help him out, and Wyatt wasn't about to pass up the opportunity. "Would you be interested, Kayla?"

"Depends," she said, her eyes fixed on her beer mug.

Great. What did that mean, and why did it feel like she was withdrawing again? He glanced at Sam and Haley. Had they noticed Kayla's noncommittal answer?

"We're in," Haley chimed.

Sam raised his brow. "We are?"

"Sure. It won't kill you to see a play," Haley said, nudging him with her shoulder.

"If you say so, dear," he teased. "So long as it's about hockey."

"Geez. It's a sign. Even my brother's favorite sport starts with an *H*. Unfortunately for you, Haley, it's clear fate meant to stick you with my big brother." Josey snorted.

Wyatt groaned. "Even by my standards, that one stunk."

"Whatever. I'm not complaining." Haley leaned in to kiss Sam's cheek.

"I see what you mean," Sam said, running his hand up and down Haley's arm. "The jokes just get lamer and lamer, and they don't seem to get when to quit."

Another one of those annoying envy pangs hit Wyatt, but this one didn't last long. Maybe someday soon, he and Kayla would tease each other the way couples did, and she'd lean in and kiss *his* cheek.

A few minutes later their food arrived, and the conversation lulled. Wyatt split the burger and made the transfers, so he and Kayla each had half the turkey sandwich and half the burger on their plates. "Anyone want fried pickles?" He took a few, dipped them in sauce before passing the basket to Kayla.

"Sure, I'll take a few," Josey said. "Pass them around."

After the table had been cleared, and they'd had one more beer, their server placed the bill in the center of the table. Kayla reached for her purse, and Wyatt put his hand on her forearm. "I've got this."

"I can put in for my share."

"You bought the pizza the other night. Remember? It's my treat." He fished his wallet out of his pocket.

"But the pizza was to thank you for helping out after the fire."

"And this is to thank you for listening to me read my comic books." He picked up the bill, did a quick tally, put in their share plus a nice tip, and handed the folder to Josey.

She wasn't acting like this was a date anymore. What had changed? This time he'd ask. He no longer felt quite so shy with her, and he had a feeling the *why* might be important.

"Wyatt has shared his comic books with you?" Sam asked.

"Yes, and I think they're amazing. His style really stands out. I suggested he look for an agent. He might have a greater chance at getting published if he has representation."

"You're probably right." Sam set his elbows on the table. "What did you think of his Mysterious Ms. M character?"

Kayla's brow rose. "The Mysterious Ms. M? I don't remember seeing her."

Oh, great. Wyatt's face heated, and he shot his idiot brother a glare. "We haven't gotten that far in the series yet." And they wouldn't for some time to come either.

"What does the *M* stand for?" she studied him.

"Ah . . . I don't know. That's what makes her so mysterious," he mumbled.

"Hmm." She turned away.

Did she suspect the *M* stood for *Malone*? "Well, this was fun, but we promised Kayla's sitter we wouldn't be out too late." He stuffed his wallet back into his pocket. "Ready?"

"I am. Tomorrow is a school day, and it's already past my bedtime." Kayla placed her napkin on the table, pushed her chair back and stood up. "Thanks for including me tonight. This was fun, and I'm glad I got to meet all of you." She smiled and draped her purse over her shoulder.

"We'll do it again," Haley said.

"And we'll plan our theater outing in the next week or so," Josey added.

"See you tomorrow, Wyatt." Sam placed a few bills with the rest of the money in the folder. "Glad you joined us tonight, Kayla."

"Me too." Kayla gave a little wave, and they started for the door.

Wyatt placed his hand at the small of her back, guiding her through the crowd, and out into the humid August evening. "I've noticed it's already getting dark earlier." He steered them down the sidewalk toward the traffic light where they needed to cross.

"Mm-mm." Kayla blew out a breath and glanced back at the door. Then she turned to him. "I thought *you* were marrying Haley."

"Me?" He stopped walking. "Why?"

"Well, you had that wedding-planning thing to go to, and I asked you when the happy day was going to be, and then I met Haley in the hall that day, and she had wedding stuff with her, and she had that glow about her, and—"

"I did have a wedding-planning thing, and it *is* a happy day. Just . . . not mine. I'm Sam's best man." He frowned. "Why would I ask *you* to go out with me if I was *engaged*?"

"I don't know." She twisted the hem of her blouse with both hands and lifted a shoulder. "I thought you were just being friendly because I'm new to the area. It was a group thing, beer and burgers with your siblings and your *fiancée* . . . who happened to be very friendly. I thought it was her idea to include me." She looked toward the park for a second before her gaze returned to meet his. "For a minute there, I even thought you might be trying to fix me up with your brother."

"Umm . . . no." He shook his head and stared. Her pretty blue eyes held uncertainty and a vulnerability that stole his breath. They stood beneath a street lamp, and the soft fluorescent glow gave her a full-body halo, turning her into a demigoddess straight out of his wildest fantasies. He reached for her. Her eyes grew wide, and her mouth opened slightly. Acting on instinct, he drew her close and kissed her. He'd dreamed of kissing her for months, and here she was in his arms.

For an instant, she stiffened. Had he made a disastrous mistake? But then she melted against him and kissed him back, and thinking was beyond him. He drew her closer, his heart pounding like crazy. He couldn't imagine any woman feeling more perfect against him. Kayla's full breasts pressed against his chest, and her arms came up to circle his neck. Desire ignited in a flash, and blood rushed to his groin. Her lips parted, and he slipped his tongue inside to taste her.

"Mmm." He pulled back, drinking in the sight of her from her slightly dazed eyes to her plump kissable lips. "Sweetest dessert ever," he whispered before going in for another taste. His breathing ragged, he deepened their second kiss, wishing like hell they were in his apartment and not standing on a corner under a streetlight.

"PDA alert! PDA alert!" someone called out, and laughter erupted behind them. Wyatt broke the kiss and stepped back without breaking eye contact with Kayla. He ignored the slightly inebriated group passing by them. "I asked you out on a date, because I wanted to spend time with you. Period."

"I can't date you, Wyatt." She averted her gaze, her voice strained.

"OK. Then we'll just hang out a lot." He ran his palms up and down her arms. "I get it. You have school and Brady. They're your priorities right now. I can support that."

"We need to talk," she said to the sidewalk beneath her sandals. "Do you want to sit on a bench in the park for a while?" Her eyes met his for a second before she scanned the park. "Is it safe?"

"I think we'll be all right." His gut churned. He'd much rather kiss. Kissing communicated plenty as far as he was concerned, and he hadn't had nearly enough practice with that kind of communication. Besides, he had no personal experience himself, but even he knew when a woman said she wanted to *talk*, things did not turn out well for the poor schmuck on the receiving end. "Sure, let's talk."

He and Kayla crossed the street and found a spot on one of the long concrete benches running along the perimeter of the small amphitheater. Wyatt searched their surroundings for any suspicious characters. They weren't the only couple in the park tonight. How many of those other conversations had begun with "we need to talk"? His heart had crawled up his throat, and he swallowed a few times in an effort to force it back to where it belonged.

"I guess by now you've figured out that I had to get married." Kayla huffed out a mirthless laugh.

"I hadn't given it any thought." He shrugged. "I mean . . . you're really young to be a mom and a widow, but—"

"Brad and I were a couple of stupid kids who fooled around and got caught." She twisted her hands together in her lap. "We started dating the middle of our senior year. Neither of us had ever had a serious relationship before. We were . . . careless. Stupid." She bit her lip for a few seconds before continuing. "The night of our senior prom, we both lost our virginity—*and* I got pregnant."

What did this have to do with them? Wyatt propped his elbows on his thighs. He had a feeling he was about to find out, and he was pretty sure he wasn't going to like where this conversation was heading. "Oh."

"More like a *BAM* than an *oh*." She raked her fingers through her hair. "Once our parents found out, they put an enormous amount of pressure on the two of us to get married. Brad's father is a minister at a church in town, and he was pretty hot under the collar about the whole thing. Brad and I were only eighteen, and under all that pressure, we caved. We got married right after graduation, and . . ." Her voice broke, and she cleared her throat a couple of times. "And right after our wedding, my husband joined the army. He was that desperate to get away from me."

He couldn't imagine anyone being desperate to get away from Kayla. "I'm sorry."

"Me too." She let out a shaky laugh. "I was the only one who behaved like a married person. On the rare occasions my husband did come home, I'd find texts and e-mails from other women on his phone, and I even found lewd pictures on his laptop. The last letter I got from him, Brad wrote to tell me that as soon as his current tour was up, he planned to divorce me. He said he'd found someone else, and they were in love. A week later, I got word that he'd died."

Her shoulders slumped forward. "I don't miss him, and it makes me feel horrible to admit it." A heavy sigh escaped. "Brad was stateside when our son was born. He could've come home, but he didn't." Bitterness tinged her words. "He wouldn't allow me to live on base, either. That's the worst of it. All Brady ever got from his dad was resentment and neglect."

"Aw, Kayla, I'm so sorry you went through all that, but it's in the past. Your life is heading in a really good direction now. Right? I'm glad you told me, but—"

"But it doesn't have anything to do with the present?" She straightened, her expression pained. "See, most kids graduate from high school and go on to college or some kind of postsecondary training. They date, travel, have fun, start jobs and spend a few years growing up and finding out who they are. *Then* they fall in love, get married and start families. I went from high school straight into motherhood, married to a boy who resented me for getting pregnant and wrecking his life," she said, her voice quavering.

"When Brad died, I swore I'd give myself back the years I'd missed. I need time to grow up and find out who I am and what I want. Besides, my heart is way too beat up to risk dating right now. I'm not going to pretend I'm not attracted to you, because I am. You're hot, funny, creative, intelligent and . . . damn near irresistible, but I'm not ready to get involved." Her expressions tightened. "I went through five years of hell, and those years pretty much reduced me to worthless. Now I'm . . . gun-shy."

The food in his stomach had turned into a lumpy mass in his gut, and the back of his throat burned. "I'm sorry you went through five years of hell. You deserve to be happy, and—"

"You deserve to be happy too, and I'm sorry I misled you. I probably made things worse when we kissed, but you're like chocolate, which happens to be my kryptonite." She faced him, her expression stricken. "Do you think we can be friends after this? I'd really like to be friends, Wyatt."

"Of course. Whatever you need, Kayla." He stood up. "But . . . just for the record, about how long do you think it'll take before you're ready to give dating a try?" He held out his hand to help her up.

She took it and rose from the bench. "I don't know, and I don't want you to wait. I couldn't bear it if I caused you any kind of heartache." With a sad half smile, she reached up and tugged at the front of his hoodie. "I don't want to be the one to prevent you from finding someone amazing, because you're amazing."

Wyatt's insides were a mess of conflicting emotions. *He was her kryptonite?* She saw him as hot, funny, all those good things, but she wouldn't date him? His heart was already aching, and he wanted to kick something, do a little demolition somewhere. Instead, he faked a smile and opened his arms. "Friends hug, don't they? I can't even imagine what it was like for you. You deserve a hug, and I could use one myself about now." Who needed a night at the theater? He was giving her the performance of a lifetime right now.

Kayla sniffed, walked into his arms and circled his waist. "It was awful," she whispered. "Nobody knows about the letter Brad sent, telling me he was divorcing me." She leaned back to peer up at him. "You'll keep that to yourself, right?"

Her eyes were bright with the sheen of tears, and a surge of protectiveness hit him square in the solar plexus. "I won't tell a soul." He cradled the back of her head and brought her close again. She relaxed against him, her cheek resting on his shoulder. She was exactly the right height, with exactly the right curves. He ran his jaw against her silky hair, and a lump formed in his throat again.

He wanted like hell to tell her he'd be there for her, that he'd be the best damned friend she'd ever had, but he couldn't. "We can be friends," he managed to rasp out.

"Can we?" She backed out of his arms. "I mean, it's obvious there's a physical attraction between us, and I—"

"I can handle it. Just have to switch gears is all." He shrugged deeper into his hood.

She studied him for a second, and then she sighed. "We should get going."

"Right." He and Kayla crossed the park and walked to his pickup in silence. He'd gone from the pinnacle—planning future dates with her, picturing them as a couple—to a major letdown in the span of thirty minutes. He'd worked extra hard today so he'd get done in time to go out, and it all caught him with him. He was wiped, emotionally and physically.

Wyatt opened the passenger side of his truck for Kayla before taking care of the meter. He climbed into the driver side and started the engine. "What do you think of Sam, Haley and Jo?"

"They're really great." She leaned her head back against the headrest. "The food was good too. I'm stuffed."

"Yeah. It always is at The Bulldog." That was the extent of their conversation for the rest of the ride home. Wyatt parked the truck in his spot. "I'm sure Brady is sound asleep. If you get the doors, I'll carry him to your apartment for you."

Her brow rose. "Really? Thanks, that would be great. I hate to wake him, but it's not easy trying to carry him and deal with unlocking and opening doors."

"No problem." He climbed out. His chest heavy, he followed Kayla up the stairs to Mariah's apartment and knocked softly.

Mariah opened the door a crack. "Brady's asleep on the couch," she whispered.

"I got this." Wyatt nodded and crept to the couch. He scooped Brady up. The kid opened his eyes, saw who had him and smiled before curling himself over Wyatt's shoulder and wrapping his skinny arms around Wyatt's neck. Wyatt hugged him tight, his heart turned over, and the back of his eyes stung. Kayla's husband had to have been a moron not to have recognized what an amazing gift he'd been given with Brady and Kayla. "Thanks for watching him," he murmured, his tone low.

"Any time," she whispered back. "How'd it go?"

Wyatt's gaze shot to Kayla.

She smiled, but it was the kind of smile that didn't reach her eyes. "We had fun." She backed into the hall. "I'll get my door."

Brady's solid warmth snug against him, Wyatt followed her through her apartment door and down the hall to Brady's bedroom. She pulled the covers back on the twin bed and stepped aside. As soon as Wyatt placed him on the mattress, Brady sighed, turned over and was sound asleep again. Kayla tucked her son in and kissed his forehead.

Wyatt's chest once again swelled with protectiveness. Not just for Kayla, but for Brady too. Kayla tiptoed out of the room, and he followed her to the front door. Pressure banded his chest. "I get how you might think you've missed out on a few things, but you're doing a fantastic job of . . . well, everything, and don't for a minute think otherwise." He fisted his hands to keep from dragging her into his arms again.

"Grandma Maggie says children are like litmus tests when it comes to their environment, and who they are says a lot about how they're being raised. Brady is polite, respectful and he's empathetic. He's a great kid."

"You know all that from the few times you've been with him?" This time her smile was genuine.

"Yes. I've spent some time playing with him and reading to him. I also watched how he played with the kids at the park the other day. He made sure everyone got their turn on the slide, and he's great with Rosie. He minds you well, and he's thoughtful."

She bit her lower lip. "Hearing you say that means the world to me." Her eyes met his for a second before darting away. "I did have a great time tonight, Wyatt. Thank you."

"Friends hang out." He should say more, much more. He wanted to reassure her, make her see things from his perspective, but the words wouldn't come.

She nodded. "See you soon."

Wyatt itched to tuck her hair behind an ear, just to feel the softness against his skin. He yearned for another kiss. Hell, he wanted so much more than friendship, but she was gun-shy, and shyness was something he knew a lot about. "See you," he whispered, turning toward the stairs to his apartment below. "Don't wait for me," she'd said. Like he had a choice.

Wyatt yawned, and blinked his bleary eyes as he crossed the Haney & Sons' kitchen to fill his thermal mug with strong black coffee. He hadn't slept much last night. Too much on his mind, and all of it had centered on Kayla.

"It's almost h-hump day," his cousin Jerry announced as he walked through the door, trailed by Uncle Dan. "H-happy Tuesday."

"If you say so," Wyatt grumbled, taking a seat at the table. Jerry was always bright and cheerful, no matter what the hour. And though he had Down syndrome, he was a productive and valuable member of their team. He sent his cousin a mock scowl. "Mornings aren't my thing, Jer."

Uncle Dan chuckled. "Mornings never have been your thing, have they? I remember when you were a baby. Even then you were a grump in the mornings."

"I guess." All this chatter made him yawn again, and he took a swallow of coffee. "I heard you have a new plumbing apprentice starting this morning, Uncle Dan. Is he meeting you here?"

"Yep. Should be here any minute." Dan filled a mug with coffee, and the door opened again.

Sam and Josey strolled in. "Hey, how'd the rest of your evening go last night?" Josey asked.

His face flaming, he pulled his hoodie lower and slumped down in his chair. "Do we have to talk about that right now?"

"Want to go somewhere for lunch today?" Sam asked. "It doesn't make sense to come all the way back to town, and I didn't pack anything."

"Sure." He, Sam and Jo were working on the same new housing development in Woodbury, a suburb west of Saint Paul. "You want to try that pizza place we've heard the crew talk about? It's not too far. I'll drive."

"Which place is that?" Sam asked.

Jo grinned. "Punch Pizza on City Centre Drive?"

"That's the one." Wyatt nodded.

"OK," Sam said. "Sounds good."

Grandpa Joe swept into the kitchen, just as the new plumbing apprentice entered. After a brief round of welcomes and introductions, Gramps asked for progress reports, and then he turned to Wyatt. "The holding company that owns your building awarded us the bid for the repairs, and I've already faxed the signed contract back to them. They're wiring the materials deposit to us this morning. I'm pulling you and Jonathan for the job starting tomorrow. I've put in an order with Viking Electrical. The supplies should be ready to pick up by this afternoon. I'll call you when I know for sure."

The news brought him fully awake, or maybe it had something to do with the coffee he'd been sucking down. "Great," he said. "I'll stop by on my way home and pick up the materials."

"You need help?" Josey asked.

"I could use an extra set of hands. You offering?"

"Yes."

"Thanks." Friends hang out, he'd told Kayla. Could he handle being around her, knowing all she'd ever want from him was friendship? He could work things out so he didn't have to be in her apartment when she was home. He and Jon, the electrician working with him, had plenty to do with the rest of the building while she was home. The entire place would be rewired, including circuit breakers in the basement, and the city would put in new meters for each of the apartments. Finally. "Anything else, Grandpa Joe?"

Gramps nodded. "Jack will take care of permits. Sam, while Wyatt starts the third floor, I want you and a crew to take care of the compromised floor joists and the door in the damaged apartment. I'll have a contract carpenter take your place in Woodbury Thursday morning." He handed him a sheet of paper from his clipboard. "Here are the measurements. I'll leave it to you to get what you need on the way to the job."

"Will do." Sam patted Wyatt on the back. "Way to go. You got us the job."

"Thanks." Wyatt rose, stretched, and picked up his thermal coffee mug. "Let's get going." Hopefully, working would take his mind off the prospect of friendship with the woman who haunted his dreams and filled his thoughts all day long.

Wyatt slid into the booth next to Josey. "Do you want to split a salad and get a couple of different kinds of pizza?" he asked, picking up a menu.

"Sure. We could do that." Sam took the opposite side. "By the way, we saw you kissing Kayla under the street light last night. Kind of a Fred Astaire and Ginger Rogers moment there, bro. Didn't think you had it in you." He chuckled. "We expected the two of you to bust out the dance moves any second."

"Fred Astaire and Ginger Rogers?" Wyatt looked from Sam to Jo. "Are they from *Dancing with the Stars*?"

Josey barked out a laugh. "You've never seen a Fred Astaire and Ginger Rogers movie? They're silver-screen icons from the 1930s and 1940s."

Wyatt tssked. "What else has Haley got you watching these days, Sam?"

"Never mind." Sam waved the question away. "Tell us how things are progressing with you and the Mysterious Ms. M?"

Groaning, Wyatt propped his elbows on the table and buried his face in his palms for a second. "*After* the kiss, she told me she can't date me."

"What?" Josey blinked. "That didn't look like an 'I'm not into you' kind of kiss at all. What happened?"

"She's not ready," he muttered, unsure how much to share before he'd cross a line in Kayla's eyes. "She wants to take a few years before getting involved again. She became a wife and mother at such a young age." He straightened and pretended to read the menu. "That's what she said *after* telling me I'm nearly irresistible and like chocolate, which is her kryptonite."

"Hmm." Jo's brow creased. "She finds you irresistible, but she doesn't want to get involved. Sounds to me like she's scared."

"I know how that works." Sam grunted. "Must've been devastating to lose her husband just when their lives were beginning. How long ago did he die?"

His older brother would know about being afraid to risk his heart. He'd almost blown it with Haley because of his fear of loss. "I don't know," Wyatt said. "I didn't ask, but I'm sure you're right. Bad timing, I guess."

Their server delivered their beverages, and they placed an order for a large antipasto salad to share, and a couple of different pizzas.

"So, what are you going to do?" Jo asked once the server left.

"What is there to do?" He tore the paper wrapper from his straw into bits. "She says she wants to be friends."

Sam leaned forward and fixed him in his sights. "So that's it? You're going to give up?"

"I have to respect her wishes, don't I?" He had no clue what to do, and his gut twisted just thinking about it. "How's your love life these days, Jo?"

"Phsssht," she hissed out. "I'm on a break from dating right now. *That's* how it's not going." She drummed her fingers on the tabletop. "Way to deflect."

She and Sam stared at him . . . and waited. "What? I guess I'll give being her friend a try, and suffer through that for a while."

Josey flashed him an "it sucks to be you" look. "Want me to fix you up with one of my friends?"

"No, but thanks."

"*You* have friends?" Sam teased. "Since when?"

"F.U." Josey picked up her soda, her middle finger sticking out from the plastic glass. "Have I ever told you you're my favorite brother, Wyatt? Because you are."

He laughed, and the three of them settled into their usual teasing and talk about work, though his mind strayed once again to his more pressing problem. Should he try to persuade Kayla to see things his way, or should he let it go? Would attempting to persuade her to his point of view only make things worse? It *did* suck to be him.

Chapter Seven

"Phew, something stinks in here." Kayla stood in her kitchen, waving her hand in front of her face. She tossed her napkin and the bit of crust left from her sandwich into the trash bin before pulling out the offending plastic garbage bag and tying it shut. "As soon as Mariah and Rosie get here, I'm taking this to the dumpster."

Brady spared her a nod and went back to slurping what was left of his tomato soup. "Can me and Rosie have ice cream when she gets here?"

"Can Rosie and *I* have ice cream," she corrected. "If it's all right with her mom, it's all right with me." Wyatt's image, the evening he stayed for her chicken noodle soup, popped into her mind. Seeing him so pleased over something as simple as Oreo-cookie ice cream had scrambled her brain. His crooked smile and the warmth in his eyes whenever he looked her way . . . damn, he got to her. She especially loved how he fist-bumped with Brady, like the two of them belonged to a private club. Wyatt was so different from her husband. Brad had mostly been annoyed and inconvenienced by their precious son. Poor Brady.

She blinked against the sudden sting in her eyes. Since she'd met Wyatt, her husband came to her mind far too frequently, which churned up all the hurt, the helpless frustration and the betrayal. She couldn't help making comparisons, and Wyatt was the clear winner in that game.

Had she been a fool to turn Wyatt down the way she had? Second- and third-guessing her decision had plagued her all day, and she hadn't slept well last night either. Reliving Wyatt's kisses and how he'd held her—as if she really meant something to him—had kept her tossing and turning until dawn. She'd had no experience with being wanted and treasured by a man, and she'd turned him away. *Because I'm not ready. I'm not.* She swiped away the few tears that had escaped.

"Hello," Mariah called through her door. "We're here."

"Come on in." Kayla shoved her roiling emotions back into the box and hefted the garbage bag. Pasting a smile on her face, she met the two at the door. "You can put Rosie's overnight bag on the couch. I have to take this down to the dumpster. Make yourselves at home, and I'll be right back. Brady's in the dining room finishing his supper."

"OK. We'll join him."

"Thanks." She slid out the door and headed for the stairs. Just as she got to the back door, Floyd appeared on the landing. "Hey, Floyd. How's it going?"

"Not good. I'm looking for a new caretaker job. Can't see paying full rent for a basement apartment in this dump."

"That's too bad." What else could she say, since she didn't hate to see him go. He followed her out the back door and to the dumpster.

"Yeah," he muttered. "I suppose you heard the guy who lives in the apartment beneath yours got the job to rewire this place, huh?"

"No. I hadn't heard." A thrill shot through her. She lifted the lid and tossed her bag inside. "That's good news."

"It would be, 'cept he's an asshole."

"No, he's not. He's a great guy." She glowered. "The code violations need to be fixed, and since Wyatt lives here, he has a vested interest. I'm sure he'll do an excellent job."

"The part about needing to be fixed I agree with, but *here's* what you don't know," he said, leaning closer like he had a juicy bit of gossip he was sure she'd want to hear. "When Haney sent the bid to the insurance company, he included copies of pictures and letters he'd sent to the owners before the fire. Haney's been complaining about code violations since he moved in." He straightened, his expression angry. "Because of him, the insurance company won't pay out on the claim due to negligence on the part of the owners."

She frowned. "How do you know all of this?"

"My uncle is an accountant for the company that owns this place and a few others in the area. He got me the job as caretaker here, but thanks to the weirdo on the first floor, they won't hire me for any of their other buildings."

"Pointing out violations was the responsible thing to do, Floyd. The owners can't pretend they didn't know, and they could've brought the building up to code at any time. They chose not to. That *is* negligence on their part."

"But—"

"Regardless of what you think about Wyatt Haney, the insurance company would've seen the code violations once they inspected the property. Chances are, they would've denied the claim anyway. The fire in my unit forced the issue; that's all. It really doesn't have anything to do with Wyatt, and you said yourself he wasn't the only one who complained about the lack of upkeep around here."

"I'll admit the place looks like crap, but the owners wouldn't spring for the materials I needed to do the job," he whined. "The vacuum cleaner I got stuck with is at least fifteen years old and hardly picks up anything anymore. The owners refused to reimburse me for paint, caulk or even concrete to patch the cracks in the stairs and sidewalk out front. And I know that has to be another code violation. After my second year here, I quit paying for supplies out of my own pocket." His tone defensive, he surveyed the cracked asphalt in the back lot. "What was I supposed to do?"

"I'm sorry. I had no idea. I don't think anyone did." She edged away from him, making for the back door. "I've got to get back up to my son. I hope you find a better place soon." She dashed inside before he could rant anymore.

She couldn't see how who paid made any difference one way or another. Had the building owners taken care of the issue years ago, they would've had to pay for it themselves then, anyway. As they should have, since they knew updates were needed. At least the citation meant the wiring would be taken care of soon, and she could stop using extension cords. She'd be able to use her window AC, which would be a huge relief.

Would Wyatt be in her apartment when she and Brady were home, or would he do the work while she was away at school? *Drat.* She'd have to get up extra early to straighten the place up and make the beds.

Kayla walked back into her apartment and to the dining area. "What time does your shift start tonight?" she asked. In trade for watching Brady the previous night, Kayla had agreed to take Rosie overnight.

"Ten. Mind if I hang out for a while?"

"I'd love it. We can catch up."

"Mommy," Brady chimed, "don't forget."

"Right. Can Rosie have *i-c-e c-r-e-a-m*?"

"Only if I can have some too." Mariah laughed.

"Of course." Kayla busied herself with dishing out four bowls of ice cream and setting them on the table. She slipped into her chair, yawning so hard her jaw made a cracking sound. "I stayed up way past my bedtime last night."

"But you had fun, didn't you?" Mariah asked. "I'm dying to hear."

Kayla glanced at the children. Both were absorbed in their dessert and in each other. She leaned closer. "Wyatt isn't engaged after all. It's his brother, Sam, who's getting married, and Wyatt is his best man."

"I had a feeling you were wrong about that. The way Wyatt looks at you . . ." Mariah cocked an eyebrow. "Not at all like a guy who's in love with somebody else."

"Hmm." She chopped at the ice cream in her bowl with the edge of her spoon. "So, last night Wyatt thought we were on a date, while I thought he might be trying to fix me up with his older brother."

"That must have been . . . interesting," Mariah chuckled. "I'm glad you two got it straightened out. Did he kiss you good night?"

"He did." She sighed. "Twice."

"Yay!" Mariah's volume shot up, and the two children focused owl-eyed on them for a few seconds.

"Can me and Rosie go play now?" Brady asked. He'd already set up an elaborate village of Lego forts, superheroes, heroines and plastic animals in his bedroom in anticipation of Rosie's arrival.

"Thank heavens for short attention spans," Kayla muttered, rising from her chair. "Sure, let's get some of the sticky off you two first." She went to the sink and dampened a couple of paper towels. After the children wiped their hands and faces, they ran off down the hall.

"So, last night was a date. That's great, Kayla."

"No, it's not. After the kisses, I told Wyatt I can't date him." She shouldn't have kissed him, but, man, she couldn't deny how much she'd enjoyed their moment under the soft glow of the streetlight. "I'm not ready."

"Girl, you are way too young to cut yourself off like that. Wyatt is one of the good guys, and you're crazy to let him get away."

"Let him get away?" She snorted. "You make it sound like I've snared him." Anger flared, and her chest tightened. Her husband had believed she'd gotten pregnant on purpose to trap him. She hadn't.

Neither of them had planned on sex that night, but there'd been drinking involved. Things just went too far, and *BAM*.

"You know what I mean. Don't let this opportunity pass you by. You might regret it later. How long are you planning to keep yourself isolated like you do? Would your husband want to see you continue to mourn him like this?"

"I hadn't thought about a specific time frame, Mariah." She wasn't mourning, more like decompressing and hibernating, but she'd keep that to herself. Brad wouldn't have cared one way or the other. "At least until I'm finished with my program." She got up to clear the table.

"Did you hear Wyatt's construction company is doing the rewiring here?" she asked, carrying the bowls to the sink.

"I didn't know he had a company." Mariah joined her in the kitchen and dropped the spoons into the sink.

"He's an electrician and a partner in his family's construction business." Kayla shared what she'd learned from Floyd, relieved that she'd managed to turn the conversation away from dating. "Dishes can wait. Let's go sit in the living room."

"Fine by me. I'm going to be on my feet all night." Mariah followed her to the couch, sat down and propped her feet on the coffee table.

She'd never told Mariah how miserable her marriage had been, or that her husband had planned to divorce her. She'd never told a soul about Brad's letter until last night. Something about Wyatt's shy, sensitive nature had gotten through her reserve. He'd listened without judgment, offering only sympathy and understanding. At least he'd agreed to be her friend.

Did I make a mistake? Her head said no while her heart argued the point. She shook the thought off. She needed time to heal before she'd be ready to open up her heart—if she ever got to that point again. Brad had made it his mission to make her feel worthless and stupid, like everything wrong between them had been her fault. He was probably on the other side right now, blaming her for the fact that he'd joined the army. Somehow, in his mind, his stupid accident would've been her fault too.

By standing on her own, finishing school and starting a career, she'd prove Brad wrong. She wasn't stupid or worthless, dammit. She needed to know she could rely on herself first, before she learned to rely on someone else. Then, if she ever did fall in love, she'd be on equal footing with her partner, whoever he might be. "Enough about me. How are things going with you and Drew?"

"Great, but he's pushing to take our relationship to the next level, and I'm not there yet."

"The next level meaning what?"

"Moving in together." Hurt flickered through Mariah's eyes. "It's such a hassle when everything falls apart. My divorce tore Rosie to pieces, and she's just now beginning to adjust to only having weekends and the occasional evening with her dad. What if Drew and I do move in together, and then we split up? I don't want to put Rosie through that again. I don't want a string of men passing through her life. When and if I commit, I need to be sure it's going to stick before taking any next steps."

"Then you get where I'm coming from. It's the same for me."

"Nuh-uh." Mariah grimaced. "You lost your husband because of an accident, not because you two split up. It's entirely different. There are no weekends with Dad without Mom for Brady. He doesn't have to say good-bye to one of his parents over and over."

"You think having no father at all is preferable to having a week-end dad? I don't agree." Brady really hadn't had much of a dad anyway. Bitterness reared its ugly head. "Have you forgotten? Brady's dad was mostly gone anyway, because he was deployed."

Mariah covered her mouth for a second. "Oh, Kayla, I'm sorry. That was insensitive."

"It's OK. You're right. Our situations are different, but I don't want a string of men passing through Brady's life either, or mine. My concerns and yours are the same, but for right now, it's . . . easier all around if I just don't date at all." *And way less painful.*

"I'm sure, but easier doesn't always mean better. It would be good for you to get out and have some fun. School and single parenting are tough, and we all need breaks. Don't you want to fall in love again? What about sex? You gotta miss sex."

"Sex is highly overrated." She snorted at her own whopper. Wyatt in all his tall, lanky sexiness had become the main X-rated feature film in her dreams lately, leading to lots of restless turning, tossing and sheet tangling. "There's nothing wrong with choosing to remain single. Lots of women are making that choice."

She and Brad had been a couple of horny teenagers with a mutual curiosity. That's all. As for loving again, she hadn't loved or been loved the first time around, so there was no *again* for her. "I'm happy with my life, and I'm looking forward to starting my career." The looking-forward part was true, but the happy part, not so much. Her life had gone into a holding pattern. "Do you want to watch a movie or something?"

"Sure." Mariah slid her a "I know you're changing the subject" look.

Kayla picked up the remote from the coffee table and handed it to her. "You choose. I'll go check on the munchkins."

She left Mariah to scroll through movies. Animated chatter and giggles, followed by a loud thump, met her in the hallway leading to Brady's room. "You two better not be jumping off the bed," she called, her spirits lifting. Her words were followed by utter silence. She leaned against the doorframe of her son's bedroom and crossed her arms. Two pairs of overly innocent eyes met hers.

"Sorry, Mommy." Brady picked up his Superman action figure, studying it closely. "We won't jump off the bed anymore." He slanted a conspiratorial look at Rosie, who covered her mouth and giggled.

"Good." She had to work at squelching a smile. School and Brady were enough for her. At least the holding pattern was a relief from the stress she'd been under with Brad. She was making a life for herself and her son and standing on her own two capable feet.

The back of her throat did that tingly, pretears thing, and so did her eyes. Had Mariah been right? Had she been isolating herself from the possibility of further hurt? Brad had run her down so many times and in so many ways. Proving him wrong had become the driving force in her life.

He was gone. She was doing really well in school, and her little boy was thriving. So, why did this need to prove herself still consume her?

Kayla helped Brady get settled into his booster seat in the back of her saunalike car. "We're hitting the nearest fast-food drive-through on the way home, kiddo. It's way too hot to cook, and I'm beat." Even leaving her car in the sun for the ten minutes it took to pick up Brady from day care had caused the interior to turn into an oven again.

"Yay!" Brady threw a fist up in the air.

The temperature had hit the midnineties, and her day had been long and exhausting. The air-conditioning had been out at school, and she'd been sweating all day. A bead of perspiration trickled from her forehead into her eye, and her scrubs stuck to her. "Yay is right."

She might even risk using the window air in her apartment this evening. When would Haney & Sons start on her apartment? It had been Tuesday when she'd heard they'd gotten the job. The permits had been taped to the front door by Wednesday, and Floyd had notified everyone in the building that work would be done in their apartments. This was Thursday. She hadn't caught even so much as a glimpse of Wyatt since she'd told him she couldn't date him. Was he avoiding her?

She mopped her forehead with her sleeve, and then retied her ponytail to keep the hair off the back of her neck. Once the car was started, she turned the AC to full blast, but the air coming from the vents was no cooler than the interior of the car. A nice cool shower once they got home was definitely a priority. She pulled out of the parking lot while planning her evening, which included standing in front of her window air for as long as she could before a fuse blew.

Turning into the McDonald's halfway between school and home, her mouth watered. A very large soda with lots of ice sounded really good right now. "Cheeseburger Happy Meal, Brady?"

"Yes, please and thank you, Mommy."

She smiled at him in the rearview mirror and pulled into the line for the takeout intercom and placed their order.

"Can I have my pop?" Brady asked, as she set their order on the passenger seat.

Kayla drove away from the window and swung her car into a parking spot. "Yes, but only if you promise not to spill. You have a tendency to fall asleep while in the car, which leads to sticky disasters."

"I promise."

She fixed their sodas, took a drink of hers and handed Brady his Sprite. "If you start to nod off, put your drink between your leg and the side of your booster seat."

He took the plastic cup from her, and she patted his knee before heading home. A large dumpster and a couple of white Haney & Sons vans were parked in front of the building. Wyatt might be working in her apartment right now. Kayla took a left at the corner, heading to the parking lot in back. His pickup truck was in its assigned spot, and anticipation quickened her pulse. She missed him—blushes, hoodie and all.

Grabbing the bag, she climbed out and set it on top of the car, so she could help Brady from his seat. With their supper in hand, she and Brady made their way into the building and up the stairs. Rock music poured into the hall from her apartment, and her door was open a crack. The ceiling in the outer hallway had been cut away, exposing the charred beams, and the plaster on her outside wall had been stripped down to the framing.

"Who's there?" Brady asked, pressing himself close to her side.

"I'm not sure, but Wyatt's family is fixing our apartment for us."

"Is he here?" Brady lit up. "Will Wyatt read to me tonight?"

And didn't that send a wrench to the gut. If Wyatt was avoiding her, there wouldn't be any more comic book readings. He'd said they could be friends, but if the tables were turned, she wasn't so sure she could switch gears so easily. "I guess we'll see, won't we?" She opened the door wider and Brady darted through ahead of her.

Sam and another guy were cleaning up debris in the dining area. The entire ceiling had been torn out, and they had positioned beams like pillars against the exposed joists. Sam glanced at her and smiled.

"Hey, Kayla. We'll be out of your way in a few minutes. This is Thomas. He'll be working with me here." Sam tipped his head in the direction of the man sweeping debris from the canvas covering the floor. "Tom, this is Kayla and her son, Brady."

"Hey," Tom said with a nod. "Do you need me for anything else, Sam?" he asked as he emptied a dustpan into a five-gallon plastic bucket.

"Nope. See you tomorrow."

"Nice to meet you," Kayla said as Tom grabbed his things and headed for the door. "Sam is Wyatt's brother," she told Brady, giving his hand a reassuring squeeze.

"Oh." Brady pressed up against her side again. "Where's Wyatt?"

He'd stolen the question right out of her mouth. The force of her disappointment at not finding him in her apartment took her by surprise. She wasn't supposed to miss him this much.

"He's either in the basement installing the circuit-breaker boxes, or he's on the third floor. Since Haney & Sons is rewiring the entire building, he and his crew are starting with the apartment above yours, and working their way down." Sam studied the support beams. "We're going to replace the burned crossbeams here tomorrow, and once Wyatt has rewired your dining room and kitchen, we'll be back to put in the new ceiling."

"Great." Kayla laid a hand on her son's head. "Let's have a picnic in the living room. I'm starving." She nudged Brady toward the coffee table. "Sorry to eat in front of you."

"No problem," Sam said, turning off the Blu-ray speaker sitting on the living room floor. "All right if I leave a few tools here since we'll be back tomorrow?"

"That's fine by me. Did Floyd give you an earful when he let you in?" She opened Brady's Happy Meal and unwrapped his burger for him. Sweat trickled down her temples. Her place was stifling.

"Uh, no." Sam chuckled. "The caretaker left an envelope full of master keys taped to the outside of Wyatt's door with *Asshole* written across the front." His gaze shot to Brady. "Oh, sorry."

"It's OK. He's heard the word before." She cast him a wry look. "Floyd is blaming Wyatt for a lot of stuff that isn't his fault. I tried to set our caretaker straight on a few things, but he wasn't real receptive."

His gaze intensified. "Thanks for defending my little brother. He's a good guy, you know. You won't find anyone nicer."

Heat rushed to her face, and she focused on setting out her meal, which was barely lukewarm now. "I know."

"I need ketchup, please," Brady said around a mouthful.

Kayla shot up. "I'm on it."

Sam trailed her to the dining area. "Is that a picture of your late husband on the living room wall?"

"Yes." She'd hung it up mostly for Brady's sake. He'd had a father, albeit not the best father, but she didn't want him to forget.

"How long has it been since he passed?" Sam picked up his power saw and wrapped the cord around the base before adding it to the pile of equipment in the corner.

"It's been about two years." No shyness where Sam was concerned. Disconcerted, Kayla grabbed the ketchup from the fridge and a small plate from the cabinet. Had Wyatt told Sam about her miserable past? She squirted ketchup onto the plate and brought it to her son.

Sam followed her into the living room. "I'm sorry. I don't know how I'd survive if I lost Haley. Did Wyatt tell you we lost our parents when we were kids?"

"He did." Where was he going with this? "Losing your parents must have been devastating."

"It was, and I'm sure losing your husband devastated you too." His blue eyes filled with sympathy. "It can't be easy for you, losing your life partner and being on your own with Brady."

She averted her gaze and swallowed against the tightness in her throat. Wyatt had kept his word. He hadn't told his brother her marriage hadn't been the stuff of fairy tales. "Brady and I are doing fine. We're a team. Right, buddy?"

Brady's head bobbed, and he shoved a fry in his mouth. "Is Wyatt gonna come see us tonight?"

"I don't think so." She smoothed back the damp bangs from his forehead. "He's pretty busy."

"Do you draw comic books too?" Brady asked Sam.

"No, but I coach hockey. Are you interested in learning how to play the game?"

"I don't know." Brady's attention went back to the toy he'd found in his Happy Meal.

"Like me, he's never seen a hockey game," she told Sam.

"We'll have to do something about that. I'll have Wyatt bring you and Brady to watch my team during one of our practice sessions sometime. The younger kids start developing their skills, the better."

"I . . . sure." She bit her lip for a second. "That would be fun."

"Look, I get you're not ready to date and all—"

"Wyatt told you that?" Her brow shot up.

"The subject came up over lunch on Tuesday because we asked." He shrugged. "Just because you're not ready to date doesn't mean you and Wyatt can't be friends and hang out now and then. No pressure."

She nodded, and her insides knotted. She followed him to the door.

"See you tomorrow," he said as he left.

"Say hello to Haley for me." Kayla shut the door behind him and went back to the couch. She plopped down next to her son and stared at her food, which she hadn't touched and no longer wanted. Her rejection had to have hurt Wyatt. Hell, she was hurting, and she'd been the one doing the rejecting, not the other way around. She groaned, closed her eyes and leaned her head back against the couch.

"What's wrong, Mommy?"

"Nothing, buddy. I'm just tired." *Tired, and I might just be an idiot.*

Chapter Eight

Wyatt's ringing phone woke him. He never slept in on Saturdays, but this morning was supposed to be the exception, because he'd had trouble falling asleep last night. He wasn't ready to get up. Grabbing his phone from the nightstand, he hit accept and brought it to his ear. "Hello," he croaked out through a yawn.

"Are you still in bed?" Sam asked. "You sound sleepy."

"I am, and you woke me. Thanks a bunch." Wyatt glanced at his clock. "What do you want?"

"For you to be less cranky." Sam grunted. "Jerry, Frank and I decided we'd head to the Men's Wearhouse this afternoon to pick out our suits for the wedding. Are you available?"

"I guess." Of course he was available. He had no social life to speak of, and the only woman he wanted badly enough to attempt overcoming his shyness had made it clear she didn't want to date him. He pinched the bridge of his nose and closed his eyes. "What time?"

"Jerry needs to be picked up, so we're meeting at Uncle Dan's at one. We'll take my SUV from there."

Wyatt pushed himself up to sitting and swung his feet to the floor. "All right. I'll see you there."

"You OK?"

"Yeah. I stayed up late working on a new idea for a comic book and planned to sleep in this morning. I'm fine, just not awake yet." In his latest Elec Tric installment, his poor superhero has his heart broken by the Mysterious Ms. M. *Go figure.*

"All right. See you later," Sam said before ending the call.

Flopping back on his bed, Wyatt stared at the ceiling. It was already nine. By now, Kayla and Brady had left for their Saturday trip to the laundromat, saving him from the painful temptation to stare longingly at her from his window. He still hadn't switched gears from *wanting* to *friendship*. How to do that eluded him.

He rubbed his face with both hands. "Coffee. Things always look better after I've had coffee." He got up and padded down the hall, making a pit stop at the bathroom before ending up in the kitchen. He set up the coffee maker, pushed the button to start it and yawned again. By the time he took a quick shower, coffee would be ready.

Showered, dressed and with a fresh mug of high-octane wake-me juice, Wyatt returned to his studio to look over the work he'd done the night before. He glanced at the shelf where he'd set the portrait of Kayla and her son, and his heart tripped.

He hadn't framed the portrait yet. Maybe he never would. He could give it to her as is, and she could do with it whatever she wanted. He swallowed against the rising tide of disappointment and rejection. No, that wasn't fair. She hadn't rejected *him*; she'd rejected the idea of dating. After hearing her story, he couldn't blame her. Still stung, though.

Sipping his coffee, he moved to sit at his drawing table and opened his sketchbook to the preliminary sketches and notes he'd made, intending to tweak and edit before beginning the actual panels. He tried to concentrate, he really did, but his gaze kept drifting back to the damned portrait. By the time he finished his coffee, he'd given up on the notion of getting anything done with the new stuff. Some days were like that. He'd used all his inspiration last night. "Screw it."

He abandoned any hope of making progress and strode for the door, grabbing his keys on the way. Might as well make the frame this morning, and tomorrow he'd take the portrait to a frame shop for glass and matting. He'd give it to her, and they'd go back to being nothing but acquaintances who lived in the same building. Unfortunately, there were no internal shutoff valves for desire or longing. He climbed into his truck and set out for his grandfather's workshop.

Ten minutes later, Wyatt parked and made his way to the gate leading into the backyard. He found his grandmother weeding the raised flower beds growing along the length of the privacy fence. "Hi, Gram."

"Wyatt. What a lovely surprise. What brings you here this morning?" She straightened.

"I have a project I want to work on in Grandpa's workshop."

"Ah. I was just going to get some lemonade. Would you like some?"

"Sure. I'll come with you."

Grandma Maggie took off her gardening gloves and patted his cheek. "Did you get things straightened out with your young lady?"

"Yes." He huffed out a breath. "No . . . *argh*. I don't know." He stuffed his hands into his hoodie pockets and matched his stride to his gram's. "Do you have a few minutes? Maybe you can shed some light on a few things for me."

"Of course."

He followed her through the sliding doors into the kitchen. "Kayla doesn't want to date me, Gram. She says she's not ready." Wyatt went for glasses while his grandmother got the pitcher of lemonade out of the fridge. He brought her up to speed on everything that had happened, including the part where Kayla told him he was her kryptonite. He even admitted that they'd shared a couple of kisses *before* she informed him she wouldn't date him.

He and Gram settled at the table. "She told me something and asked me to keep it to myself." He shrugged. "Unfortunately, that's the part I need to talk about the most. If I tell you, then I'm breaking my word to her, but . . ."

"I am the soul of discretion. Besides, who would I tell?"

"Grandpa Joe?"

"I wouldn't tell him, but even if I did, whatever I said would go in one ear and right out the other." She snapped her fingers. "Lickety-split."

Wyatt sucked in a breath. "Kayla got pregnant her senior year of high school, and she and her boyfriend were pressured by their parents into marrying, which turned out to be hellish for her. The guy was an immature, selfish ass who made her life miserable and ignored his son. He joined the army right after their wedding." His jaw tightened. "He wasn't faithful to Kayla. The last letter she got from him, he told her he'd met someone and fallen in love. He planned to divorce her when his tour of duty was up."

His heart ached just thinking about how she must have suffered through the whole ordeal. "She says she went through five years of hell, and she feels like she missed out on a lot of stuff. She's determined to get back those missing years, but I don't see how that's possible. You can't go back. The years between high school and now . . . it's all just life, and we're all just living it the best we can. Kayla doesn't realize she grew up just like the rest of us, probably faster. As far as the years between our teens and early twenties being somehow better or more fun, I don't think that's true for a majority. Not for me, anyway."

"Hmm." Grandma Maggie nodded slowly. "That poor girl. She's been hurt badly, and she's still grieving."

"But, Gram . . . she and her husband didn't get along. He was mean to her. Why would she grieve for him?"

"Miserable or not, he was a big part of her life, not to mention the father of her child. Things didn't go the way they should have between them, and that is cause enough for grief." Gram patted his arm. "Oh, she's grieving all right, but it's more complicated because her sadness is also for herself and what she perceives as her lost adolescence. She's protecting herself, Wyatt. She's reacting from a place of pain. It could be she's afraid if she lets you into her heart, she'll be hurt again."

He was the one more likely to be hurt. He already hurt, and they'd only gone out once. "OK. She's hurt, and she doesn't want to date." *Me, anyway.* Saying it brought a hollow ache to his chest. "You and Grandpa Joe always taught us to be respectful when it comes to stuff like this. So"—he pushed his hoodie back and raked his fingers through his hair—"should I just let it be? Should I leave her alone and forget about her and Brady?"

"That's up to you. She did say she wants to be friends. If you don't feel you can handle friendship, then you need to take care of yourself. Walk away. On the other hand . . ." She tapped her glass and arched an eyebrow.

"There's an 'other hand'?"

"Always. If you're there for her—as a good friend, mind—her feelings might change. She's viewing you and the situation from a perspective tainted by her unhappy past. Her husband wasn't there for her, and he certainly wasn't her friend. As she gets to know you better, she'll see you for who you are: a compassionate, reliable man who respects and values her for who she is. Become indispensible to her. She's bound to come around."

"Then again, she might not."

"She'd be crazy not to. If you really care for this girl, my advice is to be the best friend she's ever had. You know what your grandfather says: Haney men can fix anything."

He chuffed out a laugh. "Yeah, I've heard that a time or two." He gulped down the rest of his lemonade and rose from the table. "Speaking of Gramps, where is he this morning?"

"He's learning how to golf."

"Really?" He cracked a grin. "Why?"

"You know how your grandfather loves to go to garage sales, looking for tools and other crap we don't need. He found a complete set of brand new golf clubs being sold for next to nothing." She chuckled. "That man can't pass up a deal. He decided on the spot he needs a new hobby and more exercise, so he bought them. Your grandfather joined the Town & Country Club on Marshall Avenue. The great deal he got on those clubs ended up being quite expensive." Gram's eyes took on a dreamy look. "But that's my Joe for you. He'll save a penny only to spend a dollar."

His throat closed so tight he couldn't breathe. He wanted to be somebody's Wyatt. Correction. He wanted to be Kayla's Wyatt. He leaned down and kissed Grandma Maggie's cheek. "Love you, Gram," he croaked. "Thanks for listening."

"Anytime, sweetie. Your grandfather and I are very proud of the man you've become, you know. You remind me so much of your father. He was shy too. Such a sweet boy."

Wyatt wasn't sure whether she was referring to him or to his father as being sweet. Either way, the lump in his throat grew larger. "Gotta go make a picture frame. I have to be at Uncle Dan's at one," he said, putting his glass in the sink.

"Go on, then. I'll be back to my weeding in a minute or two." Gram swiped streaks through the condensation on her glass with her thumbs, her eyes still dreamy, as if she might still be reminiscing.

He left the kitchen and hurried to the workshop out back. He walked inside and something about the place settled him. The large room with its cement floor smelled of wood, stain and the tang of steel power tools with a touch of rust. Gramps collected old tools like some people collected old coins. The welcome, familiar scent was one Wyatt associated with home, family and especially with his grandfather.

He opened the windows to let in some fresh air. Then he walked to the corner where a bunch of mismatched pieces of casing and base-board had been stacked inside an old barrel. Gramps had picked up the wooden barrel at a flea market long before Wyatt was born.

As he looked through the remnants, he thought about what his grandmother had said. Kayla had been the one who'd been hurt, not him. He'd been avoiding her, but what she needed was for him to man up and be her friend. He'd been thinking only of himself. Hadn't he told her whatever she needed, he'd be there for her? Guilt wrenched at him. At the first test of friendship, he'd failed her. How could he expect more with her if he couldn't even be a friend first?

"That's changing as of today," he muttered to himself. He'd be the best damned friend she'd ever had. He'd become indispensible to her, and eventually she'd come around. After all, she had admitted he was her kryptonite. Build on your strengths, that's what Gramps would say.

His blood rushed, remembering how perfectly she fit in his arms, her lush curves pressed against him and the way she'd kissed him back. Having her in his arms had been the closest he'd come to heaven on earth, and he wanted more, much more. He groaned. Waiting just might kill him.

Forcing his mind off Kayla's curves, he focused on the remnants and chose a piece of trim that had been painted white with grayish streaks. He lifted the piece out of the barrel and laid it on one of the workbenches. Then he searched the shelves for Grandpa Joe's miter box and a handsaw. It didn't make any sense to fire up the big electric table saw for such a small project.

It took him only about forty minutes to measure, cut, glue and staple the frame together. The portrait would look great against the white and gray, with maybe red or blue matting. Satisfied with his work, Wyatt cleaned up, closed the windows, grabbed the frame and left the shop. Grandma Maggie was back to her weeding. "What do you think, Gram?" He held up the frame.

"Nice. What's it for?" She sat back on her heels.

"I did a portrait of Kayla and her son. I thought I'd frame it before I give it to her."

"She'll like that. I take it you've decided not to walk away?"

"I guess. For now at any rate." His stomach lurched at the possibility of another rejection coming at him a few months down the road.

"It'll work out, Wyatt. You'll see."

"Thanks, Gram. Do you mind if I make myself a sandwich before I head out? I skipped breakfast."

"Help yourself." She went back to pulling the weeds that had dared to infiltrate her flowers. "You're a good man, Wyatt. Any young woman would be lucky to have you in her life. Don't forget."

"You're not biased at all," he teased. "Later, Gram. I'll keep you posted."

Wyatt set the frame on the kitchen counter before scrounging through his grandparents' fridge for stuff to make his lunch. He put together two fat ham and swiss-cheese sandwiches, wrapping one in a couple of paper towels before cleaning up. The other he tore into, pausing long enough to tuck the frame under his arm on the way out.

If a friend is what Kayla needed, then a friend he would be. She'd come around eventually. After all, he was a Haney, and Haney men could fix anything—maybe even broken hearts.

"You can go, Jon. I'll clean up." Wyatt finished fastening the new outlet cover in Kayla's kitchen. It had taken until Wednesday to get to her apartment, and they'd only gotten to the kitchen and dining area.

"Thanks, man. My youngest has T-ball tonight, and I really don't want to miss it. She's a hoot to watch." Jon grinned, his tone filled with pride. "That one is determined to do everything her older brothers do, only better."

"Like my sister."

"Yeah, my little girl is a lot like Josey, and that's a good thing." Jon put his tools in his toolbox and set it in the corner. "See you tomorrow."

"See you." Wyatt had arranged things, so he'd be in Kayla's apartment when she got home, which would be any minute now. He was a mess of nerves. Should he go down to his place, get the portrait and bring it up, or wait? How would she react?

He rewound the small wooden spool of black insulated wire and taped the loose end to the wood. Then he did the same to the white, neutral wire. Gathering his tools, he caught the sound of Brady's voice in the hall. His breath hitched, and his heart knocked around in his chest. The apartment door opened. "Hello," he called from the dining room.

"You're here." Kayla came around the corner, her face flushed.

Wyatt placed the spools on end next to his tools, and then he straightened. Heat surged to his face at the sight of her. Damn, he thought he was over that. "Yeah . . . I hope it's OK. Just cleaning up. Once I'm done here, I'll run down to the basement, flip the new circuit breaker, and you'll be up and running again." He forced himself to inhale. "In the kitchen and dining area anyway. We'll be back to do the rest tomorrow, and Sam will be back to put in new sheetrock where we had to tear out the walls."

"Wyatt," Brady cried, hopping in place. "Will you read to me tonight? Mommy, can Wyatt stay for supper?"

"Honestly, I don't even know what we're having for supper yet, but you're welcome to stay." Her gaze touched his for second before flitting away.

"I was going to get Chinese takeout. If you want, you two can join me at my place for dinner tonight."

"Yeah," Brady beamed.

"Sure. I just need to change."

"What should I order for you two?"

"Brady likes chicken fried rice, and I'll have sweet-and-sour pork." She reached into her purse, pulled out a twenty and handed it to him.

He took her money. This wasn't a date, just friends hanging out. "I'll get an order of egg rolls to share too."

"Sounds great."

"Come downstairs at . . ." He pulled his phone out of his pocket and checked the time. "How about six?" That would give him time to put in the order, shower and then pick it up.

Kayla smiled, her pretty blue eyes connecting with his again. "All right. See you at six."

"All right. See you at six." Had he just repeated what she'd said verbatim? Why, yes he had. His pulse kicked into high gear, and color once again rushed to his face. He made a beeline for the door. "Later."

Wyatt took the stairs at a good clip, heading for the basement to flip the circuit breaker for her. This friend business would take some getting used to. He and Kayla were back at square one, with him sweating, blushing and his heart thumping like crazy. Not where he wanted to be with her at all. Once inside the safety of his apartment, he headed to his kitchen for his takeout menus and placed the order. Then he gathered clean clothes and took his shower.

By five minutes to six, Wyatt had the large brown bag containing their meal on the table. He left the cartons in the bag to keep everything warm and gathered plates and silverware from the kitchen. Kayla and Brady knocked on his door. *Thump-thump* went his heart, and his legs turned to rubber. He wiped his palms on the front of his cargo shorts and strode to the door. "Who's there?" he called through the heavy oak.

"It's *me*," Brady called back.

"Me who?" Wyatt grinned. The sound of childish giggles melted his heart, and he swung the door open wide. "Oh, it's *you*." He held out his fist.

"That's what I said," Brady chortled, bumping his fist back. "It's *me*."

"And me," Kayla said, smiling. "Mmm. I smell Chinese food." She put her hands on Brady's shoulders and guided him inside.

The warmth in her eyes and her high-wattage smile didn't make it any easier for him to stand on his already-shaky legs. "Let's eat, and then we can read another Wyatt R. Haney comic book."

Brady slipped his hand into Wyatt's. "I drawed a comic book at my school yesterday, and today we got to go to the Como Park Zoo."

"Wow. Sounds like you have a lot of fun at your school." He held on to Brady's hand, and when they got to the dining room, he swung him up onto a chair. "Can I go to your school too?"

"No." Brady giggled again. "You're too *old*."

"Huh." Wyatt took the cartons out of the bag and set them on the table. "Maybe the three of us could go to the amusement park at the Mall of America someday." He glanced at Kayla. "What do you think? Might be fun."

"Could we, Mommy?" Brady got up on his knees, his expression full of hope.

"That would be fun. We've never been to the Mall of America."

"Really?" Wyatt's brow rose. "You live in the Twin Cities, and you've never been to the Mall of America? Besides the amusement park in the center, there's a Lego store, a movie theater and the Sea Life Minnesota Aquarium too."

She laughed. "OK. I'm sold. We can go check it out."

A lot of the tension he'd been holding slipped away. This could work out if being her friend meant they spent more time together. He folded up the large paper bag their food had come in, set it aside and took a seat. "Do you two want to share everything?"

"Depends. What did you order?" Kayla spooned some of the fried rice onto her son's plate.

"I got the house special lo mein."

"What's that?" Brady asked around a mouthful.

"Noodles and lots of stuff mixed in, like shrimp, chicken and pork."

"I like noodles."

"I know you do, Superkid." Wyatt dumped some of his lo mein onto his plate, then added a small amount to Brady's. Kayla did the same with her order.

"How's the rewiring coming along?" Kayla paused to ask.

"The third floor is finished, and circuit boxes for each apartment have been installed. Now that we're working on the second floor, we're doing your apartment first, so Sam can get in and put the new ceiling up. He's on another job, so it might take a few days before he gets back."

"That's OK. I've grown used to not having a ceiling."

"How's school?"

"Good. The AC was out, which was miserable, but now it's fixed."

This was conversation lite, nothing too personal, but Kayla and Brady were here, and that was all that mattered. By the time they finished, cleared the table and put away the leftovers, Brady's eyes were at half-mast. "Looks like you got some sun today, bro." Wyatt tousled the kid's thick blond mop. "And I'll bet you did a lot of walking. Are you sure you're up to a comic book reading tonight?"

Brady nodded through a yawn. "Yes, please and thank you."

Wyatt chuckled. "Come on then." He picked the kid up and held him tucked against his side like a football. Wyatt bounced the kid all the way to the couch, gratified by the little boy giggles and Kayla's radiant smile. This friend thing was a chancy business. Every one of her smiles, and every time his eyes met hers, he was in a little deeper. *Heartbreak, here I come.* And willingly too if there was even a ghost of a chance she'd come around.

He tossed his human football on the couch, and Brady shrieked with glee. "I'll be right back with the next chapter in Elec Tric's adventures." He pointed a stern finger at Brady. "Don't go anywhere."

Brady pushed himself up to sitting. "I won't."

He hurried to his studio and grabbed the third comic book and the framed portrait. His breath catching, he returned to the living room. "Do you remember when I told you I made something for you and

Brady?" he asked, taking his place on the couch next to Brady. "Well, here it is. I hope you two like it." He set the framed portrait on Kayla's lap and watched her face. Her mouth formed a sweet little *O*, and she traced the figures with her finger.

"That's *me*!" Brady leaned against his mom. "And that's you, Mommy."

Kayla blinked rapidly, and swallowed. "It's . . ." Her gaze lifted to his.

Her eyes were bright with tears, and his chest tightened. "You don't like it?"

"Oh my God. I love it. It's amazing." Her attention returned to the picture. "No one has ever done anything like this for me before. Thank you, Wyatt."

His chest swelled with pride. "What about you, Superkid? Do you like it?"

"Yeah," Brady sighed. "Mommy, can I bring it to show my friends at school?"

"Let me think about that, kiddo." She swiped at her cheeks.

She wasn't looking at him, but her expression had gone all soft as she studied the picture. He'd made her happy. Score one for the friend who lives downstairs. "Ready for the story?" Brady nodded and leaned against his side.

"*A Hero Lives to Fight Another Day*," he read the title and turned to the first panel. By the time he got to the third page, his little friend was sound asleep and drooling on Wyatt's arm. "And . . . he's out." He grinned at Kayla.

"Have you been avoiding me?" she asked, her tone low.

He was about to tell her no, but she deserved honesty. "I needed time to . . . adjust. So, yes, I was avoiding you."

"I'm sorry, Wyatt." She searched his face. "Are we OK?"

"Absolutely." *Not.*

"So, this is how you see me," she whispered, reaching for the portrait where it rested on his coffee table.

Uh-oh. "What do you mean?"

"You made me so pretty in this portrait." Her eyes met his again.

The vulnerability and doubt he glimpsed in their blue depths nearly did him in. "You *are* that pretty, Kayla. In fact, you're beautiful, gorgeous, magnificent . . ." She let out a throaty laugh that sent a current of desire straight through him.

"If you say so."

"You don't believe me?" He frowned. "How could you not know you're a certified, bona-fide knockout?"

Kayla shook her head and rose from her place. "I'd better get this kid to bed. Thanks for inviting us to join you for dinner tonight, and for the amazing picture. You're a very talented man, Wyatt Haney."

"Do you want me to carry Brady upstairs?" Wyatt rose carefully, letting Brady slip down to the couch slowly enough that he didn't wake.

"No, I have to wake him. He needs to brush his teeth and use the bathroom before I put him to bed."

"I'll get your leftovers and put them in a bag for you."

"Thanks." She shook her son's shoulder. "Brady, wake up. We need to go home."

Plastic bag with her cartons of leftovers in hand, Wyatt returned to the living room to find Brady practically asleep on his feet. "Leftovers, the portrait and a sleepy kid—that's a lot to handle."

"I've handled worse." Her expression tightened.

Somehow, he sensed she wasn't referring to things needing to be carried upstairs. "I'm taking Brady. You get the portrait and the leftovers." He handed her the bag and lifted Brady into his arms. "No arguing."

Brady sighed and slid his arms around Wyatt's neck. He smelled like sunshine, fresh air and little boy. These two had already made a place for themselves in Wyatt's heart. "Ready?"

Kayla expression one of resignation, she picked up the portrait and preceded him to the door. He followed, wondering why she resisted his help. He stood back while she unlocked her door, and then he set Brady on his feet just over the threshold. "Hey, little man. Better go take care of business before you hit the sack." Straightening, he faced Kayla. "See you tomorrow."

"No more avoiding?" Her brow rose in question.

"No more avoiding," he agreed.

"Good." She nodded, moving to close the door. "I'm glad."

"Me too." He longed to draw her close, erase the shadow of hurt lurking in her eyes and kiss her breathless. He stepped away. "Good night."

"Good night," she said, easing the door closed.

Wyatt turned around and walked slowly back downstairs. Gram was right. Kayla had been hurt, and now that he'd put his own ego aside, the truth smacked him between the eyes. His gorgeous, intelligent, sexy neighbor feared having her heart broken again. She didn't see herself the way he saw her, didn't even realize how amazing she was.

He shook his head and blew out a long breath. The idiot she'd married had really done a number on her, and it only made Wyatt more determined than ever to shower her with . . . *friendship*.

Chapter Nine

Ever since Wyatt had given her the amazing portrait, Kayla had agonized over how she might repay his kindness. It had taken her two days, but she now had a plan.

"Hey, Brady," she said, sweeping into the living room with her laptop in hand. "It's time for our chat with Gammy and Pops." She set up her laptop on the coffee table and turned off the window air. Her apartment rewiring completed, she no longer had to worry about running her AC, but it was noisy.

"OK." Leaving his toys where they were, he joined her on the couch.

Every week, she and Brady shared a FaceTime call with her parents. She opened her computer and entered their number. Her parents appeared on her screen. "Hi, Mom. Hi, Dad." She waved.

"Gammy, Pops, d'you know what?" Brady slid off the couch, placed his hands on the coffee table and leaned in close to the camera lens above the computer screen.

"No, what?" They asked in unison, well versed in Brady speak.

"I got to go to Como Zoo with my school, and there are gorillas there, and tigers." He practically vibrated with excitement.

"Wow, that's great," her mom said, grinning. "Looks like you've grown since last week, Brady."

"Yep." He straightened and threw out his chest. "And I'm getting stronger." He flexed his skinny arms for them. "See?"

"Whoa," her dad chuckled. "You sure are."

"I drawed a comic book at school. Do you want me to send it to you?"

"Oh, we'd love that, sweetie," her mom said. "Sure does sound like you have a lot of fun at that school."

He nodded enthusiastically. "And d'you know what else? I'm going to stay there until I start kindagarden."

Kayla and her mom shared an amused look. "Speaking of school, how're things going with your program?" her mom asked.

"Really well. Not much longer, and I'll be finished. I found out the graduation ceremony is going to be at O'Shaughnessy Auditorium in Saint Paul, which isn't too far from my apartment."

"Good. We've already reserved our hotel rooms for the weekend of the seventeenth. Your brother and grandfather are going to make it after all. We're all looking forward to it," her dad said. "We're proud of you, Kayla."

"Thanks, Dad." She'd worked hard to pull her life together after all the *BAMs*. A rush of pride swept through her. Her parents had been so disappointed when she'd turned up pregnant, and it wasn't like they hadn't taught her about the facts of life and birth control, either. She'd let them down big time. Hell, she'd let herself down. Her gaze caught on Brady, and a flood of love and tenderness hit her system. No matter what though, she'd never regretted having her amazing little boy. She reached out and smoothed the hair from his forehead.

"Are you still planning on coming home over Labor Day weekend?" her mom asked. "We miss you two so much."

"I miss you too, Gammy, and d'you know what?" Brady launched into excitement mode again. "My friend Wyatt drawed a picture of me and Mommy. You wanna see?"

"Of course we do." Her dad flashed her a questioning look.

"Wyatt Haney is our downstairs neighbor," Kayla explained. "He writes and illustrates comic books. You'd love his work, Dad. It's very retro—late 1930s, early 1940s, similar in style to Creig Flessel."

"Oh?" That got his attention. "That's something I'd like to see."

"He's also an electrician and a partner in his family's construction business, Haney & Sons. They're the company rewiring our building." She pushed herself up off the couch. "You chat with Gammy and Pops, Brady, and I'll get the portrait."

Brady chattered on with her parents while she went to her bedroom for the prized picture. She'd left it on her dresser until she could get around to picking up one of those picture hooks to hang it on the wall. Every time she looked at the portrait, her heart turned over. No one outside of family had ever done anything so thoughtful and sweet for her. No man ever had, that's for sure, and certainly not the boy she'd married. Wyatt was special, unique.

Portrait in hand, she sat back down in front of her computer. "Here we are. Supermom and Superkid, ready to take on the world." She adjusted her computer so the illustration took up the entire screen. "What do you think?"

"Wow, that's really something." Her dad's tone was a mixture of surprise and appreciation. "He's very talented."

"Is Wyatt someone you're seeing, Kayla?" her mom asked.

"No." Her heart wrenched at the reminder of her decision, and all the second-and third-guessing came back with a whoosh of conflicting emotions. "We're just friends and neighbors. He's the one who called the fire department when my smoke alarm went off. He's done so much for us, and I want to do something for him in return. Which reminds me, could you give me Aunt Becky's telephone number? I want to ask her how to go about finding Wyatt an agent."

Her dad shifted and patted her mom's knee. "I'll go get that, honey. You stay here."

"You never did answer my question, Kayla. Are you still planning to bring our grandson for a visit over the Labor Day weekend?"

"Of course we are. Brady and I are really looking forward to our visit. I'm going to pack that Thursday night, and we'll leave right after school Friday afternoon. I'm pretty sure I'll be able to get out early that day. We don't get many clients before long holiday weekends, so we'll probably be there by dinnertime."

Her dad returned and gave her Aunt Becky's number. Kayla entered it into her phone's contacts. "Thanks, Dad. Got it."

"Why don't you leave Brady with us for the rest of that week?" her dad suggested. "We would love to have him, and I know the Malones would love to spend some time with him. It'll give you a much needed break."

"Oh, that's an excellent idea," her mom agreed. "We have a brand new donkey on the farm. Wouldn't you like to visit with the chickens, goats and all the other animals, Brady?"

Kayla's dad, a veterinarian, worked with large animals on the farms surrounding Decorah. He also cared for household pets in a clinic in town, but cows and horses made up the bulk of his practice. Kayla and her brother had grown up with a menagerie of critters and acres and acres in which to run and play.

She looked at her son. "What do you think? Would you like to spend a few days with Gammy and Pops? They'd love to have you, and you'd get to see Grandpa and Grandma Malone too." Hopefully, her in-laws would see their grandson once she was on her way back to the Twin Cities. They loved Brady, and she'd never keep him from them, but she'd never gotten along or felt comfortable around either of them.

And with their only son's death, the tension had grown worse. They blamed her for everything.

"Are you gonna be there too?" Brady asked, his tone anxious.

Kayla smiled at her parents. "Can Brady and I have some time to talk it over? He's never been away from me for more than a night." She'd miss him desperately, but there was no denying the thought of having a week to herself held enormous appeal. She hadn't had that since the day he was born. What would she do with all that extra time? "I might have to do a little convincing."

Her mom chuckled. "You do that. Your dad and I would be happy to bring him home the following Saturday. We can all go out to dinner together then and have a nice visit. We'll stay the night and drive home Sunday morning."

"I'd like that. Maybe I can get Wyatt to show you some of his comic books, Dad. He's been reading them to Brady." And to her. A wistful smile broke free. She loved the way Wyatt's face lit up when he had the two of them as his audience, his fan club of two. The way he got into his characters, taking on their roles and changing his voice for each one, tickled her. "So, what's new with you two?" she asked.

After spending another five minutes getting caught up with her parents, she and Brady said their good-byes and ended the call. "We'll get to see Gammy and Pops in a few weeks. Are you excited about that?"

"Uh-huh," Brady agreed happily before returning to his toys.

She should visit her parents more often. After all, Decorah was only a few hours away. When she'd moved to the Twin Cities, all she'd been thinking about was getting away from the reminders of every *BAM* that had hit her in the past few years. Other than the fire in her apartment, things had calmed down considerably since then. She was on a good track, and the first of her goals was within reach. Hopefully her run of things turning to hell had passed.

Kayla picked up her phone and brought up Aunt Becky's number, eager to hear what her aunt might have to offer in the way of information. She couldn't wait to see how Wyatt would react once she'd done an agent search and handed him something tangible, something that let him know how much she appreciated having him in her life. He had no idea how much he meant to her. Her breath caught, and tears welled. Just how much did she care? Her years with Brad had left her with nothing but insecurity, and until she sorted herself out, she couldn't move forward.

If only she and Wyatt had met a few years from now, once she was well into her career. Then perhaps she'd be over everything that had happened. But between now and then, he'd likely find somebody who was perfect for him, someone who wasn't a single mom with emotional baggage.

Wyatt deserved to be ecstatically happy, and thinking about him with another woman should not cause this sudden twinge of jealousy. He was a great guy, and hot. Come to think of it, it was a wonder he hadn't already been snapped up. Were other women blind?

Sweat beading on her forehead, Kayla lifted the heavy tubs of clean laundry out of the trunk of her car and set them on the asphalt. Then she handed her son the bottle of detergent. "Come on, Brady. I want to get out of this heat." The temperature had hovered in the nineties for the past few days, and the humidity wasn't far behind.

She struggled to carry the stacked tubs, Brady walking along beside her. Then the back door opened, and Wyatt appeared. He hurried toward her and took the tubs out of her hands.

"My superhero neighbor to the rescue. Thanks." She flashed him a grateful smile. "Whew, it's hot."

"It certainly is."

"Hi, Wyatt," Brady chirped. "Guess what?"

Wyatt grinned. "What?"

"I'm gonna go stay at my Gammy and Pops's farm for a whole week."

"Wow." Wyatt winked at her.

Her knees went a little wobbly. She opened the back door for him, catching a whiff of his scent as he passed. She took it in, her gaze sliding over the taut muscles of his bare arms as he carried her laundry. Her damn hormones were acting up again.

"Yep. By myself, too, 'cause I'm a big boy now." Brady hopped up the stairs, one at a time. "Gammy and Pops have a donkey"— *hop*—"goats"—*hop*—"chickens"—*hop*—"a bellied pig"—*hop*—"and a llama."

"Hold the railing, please, Brady," Kayla admonished, taking up a place behind him in case he stumbled.

"A *bellied* pig?" Wyatt raised a brow.

"A potbellied pig. Lots of people buy them as pets, and then they change their minds. My mom runs a nonprofit animal rescue organization that takes in unusual animals and finds homes for them."

"Oh. So they don't farm?"

"No, my dad is a veterinarian." They started up the second flight of stairs to her apartment, her son still hopping.

Wyatt set down the laundry in front of her door and fist-bumped with Brady. "When are you going to visit your grandparents, Superkid?"

"I dunno." Brady shrugged and peered up at her. "When am I going, Mommy?"

Kayla put her key into the lock of her door. "Brady and I are visiting my parents over Labor Day weekend. We're leaving Friday, and I'm driving home on Monday. He's going to stay with them the rest of that week." She opened the door wide, and cool air wafted over them. "Oh, that feels good," she said.

"Where do you want these?" Wyatt asked, hoisting the tubs again.

"Just inside the door is fine," she said, pointing to the spot. "Thanks again for carrying them upstairs for me."

"I was wondering if you and Brady have anything planned for the rest of the afternoon?"

"Other than staying out of the heat? Nope. Not a thing."

"Would you two like to go to the Mall of America and check out the amusement park? It'll be cooler there."

His face turned red, something that happened less and less with her. Asking her to spend time with him must still be difficult, or at least awkward. Not surprising, considering she'd told him she wouldn't date him.

"Can we, Mommy?" Brady grabbed her hand with both of his. "Please?"

"I'd love to. Can you give us twenty minutes to get ready?" Wyatt's answering smile and the warmth in his eyes stole her breath.

"I can do that. Come down to my place when you're ready."

"All right," she said. Wyatt left, and she turned to Brady. She and her son always wore bottom-of-the-drawer stuff on laundry day. "Let's change into something a little nicer for our mall adventure."

Kayla hefted one of the tubs of clean laundry and carried it back to her room. She dumped the folded pile onto her bed and found a pair of shorts and a matching T-shirt, handing them to her son. "Go. Try to use the bathroom, and change into these. You can have a snack before we leave."

"But . . . I don't hafta go."

"Try anyway. You never want to go when you're excited. Then, right in the middle of all the fun, the situation becomes urgent."

"What's *urgent* mean?" He stared up at her.

"It means you nearly wet your pants because you refused to go when I told you to."

"Mmmph." He marched off, clearly unhappy with her definition of *urgent.*

Smiling, she chose capris and a lacy sleeveless shirt for herself. The toilet flushed, and her smile widened. She met Brady just as he was leaving the bathroom, his hands still dripping. "And I suppose you left your dirty clothes on the floor for me to pick up?" Kayla placed a hand on her hip and aimed a pointed look his way.

Brady let out another huff of exasperation, turned around and stomped back into the bathroom, emerging once again with his discarded clothing clutched to his chest.

"You know where they go," she said, tousling his hair as he passed, then she took possession of the bathroom. She changed into her clean clothes, brushed her hair and put it up into a loose knot on top of her head.

"Can we go *now*? I don't need a snack." Brady stood in the doorway, his expression impatient.

Kayla laughed. "Yes. We can go *now*." She took his hand, and he practically dragged her to the door. Kayla grabbed her purse from the top of the second tub of laundry, and they made their way downstairs to Wyatt's apartment. She knocked. "I've always wanted to go to the Mall of America. This is going to be fun," she said, giving Brady's hand a squeeze.

Wyatt opened his door and stepped out into the hallway. "Do you want to take my truck or your car?"

"Let's take mine. Brady's booster is in the back. Will you drive, though, since you know the way? I get nervous when someone is telling me where to go while I drive."

"Sure." He locked his door. "Nickelodeon Universe, here we come." He held a palm low for Brady.

"Yeah," Brady said, slapping Wyatt's hand. "Here we come."

"I've taken him on rides at our county fair, but Brady has never been to a real amusement park." She followed Wyatt and her son down the stairs. "Neither have I, for that matter."

"Wow. You've missed out. We also have Valleyfair, which isn't too far from the cities. My siblings, cousins, and I spent a lot of hours at the place when we were younger."

"I checked it out online earlier this summer and decided it was too expensive right now. Maybe when Brady is a little older we'll go. I can't believe people actually buy season passes, but I suppose it's cheaper for families to go on several staycations to Valleyfair than it is to take the entire family out of town. The water park looks like a lot of fun."

"The water park is my favorite part." Wyatt opened the door to their parking lot, taking Brady's hand as they walked into the stifling heat. "Speaking of vacations, if you could take one anywhere in the world, where would you go?"

"Hmm." She hit the Unlock button before handing him the keys to her car. "I'd have to say Germany, especially Bavaria."

He opened the back door and stepped back. "It's a blast furnace in there."

"I know. Black interior. What was I thinking?" She opened the front door for air circulation and helped her son get into his booster in the back. Wyatt had the car started and the air on by the time she settled into her seat. Sweat trickled down her temples, and she adjusted the side vent to flow directly on her and aimed the center vent toward the back for Brady.

"So, why Bavaria?" he asked.

"The Alps. To get to them, you have to pass through several picturesque medieval villages along the way," she said. "I've seen pictures. I'm mostly German. My maiden name is Wagner, and mom's is Becker. I think it would be fun to visit my ancestors' country of origin. What about you? Where would you go?"

They were making small talk, like they had when they'd gone to The Bulldog together. Wyatt was more adept at social skills than he gave himself credit for, because the chatter was helping her get past the awkwardness still lingering. Besides that, she really wanted to know where he'd go and what interested him.

"I've always wanted to see the Great Wall of China, because it's so amazing, especially considering when it was built. I'd also like to visit Spain. I took Spanish in high school, and I learned a lot about the country. It would be nice to actually tour some of the places I read about, and I hear the food is out of this world." He pulled out of the lot, and they were on their way. "I hope to get the chance to travel someday. Seeing a good chunk of the world is a big on my bucket list."

"Mine too. I also think it would be fun to visit some of our national parks and give camping a try."

"You've never been camping?" He glanced askance at her.

"I grew up on a farm. We were outdoors all day long. I guess my parents never saw the need to camp out." She shrugged. "I think it would be good for Brady, though."

"Superkid, has anyone ever taken you fishing?" Wyatt asked, looking at Brady in the rearview mirror.

"Nope."

"Well, we'll have to rectify that situation ASAP. I can borrow a kid's pole from one of my many cousins, and we can hit one of the area lakes. I've heard Como Lake is a good place to fish. The city stocks the lake."

"OK," Brady said, like he had a clue.

"How about you, Kayla. Have you fished?"

"Yes, and handling slimy fish and gross worms is not my idea of fun."

Wyatt chuckled. "Let's go fishing next Sunday. I'll handle the worms and the fish for you."

Amusement park today, fishing next Sunday? That's a lot of time spent with someone she wasn't dating. "First you were avoiding me, and now we're making plans two weekends in a row? What are you up to?"

"Nothing," he replied, his eyes wide and innocent. "The conversation about camping just kind of led to the fishing suggestion—which is a good one, by the way—and we should take advantage of what remains of the summer. It's important to give Brady new experiences. This is Minnesota, the Land of Ten Thousand Lakes. Every little boy and girl should know how to fish."

"Hmm. Your words sound reasonable enough, but the blush says otherwise." She snorted. "I love that about you. It's absolutely impossible for you to be duplicitous. So, again . . . what are you up to?"

"You said you wanted to be friends."

"I do."

"Well, I'm being your friend. I enjoy spending time with you and Brady. That's all." He cocked an eyebrow and shook his head. "Fishing isn't a date, Kayla. Neither is taking a five-year-old to Nickelodeon Universe. Relax."

"OK. Fair enough. I enjoy your company too." She grinned at Brady. "What about you? Do you enjoy Wyatt's company?"

"Yep!"

Wyatt chuckled. "We're here," he said, turning into a parking ramp.

"We are? This is Mallmerica?" Brady strained in his seat to peer out the window.

"Mall of America," she corrected as Wyatt pulled into a spot and cut the engine. "But this is just the parking ramp."

"OK, Superkid. I have a job for you." Wyatt unfastened his seat belt and twisted around to face Brady.

"What?"

"Your job is to remember that we're parked in the east ramp, on Georgia level P2. Can you do that?"

"Yep. East ramp, Georgia level P2." Brady repeated, his voice laced with pride.

Kayla's heart turned over. Unlike her husband, Wyatt was great at making her little boy feel good about himself. He'd be a great dad, and for some lucky woman, a great husband. Her chest tightened at the thought.

He'd made the switch, and they were friends. You couldn't undo a rejection like the one she'd handed him, and she wasn't even sure she wanted to. Did she? *There you go, second-guessing yourself again.* Would she never get things right when it came to timing and relationships?

Chapter Ten

Oh, he was up to something all right. Wyatt held Brady's hand as the three of them walked through the parking ramp toward the doors leading into Mallmerica, as Brady had called it. He planned to *friend* the hell out of Kayla, to *not* date her as often as possible until she finally succumbed and fell madly in love with him.

He got that she'd been hurt, and he understood her reluctance to date again. But if Grandma Maggie was right, and it was fear holding her back, he intended to help her get over that hill. He'd be waiting with open arms on the other side. He figured he already had a head start. Not that he'd had a lot of personal experience, but he'd read stuff. Kayla's eyes often darkened when she looked at him—a sure sign of attraction. She went slightly breathless around him sometimes too, and he wasn't the only one whose cheeks rosied when they were together. Though he'd put a stop to his accidentally-on-purpose touches and brushes, he'd certainly noticed how flustered those touches had made her. He might have pushed that a bit, but who could blame him? He'd loved the way she reacted. His mission—and he had chosen to accept it—was to wear down her resistance. Grinning, he winked at her.

"What?" Her eyes widened.

"I'm excited. Did you know that a chaperone can accompany a child on the kiddie rides for free? Big Rigs is my favorite. What do you say, Brady? Want to ride a truck on rails with me?"

Wyatt opened the door and ushered them through. The east entrance into the mall was crowded, colorful and noisy, and Nickelodeon Universe provided a backdrop of constant motion and flashing lights. "I guess we aren't the only ones who decided to get out of the heat at the mall today." He pointed to the amusement park. "We need to go down one floor to enter Nickelodeon. He guided them to the elevator, past the floor-to-ceiling advertisements for Sea Life Minnesota Aquarium. "There's another attraction we can check out sometime."

"That would be fun," Kayla agreed.

Brady stared at the amusement park from where they stood. "Is that Nickelodeon?" he asked, sidling close to his mom's side.

Wyatt pushed the elevator button. "It is."

"Wow. There are actual trees growing inside," Kayla said, studying the park, which took up the entire center of the mall.

"Yep." The elevator door opened. Wyatt herded the two inside and hit the button for the first floor. "I figured we'd just do the kiddie rides today. Is that all right?"

"Sure, unless we find something the three of us want to go on together."

He pulled the ticket he'd purchased online from his pocket. "I already got an all-day pass for Brady. If there's something the three of us want to ride together, we can get tickets from one of the kiosks."

"You already bought Brady's pass? How much was it? I'll pay you back." She brought her purse around to the front of her.

"Less than you'd expect, since he's only five. You can buy dinner at the food court, and we'll call it even."

"All right." Her chin came up. "I will."

They got off the elevator, and Brady's eyes widened. His gaze darted all over the place, from the escalator leading down to the Sea Life

Minnesota Aquarium, to the lights, crowds and the moving rides inside Nickelodeon. The cacophony of children shrieking, coupled with the mechanical sound of the moving rides, was loud and a bit overwhelming. Brady had gone quiet, and he looked so tiny amid the teeming throng filling the mall.

Wyatt scooped him up and held him in his arms. "A little too much, huh?" Brady snuggled against Wyatt's chest and laid his head on his shoulder. "Your mom and I are right here, Superkid. I promise you don't have to do anything you don't want to. Let's go check out the Big Rigs."

Brady nodded against Wyatt's shoulder, and 220 volts of protectiveness and love sent a jolt through him. Is this what it felt like to be a dad? He wanted the world for Brady just then. Kayla moved closer and ran her hand up and down Brady's back. Her gaze met his, a half smile on her pretty face, and her expression filled with tenderness. For a second, only a second, Wyatt imagined they were a unit, a family. His family.

He had to turn away, or the force of his emotions might shoot from his eyes like Elec Tric's lightning bolts. Swallowing against the sudden tightness in his throat, he set Brady down and took his hand. "Ready?"

"I am," Kayla said, taking Brady's other hand. "How about you, kiddo?"

"You can ride the Big Rigs with me?" Brady asked, staring anxiously up at Wyatt.

"I can indeed."

"OK." The kid squared his narrow shoulders. "Let's do this thing."

Wyatt laughed. "Where'd you hear that?"

Brady shrugged, his grin wide. "I dunno."

The three of them wended their way through the crowd into the amusement park, veering toward the junior area. Curious stares came his way, as they always did when he was in public. His hoodie didn't hide his burn scars, but they did give him a bit of insulation.

"That must be annoying," Kayla said, glaring at a passerby who had stared his way.

"What's that?"

"I get why you wear the hooded sweatshirts. People are so rude," she huffed.

"I'm used to it." He couldn't help but smile at the affronted-on-his-behalf tone she'd used. They passed the Guppy Bubbler, the Hayride, Swiper's Sweeper and the Crazy Cars, Brady's excitement mounting with each ride that came into view. Finally, Wyatt led them along the wooden walkway to the Big Rigs, a small train of brightly colored cars made to look like semitrucks. "Here we are." He placed his hands on Brady's shoulders and guided him into the line. "You can watch other kids ride while we wait."

Kayla took out her phone. "I'm going to take pictures."

Brady's attention riveted on the ride, he kept a firm hold on Wyatt's hand. Finally it was their turn, and they were lucky enough to be first, which meant they got the big red truck in front. Wyatt helped Brady get situated first, and then he squeezed himself into the tight space beside him, his knees pressing against the front. "All set?"

Brady nodded, too keyed up to answer verbally. Wyatt gave Kayla a thumbs-up, and she took a picture. The ride started, and Brady gripped the safety bar. After a few seconds, he relaxed, and a wide smile lit his face. Wyatt hugged the boy's shoulders. "Are you having fun?"

"Yeah!" Other kids were holding their hands in the air, and soon Brady did the same.

Another wave of protectiveness hit Wyatt. He wanted Brady to always feel safe and hoped like hell he would grow up to be confident, thoughtful and strong enough to stand up for himself and others should the need arise. Every boy deserved a man's guidance through the perils of adolescence. Wyatt's eyes stung. He'd had his dad during his formative years, and then he'd had his uncles and Grandpa Joe. They were the best, and he wanted to pay it forward with Brady.

He glanced at Kayla, and she sent him a little wave, her face radiating happiness. His poor heart slammed against his sternum, stealing his ability to breathe. She had no idea how she affected him. Nudging Brady, he directed his attention to his mom. Brady beamed and waved at his mom. Kayla took another picture, and shortly after that their ride came to an end. They got off and joined the milling crowd of parents and children on the main path through the labyrinth of bright colors and movement.

"What can I ride next? Can we do the cars?" Brady pointed to the junior-sized bumper cars. "Mommy, will you go on them with me?"

"Sure, if Wyatt's feelings aren't hurt that you don't want him to ride with you again," she teased.

"Oh." Brady stopped, his face falling. "You can go with me on the ride *after* the cars. OK?" He peered up at Wyatt, concern suffusing his features.

He feared the lump in his throat would become a permanent fixture. Wyatt squeezed Brady's hand. "I'm all in favor of taking turns."

It hadn't taken Brady long to get over his initial nervousness, and then Wyatt and Kayla could hardly keep up with him. They spent the next couple of hours bouncing from ride to ride, going on Brady's favorites again and again.

"Can I go on that one by myself?" Brady pointed to the Flyboat, a row of seats that took the riders up to the top and dropped them repeatedly, to be caught and bounced by a cushion of air.

"Sure, and let's make that the last ride for today. I don't know about you, Superkid, but I'm starving," Wyatt said.

"I'm hungry too. Aren't you, Brady?" Kayla asked.

"I guess." He tugged them both toward the line for the Flyboat.

When it was Brady's turn to be loaded into a seat, he cast an anxious look over his shoulder. "You won't go anywhere?"

"Nope. We'll be right here." Wyatt held out his fist. Brady bumped it and went off with the teenager working the station.

"He's having a blast. Thank you for suggesting this." Kayla leaned against the log railing in front of the ride. "I need to do more stuff like this with him."

"I'm having fun too. Brady is such a great kid."

"He is, isn't he?" Kayla sighed. "I've been lucky."

"Luck doesn't have anything to do with it, Kayla. You're a great mom, and he's a lucky little boy to have you."

"Thank you," she murmured, averting her gaze.

His heart turned over. "I've been thinking a lot about what you said."

"When?" Her brow creased.

"The night we went to The Bulldog."

"Oh?"

"I know you think you missed out on a whole lot of who knows what, but you didn't. Not really. After high school most of us were struggling, broke, going to school and trying to get our shit together. Not a lot of fun, if you ask me. You did basically the same thing, only you happened to have a child at the time." He shook his head. "There is no going back, you know, and why would you want to?" He studied her, gauging her reaction. "Early adulthood, being on your own . . . it's exciting, but it's also tough."

Kayla kept her eyes on her son. "I know you can't go back, but a person can decide to take a time out to regroup after a disaster. You don't know what it was like for me. While my friends were in college, partying and going to Cancún for spring breaks, I was changing diapers and working a boring factory job."

"That's what you think you missed out on, partying and spring breaks somewhere tropical? Because I gotta tell you, the majority of us didn't party much or go to Cancún on our spring breaks. Personally, I worked during my time off from school, and it never occurred to me that I was missing anything." Except maybe dating, but that had everything to do with his shyness, and nothing to do with school or work. "I'll bet if you talked to some of your friends who drank their way through breaks, they'd tell you they have a few regrets. I'll bet a lot of them wish they hadn't wasted the time."

She straightened away from the railing. "It's not about parties and spring breaks," she said, her expression tight. "It's about *vitae interruptio*. You don't know what—"

"I lost my parents when I was a little kid, Kayla. You're not about to tell me I don't know what it's like to have my life interrupted." His brow rose. "Are you?"

"I forgot." She bit her lip. "I'm sorry."

"No need to apologize." He jutted his chin toward Brady. "Being here with your son . . . *this* is fun, the kind of fun that counts. I know you feel like you didn't get the chance to grow up before becoming a wife and mother, but you know what I think?" He leaned closer. "Raising Brady the way you are, to be the great kid that he is? Now that's grown-up in the very best sense of the word. Life moves on. We grow up and grow older no matter what."

"So, are you trying to convince me I don't need a few years to figure myself out?" Her lips compressed into a tight line again. "Because—"

"No. I'm not trying to convince you of anything." He needed to beat a hasty retreat, or she'd do the withdrawal thing again. "I'm suggesting you give yourself some well-deserved credit. As your friend, I'm trying to point out that you may have romanticized those missing years a bit." His face heated. "Do you think that's possible?"

She turned back to watch Brady. He and the other children threw up their hands and shrieked as the ride dropped, bounced and rose again and again. "Any idea when your brother will be back to finish my apartment?"

"Soon. I'll ask him on Monday and let you know." He clamped down on the urge to say more. He'd made his point, and he had no doubt she'd mull it over.

With Brady's last ride over, the three of them headed to the food court and decided on burgers and fries. By the time they were finished, Brady had already nodded off over his food a couple of times. Kayla gathered up the trash and shoved it into a bin near their table.

"Time to go home, buddy." Wyatt lifted Brady off the bench and set him on his feet.

"I don't want to go home. I want to go to the Lego store." Brady's face puckered. "We never got to go there."

"Well, we have a reason to come back another day then, don't we?" Kayla tried to take his hand, but Brady jerked away and put them both behind his back.

Then he burst into tears. "I want to go to Legos *nowww*, not another day," he wailed.

"I'm sorry, kiddo. Not gonna happen. You're practically asleep on your feet as it is," Kayla told him in a soothing voice. "We'll come back."

"Promise?" he asked, wiping his eyes.

"I promise."

"Want a ride back to the car?" Wyatt asked.

Brady nodded, his tears still flowing over having to walk anywhere at all for any reason, especially if it meant leaving the mall. Wyatt lifted the exhausted boy into his arms, and by the time they reached the doors leading to the parking ramp, Brady had fallen asleep against his shoulder. Wyatt glanced at Kayla as she opened the door for him. "That was the first time I've seen Brady kick up a fuss over anything. I was under the impression he was the perfect kid."

"Oh, believe me, it's not the first time he's thrown a fit." She snorted. "Be glad you weren't around during the terrible twos, because that year almost did me in."

He couldn't be glad about not being there for her and Brady and wished he had been. He would've seen to it that she didn't give up her goals just because they were parents. He certainly wouldn't have left her to handle everything all on her own, which forced her to work at a boring, dead-end job. His jaw tightened, thinking about what a jerk her husband had been. Kayla deserved so much better, and he admired the way she'd handled things and moved forward with her life.

"This was fun," he said. "I'm looking forward to fishing next Sunday. Do you want to go out for breakfast first?"

She studied him for a few seconds, her expression inscrutable. "Sure. I'll bring stuff to study while you two play with hooks and worms. Where do you want to go for breakfast?"

"Louisiana Cafe is my favorite place. Have you been there?"

"No." One side of her mouth quirked up. "McDonald's is our usual breakfast spot. It'll be nice to try somewhere different."

"Great. I'll round up a fishing pole for Brady this week and pick up bait and a license Saturday afternoon." Satisfied, he grinned. They'd had a great day, and he'd made progress.

"These aren't dates," Kayla blurted. "We aren't dating."

"Course not." His smile grew. She wouldn't have blurted that if he weren't getting to her. Yes, indeed. He was making inroads into her defenses and hopefully into her heart. "Just friends hanging out."

Kayla hadn't been able to take her eyes off Wyatt's bare arms and flexing muscles all morning, as he taught her son how to fish. The man fascinated her, and more than anything, she longed to run her hands over the smooth contours of those muscles. She tried for the umpteenth time to focus on studying for her upcoming national exam, but her gaze kept straying from her notes to settle once again upon hot-hoodie-guy. She gave up the fight, stretched out her legs on the blanket she'd laid under a large oak and set aside her notebook.

Wyatt had spent time with her every day since their trip to the mall, even if that time only added up to a few minutes. He'd rushed out the back door to help her carry in her groceries on Tuesday, and he did the same Saturday morning with her tubs of laundry. He kept popping up, coming around the corner from wherever he'd been working in their building. They'd chat about their days, a couple of times sharing a meal, and then he'd read a comic book to her and Brady. But never once did he touch her. Nope. The inadvertent and not-so-inadvertent touching had come to an abrupt end. Wyatt kept their conversations light and friendly while being very careful to keep his physical distance. When he read his comic books, he even made sure Brady sat between them. She wasn't sure how much more of this new torture she could take. Sighing, she leaned back, propped herself up with her arms and gave in to the urge to stare at him.

He helped Brady cast his line into the lake. The red-and-white bobber landed with a *plop* and floated on the surface. Fishing pole in hand, Brady sat down at the end of the dock, while Wyatt cast out his line. He lowered himself to the spot next to her son, and Brady leaned companionably against him. Her heart fluttered. Who knew the way he was with her son would be such a turn on? *He's a friend.* She reminded herself for the thousandth time, lusting after him all the same.

Desperate for a distraction, she scanned the area. Como Lake had a pavilion on the western side, with paddleboats to rent and a food booth in the lower level facing the lake. A walking path and a biking path encircled the perimeter of the lake, and the fishing dock had been constructed on the southern side. Brady had gotten a thrill out of seeing painted turtles, an egret and a blue heron as they'd walked from the parking lot to the dock. A nice breeze ruffled her hair. The long stretch of hot days had finally eased.

"Mommy! I got one." Brady's excitement rang through the air.

Kayla sprang from her place and hurried to the end of the dock. By the time she reached Brady, he was standing. "You sure did," she said. The bobber disappeared under the water, and the line was taut.

"OK, Brady," Wyatt said. "Reel it in like I showed you." He kept his hand on the pole while Brady turned the reel. "That's it. You're doing great." He grinned at her over his shoulder. "Take my pole, would you?"

"Sure." She took it from him and moved out of the way so the lines wouldn't get tangled. Brady continued to bring his catch closer, and Wyatt reached for the net with his free hand. Finally the fish splashed around at the end of the dock, and he scooped it up.

"Wow." Wyatt pulled the fish out and held it up by the gills. "Look at that. His very first time fishing, and he catches a walleye big enough to keep. Way to go, Superkid."

"What do I do now?" Brady asked, leaning close to get a better look at his fish.

Wyatt pulled a pair of needle-nosed piers out of his tackle box. "You can watch while I take him off the hook. See how I slide my hand down from its head? That's to keep from getting poked by the fins."

"OK." Still holding onto his pole, her son grinned at her before focusing his attention upon the lesson at hand.

"The hook is deep, otherwise I'd pull it out by hand." Wyatt gripped the hook with the pliers, worked it out and dropped the fish into the bucket he'd filled with lake water earlier. "There. Two more, and we'll have caught tonight's dinner. You want to bait your hook, Brady?"

Brady nodded. Wyatt took a fat earthworm from the plastic tub and handed it over. The tip of Brady's tongue poked out as he concentrated on getting the worm onto the hook.

"Gross," she said with a laugh.

Wyatt took the hook from Brady. "I'm going to finesse this for you, buddy."

"Can I cast it by myself?" Brady asked, wiping his dirty hands on the front of his shorts.

"Of course." Wyatt straightened, took up a place behind him, and positioned the fishing pole in Brady's small hands. "Go for it."

Brady brought his pole back and swung it forward. His bobber splashed in the lake right in front of the dock. Wyatt chuckled and helped him get set for another try. "Release earlier this time."

"OK." His face scrunched with concentration, he tried again. This time his bobber landed a good distance out into the water, and his expression turned triumphant.

"Way to go." She reached out and squeezed his shoulder. "You're really good with him, Wyatt. Thanks so much for . . . for . . ." *Damn.* Her throat closed up.

"You're welcome . . . welcome. I don't know about you, but I'm having fun. Fishing with my friends on a Sunday morning is hardly what I'd call a sacrifice, believe me." His brown eyes filled with warmth and amusement.

Friends. That word again. It had taken him days of avoiding her to switch gears on her account. To expect him to switch back now would be unfair, not to mention unkind. Nobody liked to be yanked around, and she couldn't do that to Wyatt. She cared too much about him . . . as a friend, and she didn't want to mess that up. *Gah.*

He might've been right about how she'd romanticized the time she'd missed after high school. She'd never been a partier. Despite the way things had happened, she had grown up, probably faster than her high school friends. You can't go back; you can only move forward.

Did that mean she couldn't change her mind about dating, because the more time she spent with Wyatt Haney, hoodie-wearing, comic book writer extraordinaire, the more she wanted him. The more she wanted him, the more she regretted telling him she couldn't date him. She ought to be one of his comic book characters, the one who always made the wrong decision, took the wrong turn and ended up being her own worst frenemy.

Kayla's phone rang just as she was leaving school on Tuesday afternoon. She fished it out of her bag, checked caller ID and answered. "Aunt Becky, hi."

"Hey, Kayla. How are you and Brady? How's school?"

"About the same as when we talked a couple weeks ago." She grinned. "We're great."

"Good. The reason I'm calling is because I spoke with my agent about your friend and his comic books. Turns out, Angie represents graphic novels and comic books too. Here's the deal. I'm going to New York for a children's book fair the Thursday after Labor Day. My agent will be there, and she's willing to take a look at his work if I bring samples with me."

"Oh my God. That's great! Thank you so much for talking to her."

"You're welcome. Your dad mentioned you'd be home this weekend for the holiday. Can you bring Wyatt's comic books with you? I'll stop by the farm and pick them up if that works."

"I can do that. Wyatt makes color copies of every one of them. I'll ask him for all the Elec Tric series. Those are the stories he's been reading to us, and they're wonderful. Just wait till you see them, Aunt Becky."

"I hope you're right. I've never asked my agent to take a look at someone else's work before."

"I am. Don't worry." She practically floated through the parking lot to her car. "I'll see you this weekend."

"See you then, Kayla."

She put her phone away and got into her car. Her mind racing, she drove to Brady's day-care center. Finally she had the opportunity to do something nice for Wyatt. Of course, nothing might come of it, but she didn't see how that was possible. His work was good, as good or better than any of the comic books she'd read, and she'd read plenty.

She parked in the day-care lot and rushed through signing Brady out and getting him into the car. "I can hardly wait to get home," she said, fastening Brady's seat belt. She couldn't wait to tell Wyatt the news.

"Are we going to go see Gammy and Pops now?"

"No. This is only Tuesday. We aren't leaving until Friday." She had him recite the days of the week with her a few times as she buckled her seat belt and drove out of the lot.

What if Wyatt didn't appreciate her intrusion into his comic book writing career? Had she stepped over a line by interfering? He might not appreciate that she'd taken it upon herself to find him an agent. Frowning, she parked in her spot, her heart fluttering at the sight of his truck. "Come on, Brady. I want to find Wyatt."

"Is he going to read to me tonight?"

"I don't know. I guess we'll find out." She hurried her son through the door and up the stairs to the first floor. No sign of him there, so she continued on to the second floor. Rock music and deep male voices came from her apartment, and her door was slightly ajar.

"Smells funny," Brady said, his face scrunching up.

"Our apartment is being painted. It's not as bad as the smoky smell, is it?"

"I guess." Brady preceded her into the apartment.

Wyatt and his brother were in her dining room. Sam was on a ladder, painting the last corner of her ceiling.

"Wow, it looks really good in here." She admired her new ceiling, light fixture and walls. "The fresh paint really makes everything look nice and new."

"Hey," Sam spared her and Brady a smile before turning back to painting. "We were just talking about theater night. Josey says *The Lion King* is coming back to Minneapolis in October, and she wants to know if we're all still interested."

"Oh." The tickets had to be expensive, but seeing such a popular musical would be fun. If she did go, would it be too date-like? Not if she paid for her own ticket. She glanced at Wyatt, who was chatting with her son about his day. "Sure. I'm still in."

"Good. Josey will buy the tickets and let us know how much we each owe her."

"Great." She set her purse down on the kitchen counter. "I have news, Wyatt."

"News?" His brow rose.

"Yes. Remember I told you about my aunt who writes middle-grade novels? I talked to her about your comic books."

"You did?"

"I did, because I wanted advice for you about finding an agent." She sucked in a breath. "Turns out her agent represents comic books, and she'd like to take a look at your work."

"Really?" Wyatt's face lit up, and his smile did all kinds of wonderful things to every one of her major organs—her heart in particular.

She nodded, her own smile so big her cheeks hurt. "Aunt Becky wants me to bring the Elec Tric series to her when I go home this weekend. She's meeting with her agent next week at a book fair, and she'll give them to her then."

"That was nice of you, Kayla," Sam said, flashing her an appreciative look.

"I wanted to do something to thank Wyatt for everything he's done for us. I can't promise that this will lead to anything, but—"

"I can put together a portfolio right now." Wyatt started for the door.

"Can we come too?" Brady asked.

"I would love to see where you work," Kayla added.

"Of course you can come too," Wyatt said, lifting Brady into the air and swinging him around in a wide arc. He set him down again by the door. "And we can pick out a new adventure to read tonight." He glanced at her. "Unless you have plans, that is."

"Nope. No plans." She'd made Wyatt happy, and the thrill was like nothing she'd ever experienced before. Giddy with pleasure, she followed him downstairs and through his apartment to the back bedroom.

Shelves lined one entire wall of his studio, and they held all kinds of art supplies and paper. His drawing table had been positioned between the east- and south-facing windows. Wyatt opened a cabinet positioned by the door and reached for a stack of color copies of his comic books.

"Mommy, it's you!" Brady cried, pointing to the work sitting on the drawing board.

She crossed the room to the drawing table, Wyatt converging with her at the same time. He made a move to reach for the illustrations sitting on the table, but she got there first, placing her hand on a corner. Wyatt groaned, and her gaze swung to him.

His face had turned a deep red. "It's . . . uhh."

Kayla studied the cover. A female figure, dressed in purple and black, graced the cover. The woman looked exactly how Wyatt had depicted her in the portrait he'd given her. Only in this version, she'd been portrayed as sinister, with the black eyes of a demon.

Diabolical Delilah, Elec Tric's archenemy, stood in the background, her expression a definite gloating smirk. Kayla read the title, *A Hero Has His Heart Broken*. Her stomach dropped like a bag of sand, and all her happiness evaporated. Her chest tight, she flipped through a few pages. "The Mysterious Ms. M," she muttered to herself, trying like hell to draw a breath. She was the Mysterious Ms. M, and she'd broken Wyatt's heart. She didn't know how to react and reeled from the impact.

Wyatt didn't say a word. It was just a comic book. Writers and artists drew their inspiration from life. She knew that, but it didn't help. This hurt. This hurt a lot. *Silly.* She was being silly, and the important thing was getting his work to her aunt's agent. "Becky said to send everything you have on Elec Tric. Will you have time to make a color copy of this latest installment?"

She couldn't look at Wyatt. He'd put the heartbreak of her rejection into his comic book, and there it would remain for all the world to see. Would a friend do that? Had he really switched gears? Even more important, it was obvious she'd hurt him way more than he'd let on.

He gathered a pile of his work and put it in a large white envelope, then he grabbed a marker and wrote his contact information across the front. "Um, sure," he muttered.

"I can't wait to read through all of these," she managed to say. Especially the latest issue, the one where she'd chosen to cross over to the dark side.

"Can we read this one tonight?" Brady asked, peering up at Wyatt.

"It's not finished."

"You know what? Brady and I have a lot to do before we leave on Friday. We're going to have to read another comic book some other time."

"How about tomorrow night?" Wyatt asked.

"I'm going to the laundromat then, since we'll be in Iowa on Saturday."

"If you want, I can watch Brady for you while you're at the laundromat."

"I've already asked Mariah to watch him, and Rosie would be disappointed if I canceled."

"Right." Wyatt handed her the envelope. "It's just make-believe, Kayla. My comic books are fiction."

Finally she managed to look at him and wished she hadn't. His wonderful brown eyes were filled with hurt. "I know that," she said. Forcing a smile, she took the envelope from him. "Just kind of took me by surprise is all."

His Adam's apple bobbed. "Then we're OK? You're not upset?"

"No," she lied. "I'm not upset. I just have a lot on my mind." *Like all this remorse over breaking your heart I need to process.*

"If it would help, I can watch Brady for a while right now. He and I can read, and you'll have some free time."

"Can I stay, Mommy? Please?"

"Please," Wyatt echoed.

"That would be great, and it'll keep him out of your brother's way while he's cleaning up. I'll come get him in an hour or so."

"That would be fine, or I can bring him up to you."

"No. I'll come get him." Her poor son looked completely confused. Kids were barometers when it came to tension, and she was feeling plenty. "Well, I am going to go start organizing for our trip. You be good for Wyatt." Brady made a face at her, an expression that said he didn't need the reminder. She leaned down and kissed his forehead. "See you later, kiddo." She forced another smile. "Thanks, Wyatt."

She left them and made her way slowly back up to her apartment. Sam was removing trim tape from the baseboards. The drop cloths had already been folded into a neat pile, and the paint rollers and brushes had been placed in a bucket. The work on her apartment had been completed.

He glanced at her. "Where's Brady?"

"I left him downstairs. Wyatt is going to read him a comic book." She bit her lip.

Sam stopped peeling trim tape and straightened. "What's wrong?"

She blinked and averted her gaze. "I just met the Mysterious Ms. M."

"Ah," he chuckled. "So, what do you think? The resemblance is uncanny, isn't it?"

"She . . ." Kayla cleared her throat. *I hurt that wonderful, sensitive, amazing man, and now I hurt.* "Ms. M broke Elec Tric's heart, and Wyatt turned her into a *demon.*"

"Well, damn."

"No." She muttered to herself. "More like . . . well . . . BAM."

Chapter Eleven

Panic swamped Wyatt. Why hadn't he remembered he'd left Elec Tric's latest installment on his drawing board? He could've put it away the second they'd entered the room. Kayla wouldn't have seen her demonized image or the title on the cover, and everything would be fine. Despite the fact that she'd said they were good, her expression said otherwise.

Choosing a comic book from another series he'd written a while ago, he turned to Brady. "Ready to read, Superkid?"

Brady nodded and reached for Wyatt's hand.

Wyatt led his audience of one to the living room, when what he really wanted to do was rush upstairs to talk it out with Kayla. But what could he say? *Yeah, your rejection hurt, and writing is how I process shit like this.* Somehow he had a feeling that wouldn't help matters.

He and Brady settled on the couch, and Wyatt forced his mind away from what troubled him. "This is a story about a hero whose superpowers include turning into fierce animals when the need arises."

"What kind of animals?" Brady asked, leaning against Wyatt's side like he always did when they read together.

Wyatt's chest tightened. He put his arm around his little buddy and gave him a quick hug. "Sometimes a wolf, other times a huge bear with paws the size of truck tires. And when he shifts, he's super, super strong."

"Cool," Brady said with a nod. "What's his name?"

"The Mighty Bane. He fights bad guys in his city." Once he began reading, he got into the story and the characters, and he caught a break from worrying about what might be going through Kayla's mind.

"Help! My purse," Wyatt cried in a falsetto voice as an elderly woman's purse was snatched by a punk.

"Don't worry. I'll get it back for you, ma'am." Bane changed into his wolf even as he spoke.

"It's a trap," he explained to Brady as he turned the page. "But of course our hero has no idea."

"We have you, Bane, the not-so-mighty, now," said the thug. "See how the head of the gang smacks a baseball bat against his palm?" Wyatt asked. *"SMACK, SMACK, SMACK.* That's the sound of the bat against the thug's hand while ten lowlife gangsters circle the Mighty Bane."

"When we're through with you, there won't be nothin' left." The creep's evil laughter sets Bane in motion. See here where he shifts again, his bones crackling and lengthening. Where the wolf stood but a moment ago, now a twelve-foot-tall bear faces the angry gang members. His ferocious growl rumbles and echoes against the surrounding brick buildings. *SNARL! RIP! THUD!* The sounds of battle reverberate off the alley walls, Brady. Bane's huge claws swipe left and right and his jaws snap."

"Does Bane beat the bad guys?" Brady asked, peering up at Wyatt.

"We'll see." Wyatt turned the page and continued to tell the story.

"I want to draw comic books when I grow up," Brady announced once they'd finished reading how the Mighty Bane had once again defeated the criminal element of his made-up city.

"Why wait until you grow up? I have lots of paper and colored pencils. Do you want to draw right now?"

"I already drew one at school, and I sent it to Gammy and Pops. Can I have a snack too?"

Wyatt's heart melted. Brady trusted him. They'd bonded, and he'd walk on hot coals followed by a bed of nails before he'd break that bond. "Of course. Let me get the paper and pencils, and then I'll see about a snack."

He left Brady sitting on the couch and strode to his studio to put the comic book away. His gaze lit on the Elec Tric cover still sitting on his drawing table. He wanted to rip it to shreds. Frustrated, he blew out a breath and headed back to the living room. At least he had no doubts about where he stood with the five-year-old.

After he set everything up for Brady to color, Wyatt went to his kitchen and opened his fridge. "You want a pear, Brady?" he called.

"Yes, please," Brady called back, his tone already distracted.

Wyatt washed and cut the pear into bite-sized pieces. He tossed them into a bowl, grabbed a couple of napkins and brought them to the coffee table. "Let's see what you've come up with so far," he said, taking a seat. "We comic book writers can bounce ideas off each other. What do you say?"

"Uh-huh." Brady showed him his childish figures with their round bellies and sticklike limbs. "This is the good guy," he said pointing to one of the figures. "And this is a monster."

"Ahh, I see. Nice job." The monster's only distinguishing feature was a set of horns—or were they ears?—on top of its head. "Here's your pear."

Brady took a piece and popped it into his mouth. Pear juice dampened the paper where he set his hand to color in the rounded bodies of his hero and monster.

"So, tell me what your monster is up to?" A knock on his door sent Wyatt's pulse skyrocketing. "That'll be your mom." He shot off the couch. "I gave Brady a snack," he murmured, as he opened the door wide to let her in. "I hope that's OK."

"Oh, thanks," she said, not meeting his eyes.

Great. Back to that, are we?

"Mommy, I'm drawing another comic book," Brady announced.

"That's nice, but it's time for supper." She moved to stand beside Brady. "Wow. Awesome pencils and paper, there, buddy. Did you thank Wyatt?"

Brady shot him a "back me up, 'cause we're guys" look. Wyatt winked. "He did thank me, and he also said please when he asked for a snack. He can take the extra sheets of paper and the pencils with him if he wants. I have plenty."

"Can I, Mommy?"

"You have crayons and colored pencils upstairs. You can finish your picture with your own supplies." She glanced at Wyatt. Finally. "Your paper must be expensive. He has plenty of stuff he can use. Thanks for watching him and for letting him color."

"Kayla, I can tell you're upset." Had that come out of his mouth, past the dryness and his pounding heart?

"I'm not." She shook her head. "It's just that . . ." Her expression tightened. "I feel bad, because—"

"I only suffered a very temporary and topical sting to the ego. I'm way past it now." He waved a hand in the air, going for dismissive. It came across more as a lame demonstration of just how far past it he really wasn't.

Her brow rose slightly. What did that mean? What would she do if he told her the truth? The closer they became, the more time they spent together, the more he wanted her. What if he admitted that standing this close to her drove him crazy with the need to have her in his arms? He couldn't say any of that.

"Writing is the way I process things, and of course I dramatize for the sake of the story. That's all. I don't want this to come between us. I don't want this to jeopardize our friendship. I'll tear up that episode, I swear."

"Don't tear it up." She let out a shaky breath. "Finish it, make a color copy, and give it to me before I leave on Friday afternoon. It's part of the Elec Tric saga, and I want to give as much as I can to my aunt, so she can give it to her agent."

"All right. I'll work on it tonight if you promise me we're OK."

"We're fine. Friendship intact." Her eyes were a little too bright, and her smile a little too forced.

He reached for her and drew her close. She was stiff in his arms, and she patted his back. Clearly they were not OK, and he'd just turned things awkward to the nth degree.

She stepped away and offered him another unconvincing smile. "Brady and I are heating up leftovers for supper. You're welcome to join us."

"Umm . . . I think I'd better work on that last installment of the Elec Tric series." He raked a hand through his hair, knocking off his hood. He started to pull it back up.

Kayla caught his hand and brought it down. "Don't," she said, her voice a rasp. "Don't feel like you have to cover up—not with me." Her gaze roamed his face, her expression intense and imploring.

She still gripped his hand. Instinct took over, and he tugged her close again. This time she wrapped her arms around his waist, laid her head against his shoulder and hugged him back for real. Enveloped in her warmth, her scent, it was all he could do not to kiss her crazy and back her up against the nearest wall.

She swallowed a few times, and it registered in his lust-fogged brain that she really was upset. He nuzzled the softness of her temple, inhaling her essence, and she shivered against him. That small movement sent him tumbling across that line he wanted so badly to cross. He angled his head to capture her mouth with his, but she pulled away, leaving him with empty arms and a raging hard-on.

"We'd better get going," she chirped in a strained tone. "Come on, Brady. Dinner and a bath, and then bed. Tomorrow is a school day."

Brady popped the last piece of pear into his mouth. "OK."

Wyatt followed them to the door, mortified that he'd almost lost control right in front of her son. Heat surged to his face. Kayla had to be aware of the way her closeness affected him. Their bodies had touched from chest to toes. Still in a haze of desire, his brain wouldn't sync with his mouth. He couldn't string together a sentence if his life depended upon it, and the tension definitely needed cutting.

"Bring a copy of that latest installment up to my place when you have it," Kayla said, with yet another artificial smile plastered on her face.

Still on involuntary mute, Wyatt nodded, and the two left. He closed the door behind them, wishing like hell thought balloons would appear over Kayla's head so he had a clue what was going through her mind. What a superpower that would be.

Humph. He'd have to create a new comic book character who could do that visible thought bubble thing, since he couldn't. Too bad life wasn't like his comics. If it were, he could concentrate really hard and develop the power. Sighing, he plodded into the kitchen and grabbed a beer from the fridge. Then he headed for his studio to work on finishing the latest Elec Tric disaster—or rather, his latest disaster, another setback in the Wyatt and Kayla saga.

Kayla had bought a small suitcase for Brady at a discount store the night Wyatt watched Brady for her, and she'd dug out her hand-me-down suitcase from her closet. All she had left to do was the laundry tonight and packing tomorrow night, and they'd be ready to head out on Friday. She led Brady across the hall to Mariah's apartment, leaving her one tub of laundry in the hallway by her apartment.

The door opened before she could even knock. "Boy, are we glad to see you two." Mariah grinned, placing her hand on the top of her daughter's head. "Seems like you've been awfully busy with our downstairs neighbor lately."

Kayla sucked in a breath. She longed to talk to someone about Wyatt, but she wasn't ready to give voice to her obsession. Had he almost kissed her yesterday? She wasn't sure, especially after his "it was only a topical sting to the ego and I'm way past it now" speech.

She may have imagined he'd intended to kiss her, but she hadn't imagined his hard length pressing into her. She needed space, time to think. He meant way too much to her to complicate their friendship with sex, but damn . . . she wanted him.

"So. What's going on with you and Wyatt?"

"He and I are friends." Man, she was tired of that word, which didn't begin to encompass what she felt for him. Where her husband had run her into the ground, Wyatt encouraged and praised. He helped her to feel good about herself and the choices she'd made . . . with the exception of her choice *not* to date him, that is. Too late now. He was over her.

"Friends with benefits?" Mariah waggled her eyebrows.

Her heart thudded. There was no mistaking the way his body reacted to hers when they hugged. Even thinking about him brought a throbbing ache to her core. "Not that kind of deal," she muttered.

"Rosie, you know what?" Brady jumped over the threshold. "I caught a fish, a . . . what kind was it, Mommy?"

"A walleye, and we fried it up for dinner, along with a few other fish Wyatt caught," she said. "Wyatt and I also took Brady to Nickelodeon Universe at the Mall of America. You and I should take the kids there together soon."

"Yay! Mall of America." Rosie grabbed Brady's hand. "Can we, Mama?"

"Sounds like a good idea. We'll plan something when Brady comes home from visiting his grandparents." She flashed Kayla a pointed look.

"We'll have time to get caught up while you're child-free next week. Let's plan a girls' night out or something."

"Sure." By then she'd have had time away, which would give her some objectivity. Hopefully her raging hormones would settle down.

"Hi, Mariah, Rosie."

Kayla gulped. There he was, once again managing to pop up out of nowhere, looking tall, lean and gorgeous.

"Hey, Wyatt," Mariah said. "You're still a hero in my book. I'm loving not having fuses blow all the time. Are you about done with the building?"

"Almost. We're working in the basement now." Wyatt held a large white envelope. "I'm glad I caught you, Kayla. Here's the finished Elec Tric episode."

Mariah's gaze bounced from her to Wyatt and back again. "Electric episode?"

"It's Elec *Tric*, which is the name of his comic book hero. My aunt is going to show Wyatt's work to her agent next week."

"Oh." Mariah nodded slowly, her gaze once again darting between her and Wyatt. "Well, we'll definitely have to get caught up soon."

"Absolutely." Rose and Brady had already disappeared, and Kayla jerked her thumb over her shoulder. "I'd better go get that laundry done."

"I'm on my out anyway. I'll carry the tub down for you." Wyatt didn't wait for her response. He handed her the envelope and trotted off to grab her dirty laundry before disappearing down the stairs.

"There's nothing going on between you, eh? Wish I had a neighbor to carry my stuff like that." Mariah smirked. "You will tell all. Either later tonight or after your weekend in Iowa."

Would she? "See you later." Kayla walked across the hall and unlocked her door. She set the envelope on the dining room table, alongside the other one containing Wyatt's comic book copies. She was itching to read all about the Mysterious Ms. M.

Tonight, once Brady was in bed, she planned to go through everything in those envelopes, dammit. They taunted and teased her, but she'd been too busy preparing for her trip to get into them.

By the time she made it to her car, Wyatt and his truck were gone. He'd set her laundry tub next to her car, not even sticking around for a minute so she could thank him for his help. Maybe he was avoiding her again. Disappointment tugged at her, and a lump of sadness settled in the pit of her stomach.

Was he off on a date, or to meet his siblings at The Bulldog? Either way, tonight could be the night he'd meet someone who wouldn't turn him down, and why wouldn't he? He'd gotten way past her. Yep. She definitely needed space to unravel the tangled thoughts and feelings she carried for Wyatt Haney.

Chapter Twelve

"Too early in the morning for a meeting," Wyatt muttered to himself Friday morning as he pulled his truck into the lot at Haney & Sons. Grandpa Joe had texted the night before saying he wanted all the partners present for a meeting at seven sharp. The last time Gramps had called a meeting like this, they were in trouble because of the collapse of the housing market. They couldn't be in trouble now, could they? They were barely keeping up with all the work coming in. So, what was up?

Josey drove into the lot while he was still sitting in his truck, trying to wake up. He climbed out and walked over to meet her. "Any idea what this is about?"

"Not a clue." She shook her head, her expression tinged with worry. "I hope Grandpa Joe isn't sick or something—or Grandma Maggie."

"That hadn't even occurred to me." He scowled at her. "Thanks a lot."

"It might be nothing. Maybe we have a big project coming up, and he wants to talk about scheduling." She nodded toward the door. "Come on. Let's get coffee before this thing starts."

Wyatt opened the door, and the smell of fresh medium roast wafted over him. He followed his sister inside. "Whoa. Must be serious," he said, eyeing a large white pastry box on the counter. "Gramps sprang for doughnuts."

Jerry strolled into the kitchen from the hallway. "G-good m-morning."

"Morning to you too, Jer. Do you have any idea what this meeting is about?" Wyatt asked, helping himself to coffee.

"N-nope." Jerry opened the lid on the pastry box. "Gramps said we could have a doughnut n-now, though."

"Good, I'm starving," Jo said, setting a pile of napkins next to the treats. "What have we got here?" She peered inside. "Mmm. Old-fashioned glazed and crullers. Tough choice."

Sam strode through the door, followed by their cousin, Jack Junior. "Do any of you know why we're meeting this morning?" Sam asked.

Josey chose a glazed doughnut. "No clue."

Once the other two cousins trickled in, and everyone had helped themselves to coffee and treats, Grandpa Joe, Uncle Dan and Uncle Jack entered the kitchen from the offices in back. All three wore similar expressions—solemn. Wyatt's anxiety kicked up. *Oh, God. Somebody is sick. Grandma Maggie?*

"Good morning. Thanks for coming in early," Grandpa Joe said before placing his clipboard at the head of the table. He chose a doughnut, helped himself to coffee and settled into his chair. He spent a few minutes passing out jobs and bid requests before starting. "I'm sure you're all curious to know why I wanted you to come in a bit early this morning, so I won't keep you in suspense." He looked around the table at each of them from under his bushy eyebrows.

"I'm retiring at the first of the year. Jack and Dan will take over running the business, and things will continue on as they have. Any questions?"

"You're both in good health though, right?" Josey asked, her eyes narrowed.

Grandpa Joe chuckled. "Healthy as can be, which is one of the reasons I've decided to retire. Your grandmother and I want to do some traveling while we still can. We want to do a few of the items on our bucket list sooner rather than later."

Stunned, Wyatt sat back. He didn't like change. Never had, at least not since he'd lost his parents. Were his grandparents planning to stay in their house, or would they move to Florida or somewhere where winters were mild? His gut churned. Josey was talking, her tone adamant, but Wyatt had checked out. The only thing he heard was the ringing in his ears.

"Are you about finished with the rewiring in your building, Wyatt?" his Uncle Dan asked. He'd taken the seat next to Wyatt's.

"Huh?" He blinked. "Oh. My building." He forced himself to concentrate. "We'll finish up today, and I've arranged for the city inspector to come by this afternoon."

"Good. Right after Labor Day, we'll put you back on the Woodbury Hills development."

Wyatt nodded. Josey headed down the hall to the office on Grandpa Joe's heels, and just like that the meeting was over. He, Sam and their cousins stared at one another, the shock of Grandpa Joe's announcement still settling.

"Does anybody want to meet at The Bulldog after work today?" Sam asked.

"Definitely." Wyatt got up from the table, wrapped his doughnut in a napkin and drained his coffee cup. "I'll text Josey. See you there around five?"

"Yep."

Still a bit gob-smacked, Wyatt walked out of the building and climbed into his truck. His grandparents were in their early seventies. He'd known this day would come, but still, he couldn't imagine not having Grandpa Joe running things at Haney & Sons. He just couldn't wrap his head around what that might be like. He pulled out of the lot and turned toward home, wishing he could talk to Kayla about what he'd just heard. She'd be at school now, but maybe he'd catch her before she left for Iowa.

Thinking of Kayla brought her image to mind, especially the way she'd held his hand and told him he didn't need to cover up with her. Her warmth, and the concern in her pretty blue eyes when she'd looked at him, had given him hope. He was certain she had feelings for him, but he was just as certain those feelings were conflicted.

Since their almost kiss, he'd been giving her space. Or maybe he'd been giving himself space. The distance separating them chafed, but what else could he do? If he pushed, she might shut him out completely, and that would be the end of something good, even if it was only a friendship.

He turned off Marshall Avenue onto his street and frowned. A man was putting up a sign in the front yard of their building. As he passed, he was able to read what it said: *for sale*.

"What the hell?" He frowned. What would this mean to the current residents? Given the great location, their rent could rise to an astronomical amount. The new owners could turn the place into expensive condos, or worse—the building might be razed to build a new luxury development on the spot.

He'd seen that happen to a few other old buildings in their neighborhood. And even two-bedroom condominiums were priced high. The new condos in their area went for close to half a million. Of course they had all the amenities, including more than one bathroom, and their old building didn't, but he could see their apartments-turned-condos going for three to three-fifty.

He parked his truck and headed for the basement. Jon was already there and working. "Morning," Wyatt said, getting to work himself.

His mind still spinning from the changes hurled his way, he somehow made it through the morning without making any mistakes. He kept his eye out for Kayla, hoping to catch her before she left for Iowa. How would she react to their building being for sale? Would she start looking for a new place right away? He needed to do something, but what?

The back door from the parking lot opened, and he heard Brady's familiar chatter. He couldn't keep the grin off his face, and already his outlook improved. "Let's break for lunch," he told Jon. "We can clean up while we're waiting for the inspection."

"Sounds good. I'll be back in an hour." Jon tossed a screwdriver into his toolbox.

Wyatt took the stairs two at a time to catch up to Kayla. "Hey, are you two ready for the big trip?"

"Yeah," Brady chirped. "I get to see Gammy and Pops and Grandpa and Grandma Malone."

"I'm going to make a pot of coffee and some peanut butter and jelly sandwiches before we go. Are you hungry, Wyatt? Would you like to join us for lunch?"

"Sure. I have a bag of chips I can contribute. I'll be right back." He ran down to his apartment to his kitchen and grabbed the bag of potato chips from on top of his fridge, returning to the second floor just as fast. She'd left her door open for him. Taking in a breath, he walked in, closed the door behind him, and strode to the dining area. Kayla stood in front of her coffee pot, scooping fresh grounds into the filter.

His breath caught at the sight of her. The way she stood, her generous curves, her hair in a loose knot at the back of her head . . . until now, he'd never considered scrubs sexy, but on Kayla? *Hot.*

Reining back on his X-rated thoughts, he schooled his features to what he hoped came across as a neutral, friendly-neighbor look. Maybe he'd caught a break the other day, and she hadn't picked up on the fact that he'd been about to kiss her. Friends don't make out with friends. She hadn't said anything. If she was willing to ignore the breach, so was he.

"So, I got a shock this morning," he said, opening the bag of chips and placing them on the table next to the paper plates already there.

"The for-sale sign out front?" She glanced at him over her shoulder.

He grunted. "That too, but no. This morning my grandfather announced he's retiring at the first of the year."

"Oh? How old is he?" Kayla laid slices of bread on a cutting board.

"Seventy-two, but you wouldn't guess it to look at him. He could pass for sixty easy. He's in great shape, and so is my grandmother. They stay active." He suspected the love they had for each other and for their family helped them stay young.

Brady appeared, wiping his wet hands on his shorts. "Mommy, can I have one side with strawberry and one side with grape jelly on my sandwich?" He climbed up on his chair and offered Wyatt a wet fist.

"Of course." Kayla took two jars from the fridge.

"Come here, kid." Wyatt opened his arms. "You're going to be gone for a whole week. I need a hug."

Giggling, Brady stood up on his chair and took a flying leap into Wyatt's arms. "I am definitely going to miss you, Superkid." Wyatt held the little boy close. "Who's going to listen to me read my comic books while you're away?"

"Mommy."

Wyatt peered at Kayla over Brady's head. She tucked her bottom lip between her teeth and kept her eyes on the PB&Js. Was she blushing? Maybe it was the thought of being alone with him, so . . . yeah. The near kiss thing got to her, or it might still be fallout from the Elec Tric comic book where he'd turned her to the dark side. *Oh, wait.*

He stifled a groan. He'd been so wrapped up with the changes coming his way it hadn't occurred to him until now that Kayla had probably read through *all* of the comic books he'd given her. Hadn't she said she couldn't wait to read them?

What must she think of the Mysterious Ms. M, since he'd created her shortly after Kayla had moved in? More important, what did she think of him? All the episodes were numbered and dated, so she'd know he'd been watching her. What if she viewed his using her image as creepy? Worse, what if he'd strayed into stalker territory in her eyes?

"What kind of jelly do you want, Wyatt?" Kayla asked without looking at him.

He tried to swallow against the desert the inside of his mouth had turned into. "Half and half like Brady's sounds good. Thanks." He set Brady back on his chair.

"Hearing your grandfather is retiring upsets you?" Kayla smeared peanut butter on the slices of bread.

"It shouldn't, but yeah, it hit me pretty hard." He raked his fingers through his hair, pushing his hoodie off in the process. "I remember being a little kid and playing with hand tools in his office while he, my dad and my uncles talked about jobs. Gramps has been a permanent fixture at Haney & Sons since the day the company started." He blew out a breath. "Honestly, I can't imagine the place without him."

"Change is always unsettling, but you'll be fine. You'll adjust, and it's not like he's disappearing from your life." She brought the sandwiches to the table, still on the cutting board, and put two halves on each of their plates. Then she went back to the fridge and took out an individual box of chocolate milk.

"You're right. They want to travel, and I'm happy for them."

"Who will run the place after he retires?" She stuck a straw into the milk for Brady.

"Two of my uncles." Wyatt put chips on Brady's plate before adding a pile to his. "Can I have one of those boxes of milk?" Wyatt shot Kayla a hopeful look. "I love chocolate milk with a good PB&J," he said.

"Of course you do," she said with a laugh. "Help yourself. They're on the bottom shelf of the fridge." She took the bag of chips from his hand.

Their fingers brushed, her fault this time, and an electric current shot through him, causing his heart to pound. Visions of more skin-on-skin contact with her flooded his imagination. His desire for her had grown with each passing week. He'd probably go up in flames if they ever did get naked together. He bit the inside of his cheek in an effort to squelch his lust and crossed the kitchen to the fridge for a chocolate milk.

"I'm not happy to see this building for sale. Moving is such a pain, and Brady and I like it here."

"You're not going to do anything right away, are you?"

"I don't know. I should at least start looking, since most places aren't available for months in advance anyway." She shrugged. "I just hope nothing here changes too drastically until after I finish my program."

"I don't wanna move," Brady added around a mouthful.

"I don't either." Wyatt frowned. "Hopefully it won't sell for a while, and even if it does, it takes months for anything to happen. Maybe things won't change at all, and we'll just send our rent checks somewhere new."

"Not likely." Kayla huffed out a breath.

What if Kayla and Brady moved away? Sure, they were *friends*, but friends often drifted apart, lost track. He couldn't let that happen. He wanted so much more with her. His stomach clenched. Torn between caution and the need to tell her how he felt, Wyatt struggled. "Kayla . . . I need to tell you . . . what I *want* to say is . . ."

"Hmm?" A smile graced her face, and her brow rose slightly.

She stole his breath when she looked at him like that. The words he needed to say wouldn't come. He swallowed a few times. "I hope you have a great visit home this weekend." Her smile disappeared, and her expression fell. Was that disappointment flickering through her eyes?

"Thank you. We're looking forward to our visit. Aren't we, Brady?" She rose from her chair. "Would you like a cup of coffee?"

"I'm good with chocolate milk, thanks." Wyatt took another bite of his sandwich. Had Kayla been disappointed? What had she been hoping he'd say?

"Wyatt, d'you know what?" Brady popped a chip into his mouth.

"No, what?"

"I know a joke. D'you wanna hear it?"

He nodded. "Can't wait."

"Knock, knock."

"Who's there?" Wyatt asked, already chuckling.

"Cow says."

"Cow says who?"

"No, silly! A cow says moooo!" Brady dissolved into giggles.

"All right, I've got one." Man, he really would miss Superkid this week. Nobody knew how to lighten the mood like this happy five-year-old boy. "You ready?"

Brady nodded.

"Knock, knock."

"Whooo's there?" Brady called.

"Wooden shoe," he answered.

"Wooden shoe who?"

"Wooden shoe like to hear another joke?"

Brady laughed again, and Wyatt shared a grin with Kayla.

"All right. My turn," Kayla said, her expression once again open and bright. "Ready?"

"Yep." Brady popped another chip into his mouth.

"Knock, knock," she said in a singsong voice.

"Who's there," he and Brady said in unison.

"A little old lady."

"A little old lady who?" Brady's voice rose with his excitement.

"I didn't know you could yodel," she said, a look of surprise on her face.

Brady's childish laughter lit Wyatt up, while Kayla's open smile and the sparkle in her eyes as their gazes met sent a thrill straight through to the core of his being.

"Mommy?"

"Yes?"

"What's *yodel* mean?"

Kayla laughed, and then she did some pretty hokey yodeling. "That's what yodeling is." She reached over and tousled Brady's hair.

Wyatt wanted more lunches like this, the three of them being goofy, laughing together. He wanted dinners too, and bedtimes. Especially bedtimes. His gut wrenched. He couldn't let Kayla and Brady slip out of his life. He just couldn't. Their apartment building would sell quickly, and Kayla had said she'd start looking for a new apartment right away. He dreaded the possibility that she'd drift out of his life.

When things had looked their bleakest for Sam and Haley, he, Josey and Sam had hatched the perfect plan to help his brother win back the love of his life. Tonight he'd ask Sam and Josey for help, and together they'd come up with a plan—something that would finally break through Kayla's defenses and force her to see how perfect they were for each other. He thought so, anyway. How to convince her was another matter entirely.

With their silly knock-knock jokes still hanging in the air between them, Kayla lost herself in Wyatt's warm brown eyes, and a rush of longing nearly ripped her heart in two. She'd read through all of the Elec Tric comic books the other night. With the world of demons on the Mysterious Ms. M's heels at every turn, and Tric's archenemy DD urging her to join their ranks as her second-in-command, Ms. M found herself in desperate straits in each issue. Wyatt's alter ego had been so tender and protective toward the Mysterious Ms. M, rescuing her again and again.

Clearly the superhero had fallen for his damsel in distress. He believed fate had brought them together, and he'd done everything in his power to keep her safe. Wyatt's Elec Tric character had been solid and constant. He'd never let Ms. M down, never got on her case for putting herself in harm's way.

He was just . . . there for her, wearing his heart on his stretchy blue superhero sleeve. And what did the poor guy get in return? The Mysterious Ms. M rejected him and crushed his heart, that's what. Yep. Pretty sure his art imitated his life. Oh, the remorse—how it bit, and so did its bitchy sister, Regret. Ms. M had made the biggest mistake of her life. Had she made the biggest mistake of her life too?

"We have to get going," she said, rising from her chair. "It's a three-hour drive, and I told my folks we'd be there for supper."

"Do you need help carrying your bags to the car?" Wyatt gathered their empty paper plates, napkins and milk boxes.

"I don't want to take you from your work." His offer nearly brought tears to her eyes. Wyatt always carried her tubs of laundry and helped her with her groceries. He helped her with Brady, and he was providing her son with the most excellent male role modeling possible. Like Elec Tric and the Mysterious Ms. M, Wyatt was her go-to guy, even though he didn't get much in return.

"It's no trouble, and I'm heading downstairs anyway. All we have left is to gather our tools, sweep up the remnants and do a final check while waiting for the inspector." He stuffed the trash into the bin.

"I need to change my clothes, and then we're ready." Kayla filled her thermos with coffee and flipped the off switch. "Try to use the bathroom, Brady, and then go get your backpack with your books and toys. I left it on your bed."

"OK." He shot down the hall toward his room.

"Wyatt, everything is going to be fine with your grandfather retiring." She wiped down the counter and straightened up. "When your grandparents aren't traveling, I'll bet your grandfather will hang out at your office a lot. I'm sure it's not an easy change for him either."

"You're probably right. He'll get bored without us to boss around." He shot her a wry grin. "I should've known something was up when Gram told me Gramps was learning to golf."

Kayla scanned her tiny kitchen. "Brady is going to miss you while he's gone," she told him. *I'll miss you.*

"I'm going to miss him too."

"Leaving him there is going to be weird. I've never been separated from my son for more than a night since the day he was born." She sighed. "This place is going to seem so empty without him."

"We can hang out," he said, his face flooding with color. "If you want to, that is."

"I'd like that."

Brady bounced back into the dining room with his backpack slung over one shoulder.

"I'll be right back," she said. "We'll get out of your hair in a few minutes, tops." Kayla hurried to her room and changed into jeans and a T-shirt. Then she rolled their suitcases to the living room.

Wyatt took the two bags out into the hall. She locked the door and took Brady's hand, and they followed Wyatt down the stairs and out the back door. The impulse to throw herself into Wyatt's arms to kiss him good-bye nearly overwhelmed her. After she popped the trunk, and he hoisted their bags inside, an awkwardness filled the space between them. "Well, have a great weekend, Wyatt."

"You too." He stuffed his hands into the front pockets of his jeans and took a step back. "Drive carefully."

Brady threw himself at Wyatt. He lifted her son and tossed him into the air before giving him another hug. "Mind your mom, Superkid, and no backseat driving."

"OK," Brady said, grinning. "Are you gonna read comic books to Mommy without me?"

Wyatt winked at her, and her pulse skyrocketed. "Maybe, but I can always read them again with you when you come home." He set Brady on his feet and opened the back door of her car.

"Gammy and Pops are going to bring me home." Brady climbed into his booster. "You can read to Pops too. Pops likes comic books, and d'you know what?"

"What?" Wyatt asked, leaning into her car to buckle her son's seat belt.

Oh, boy. Wyatt's jeans fit so perfectly over his very fine backside. Kayla forced her gaze away from the enticing sight and opened her car door.

"I have a *great* grandpa too." Brady threw up his hands, like that was the coolest thing ever.

"Wow. You're one lucky kid."

"Uh-huh." Brady nodded. "Bye, Wyatt."

"Bye, Brady. See you in a week."

Wyatt straightened out of her car and faced her. "Do you want to catch a movie one night next week? There are some good ones out right now."

"Sure. That would be fun. I haven't been to a movie that wasn't animated for I don't know how long." Her voice came out all breathy. A kiss. All she wanted was one stupid kiss—well, that and his arms around her—but until she'd worked through her own mixed-up feelings where Wyatt was concerned, she'd keep her hands to herself.

"We'd better be off. Thanks for carrying our bags for us." She slid into the driver's side before she did anything foolish.

Wyatt held the top edge of her car door and peered at her. "Thanks for lunch."

She snorted. "Peanut butter and jelly sandwiches isn't much of a lunch, but you're welcome."

He opened his mouth as if he wanted to say something else, but then closed it again. His hood still hung down his shoulders. He must've forgotten to pull it back up, and that, along with his blush, sent her heart aflutter. "See you, Wyatt."

"See you back." He shut her door and stepped away.

Kayla pulled out of her parking space and turned down the alley toward the street. She glanced into her rearview mirror. Wyatt still stood in the lot, watching her drive away. Her eyes welled, and she held her breath. Why, she had no idea. Never before had she reacted this way with anyone other than her son. She didn't want to leave Wyatt, not even for a three-day weekend, and they weren't even dating.

"Mommy, can we have McDonald's for supper?"

She huffed out a laugh. "You *just* had lunch, and you're already thinking about supper?"

"Uh-huh. Can we?"

"Not tonight. We're having supper with Gammy and Pops."

"Tomorrow can we?"

She grinned at him in her rear view mirror. "I love you, Brady." Once again her son saved her from the morass of her own tangled emotions.

"Love you too, Mommy."

By the time she pulled onto 35W South, Brady had fallen asleep with a picture book against his chest, and Kayla was left alone to think. She planned to do a lot of serious thinking in the next couple of days. Her outlook on love and life had been seriously tainted by her unfortunate *BAMs*. When she got right down to it, she lacked experience when it came to relationships. Maybe she needed an outlook makeover. Too little, too late?

It would take all her courage and more to ask Wyatt for a do-over. How would he react if she tried to seduce him? After the way she'd kissed him, then informed him they couldn't date, he might see her as flighty and indecisive. As sensitive as he was, fear that she'd change her mind again could lead him to reject her. Maybe, but she might risk it anyway. At the moment, not taking a chance scared her far more than the possibility that she might be too late.

Chapter Thirteen

Wyatt kept his tone low and leaned in toward Josey and Sam. "It's my turn to ask for help." Their cousins had joined them at The Bulldog, and they shared a high-top table next to the bar. The cousins had moved on from discussing the shocking news of Grandpa Joe's retirement to talking about CHS Field, the new Saint Paul Saints baseball stadium a few blocks away.

"Help with what?" Sam's brow creased.

"Seriously?" Josey smacked Sam's shoulder. "With Kayla, of course."

Wyatt flashed his sister a grateful look. "Exactly."

"Hey, we're heading out," Jack Junior said, rising from his spot. "My wife will be fuming if I don't get home soon. We're going to her parents' lake home early tomorrow morning, and I have items on the honey-do list that need to get done tonight."

"OK. Say hi to her for us, and give that baby of yours a squeeze for me," Josey said. Wyatt waited until good-byes were said and the cousins were gone before he turned back to the issue at hand. "My apartment building is for sale. The sign went up this morning."

"I kind of figured that might happen when you told us the insurance company wasn't covering the rewiring. I'm sure the owners realize that old building will need a lot more work in the near future, and it's all the expensive stuff." Sam fixed him in a pointed gaze. "So, what kind of help do you need with Kayla?"

"I'm . . ." Heat rose to his face, and he tugged his hoodie forward. "It's just that—"

"Wyatt is in love," Josey scowled at Sam. "Kayla *said* she doesn't want to date him, but he's been wheedling his way into her life in the hopes she'll change her mind. And now that his building is for sale, he's afraid she's going to move away before he can get through to her."

"Wow." Wyatt's eyes widened. "You got all that from . . . 'I'm' and 'it's just that'?"

She shrugged. "I'm really good at deductive reasoning, and Gram might've said something."

"Mmm? What did Gram tell you exactly?" His grandmother had said she was the soul of discretion when he'd shared Kayla's personal history. Kayla wouldn't appreciate it if she found out he'd talked about her with his grandmother.

"Only that you found someone you were interested in who happens to be recently widowed. Gram mentioned your *young lady* might still be grieving, and she hoped you wouldn't give up on her." She patted his arm. "No names were shared, and that's all she said. But you mentioned taking Kayla and her son to the mall and fishing, so I know you've been spending time with her. Besides that, Kayla is the only girl you've ever included in one of our nights out. So . . . duh."

"What Jo said pretty much sums up my situation. I don't even have Kayla's telephone number. She's going to start looking for a new apartment right away, and you know how it goes. People move away and lose touch."

"You could just ask her for her number, Wy," Jo frowned.

"I know. That's not the point. Realizing I don't have her number brought home to me just how tenuous our relationship is. That's all. I've been working on getting her to see how perfect we are for each other, and now I need to up my game plan. I need a grand gesture here, or at least something that will keep her around for a while, so I can keep—"

"Wheedling your way into her heart?" Josey said with a laugh.

"Exactly." He tugged his hoodie forward again.

"Yep. You need to do something, especially since you turned the Mysterious Ms. M to the dark side." Sam grunted. "Kayla looked a little rattled by that."

Wyatt groaned. "I know. We talked, and she said we're OK, but I'm pretty sure it still bothers her. See why I need help?"

"The Mysterious Ms. M? What are you two talking about?" Josey looked from Sam to him. "Oh, wait. Never mind. Sam told me about how you turned Kayla to the dark side in your Elec Tric series. Smooth move, dumb ass."

"Yes, and Kayla saw the title page, *A Hero Has His Heart Broken*, which I'd left on my drawing board."

Josey's eyes filled with sympathy. "You're screwed."

"Yeah, I know." He shifted in his seat. "So can we get back on task? Grand gesture, people. I need a plan."

"That's easy." Sam sat back and crossed his arms. "Buy the building. Become her landlord, and you can keep the rent the same as it is now. Then she won't have to move."

"Be serious." Wyatt snorted and glared at his brother. "I mean something that isn't crazy, something I can actually do."

"Do you know how much the owners are asking for the building?" Josey's expression turned thoughtful.

"No, but I'm pretty sure it's a million or two out of my price range." Wyatt rolled his eyes. "Come on, guys. I'm counting on you here."

"Just think for a minute," Josey's eyes took on an excited glint. "The income from the current renters will figure into what you can afford, and given the building's location, it's an excellent investment."

Wyatt shook his head. "It's a money pit is what it is. You *know* what it cost the current owners to rewire the entire building. Rewiring is only the beginning." He held up a hand and began ticking items off his mental list. "It needs a new flat roof, tuck-pointing, new concrete work in front and in back, new energy-efficient windows . . . Come to think of it, a twenty-first-century boiler and ductless air-conditioning would be nice. Hell, it needs to be replumbed, Jo. That's a lot of copper pipe we're talking about, and copper is damn expensive. Then there's—"

"OK, I see your point, but Wyatt"—Josey's brow rose—"it's also two blocks from the Mississippi River parkway, trendy restaurants, shops, parks and good schools. The property would be an excellent investment, and the interest rates are still really low. That area has always held its value, even during the housing market crash, and right now the property values in the Mac-Groveland neighborhood are on the rise. Say we bought it and fixed it up. We could turn the apartments into condos, sell them and double our money."

"We?" Wyatt's brow rose. "Our?"

"Hmm. Josey makes a good point, and don't forget we can call in some favors, get materials at wholesale and do a lot of the work ourselves. We are a construction company, after all."

"Wait." Wyatt propped his elbows on the table and buried his face in his hands for a few seconds. "Are you two suggesting the three of us buy my building, bring it up to date, and then sell the units off as condos? I asked for a freaking gesture, and you two turn it into . . . a business proposition and a project?"

"Exactly." Josey canted her head. "Is that third-floor apartment still vacant?"

"Yeah, why?"

"My lease is up in a couple of months. I was going to renew it, but now I'm thinking that third-floor apartment in your building might just be my new place."

"You two are serious about this?" He looked from his sister to his brother. They both nodded. "I don't know. A conventional loan would require at least five percent down, if not more. Do either of you have that kind of cash?"

"We don't know what kind of cash we're talking about without first knowing how much the owners are asking," Josey said, her tone a little exasperated. "But, if you don't want to buy it outright, here's another thought. You could talk to the current residents and see if any of them are interested in turning the place into a cooperative. That way, you wouldn't have to come up with as much cash on your own. The down payment would be divided among those who want to stay."

"Or, turn it into condos." Sam leaned forward. "You and the other renters could get together, figure the cost per unit, plus enough for the start-up of a general upgrade fund, and form an LLC as a holding company. At least find out what the building's listing price is. It wouldn't hurt, and if we do decide to go for it, I think we'd better act fast."

"Can you get me in to take a look at that empty apartment on the third floor?"

"Sure. I still have the keys. Our caretaker moved out last week and didn't bother to get them back from me. We can head over there right now if you want." The possibilities crowding together in his brain ignited a spark of excitement. He had some research to do.

"I think I'll head home." Sam checked his phone. "Haley should be finished with her book club by now. And by 'book club' I mean the opportunity to get together with her girlfriends, drink wine and gab." He stood up and stretched. "Think about it, Wyatt. I'd be interested in investing, and I'm sure Haley would be cool with it too. Things slow down considerably for us during the winter, which would give us time to work on the place ourselves. Between the three of us, we have a lot of skills. Sweat equity, bro. The best kind."

"I will think about it." What would Kayla make of the plan? Would she stay if he bought the building? There wouldn't be anything in it for her, but if the residents turned the place into condos and they all owned the building collectively, then it would be a good investment for everyone involved. Did Kayla have the cash to buy in, though? Maybe she did. She did mention an insurance payout connected to her husband's accidental death.

He and Josey walked out to the sidewalk together. He pulled his car keys from his back pocket. "Where are you parked, Jo?"

"I'm a few cars down from your truck." She pointed toward Mears Park as they walked. "I'm excited about this, Wyatt. I've been thinking about investing in property for a while, but I don't really want a house with a yard."

"Why not?"

"I don't like yard work or gardening. Probably because I work with my hands all day, and I'm on my knees on the job enough as it is. When I get home, all I want to do is relax."

"I get it." Wyatt got to his truck and took care of the meter. "I'll see you at my place in a few."

"I'll be right behind you."

Did he want a house with a yard? Maybe not now, but someday, like when—make that *if*—he ever had a family of his own, a family that included Kayla and Brady. He might never get there with her, and that thought brought a hollow ache to his chest. He could jump through burning hoops for Kayla, and she still might not want to be with him as anything other than a friend.

And what about his comic books? Did he want to take on a huge project like a twelve-unit, turn-of-the-century building? Doing so would seriously cut into his creative time. On the other hand, the work on the building didn't need to be done all at once. They could take care of things one project at a time, and Sam was right. The winter months were slow for them. It wouldn't hurt to check things out, and if he could muster up the nerve, it wouldn't hurt to talk to his neighbors. Not exactly the kind of grand gesture he'd been hoping for, but Gramps always said property was the best investment.

Tomorrow he'd call the listing agent for their building and ask questions. He'd also look into what it might take to turn the place into a cooperative or condos. At any rate, it would give him something to occupy his mind while Kayla was away. Which would be a good thing, since he'd started missing her and Brady like crazy the second their car disappeared from view.

"Mind your grandfather, Brady," Kayla said, while clearing the dinner dishes from the table. "And be gentle with the animals."

"I will," Brady replied, his eyes sparkling with excitement. He slid off his chair and placed his napkin on the table.

"Well, come on then, biddy-buddy." Her dad reached out a hand. "Let's go see the menagerie."

Brady took his grandfather's offered hand, and the two started for the door. "What's a menageree, Pops?"

Kayla shared a grin with her mom and carried the dirty dishes to the sink. "Thanks for dinner, Mom. As always, it was delicious. I don't remember the last time I had your famous fried chicken."

"I haven't made it for quite some time, but I remembered how much you love my recipe." Her mom busied herself with putting away the leftovers. "We miss you and Brady so much, Kayla. Have you given any thought to looking for a job close to home once you've graduated? You'd have help with Brady, you know. Since my job is here on the farm, he could stay here with me while you're working, and it would save you the cost of day care."

"I'll think about it." With her apartment building up for sale, where she'd be living in the near future was suddenly up in the air. Moving back to Decorah didn't appeal to her, though, even with her family here. She didn't want to be anywhere near the Malones with all their guilt- inducing judgmental attitudes.

"Good. That's all we can ask." Her mom shut the refrigerator door and glanced at her. "Besides all the relatives, we've invited the Malones over for the barbecue Sunday evening. They're excited to see you and Brady."

"Great." She couldn't help the bitterness in her tone. "I wish you'd talked to me first. I'd rather have them visit with Brady while I'm *not* here."

"But why, Kayla?"

"You know how they are. They blame *me* for everything, including the fact that Brad joined the army and died." Just thinking about her in-laws brought back all the humiliation and hurt of being married to a boy who hated her, a boy she'd been pressured into marrying. "But you know what? It wasn't my fault. Brad and I were a couple of stupid kids who made a mistake. We didn't love each other. We didn't even know what love was at that age. Neither of us wanted marriage, but did anybody listen to us? No."

"We *all* thought it would go easier on both of you if you married and shared Brad's last name. After all, this is a small town, and you know how people talk."

"Yeah, well, Brad gave his son his name, but that's all Brady ever got from him. Brady and I would've been better off without him. I could've found a way to go to college instead of wasting time working at a crappy job and waiting for my *husband* to come around."

"Oh, honey . . ."

"We *are* better off without him." Guilt burned through her. "I know it's awful to say that, and I never wished him any harm. But . . . Brad was *not* nice to me, Mom. He was a verbally abusive, unfaithful bully. I could accept his bitterness and abandonment of me, but I couldn't bear the fact that he didn't love his own son. Brady is an intelligent, sweet, amazing little boy, and he didn't deserve to be treated so poorly." She shook her head. "How I got so lucky with my son when his dad was such a selfish, immature jerk, I'll never figure out."

"We had no idea. We thought we were doing what was best."

"I don't blame you and Dad. The good Reverend Malone can be very persuasive. I'm sure Joyce and David thought they were doing what was best, too, but . . . My baby and I were the ones who suffered. There was nothing *best* about any of it, and my *husband* just up and left." Her throat tightened. "He didn't have to deal with anything beyond sending the occasional check home."

Kayla turned to face her mother. "Brad planned to divorce me after his last tour of duty was up. He'd found someone else and told me he was in love. Actually, he found several someones during our short and miserable marriage. He made no secret of his affairs either, and I'm sure that was another way to get back at me."

Wow. She'd lost control, and all of the ugly she'd kept bottled up for years just spilled out of her. "Being married to Brad left me scarred, and it left me scared. I'm not sure I'll ever trust anyone enough to completely give my heart, and that just sucks, because I'm only twenty-four."

Suddenly, her outburst became all about Wyatt. Oh, God. She'd hurt him because of the scars from her past. Wyatt wasn't anything like Brad, yet she hadn't been able to see past her own pain long enough to give them a chance. "I need to clear my head. I'm going for a walk."

"Honey, wait. Let's talk about this," her mom called after her.

She shook her head and kept on going. Her hands fisted by her sides, she strode down the long gravel driveway to the two-lane country road leading into town. This was the path she'd always taken when she'd been upset as a teenager—like when she'd figured out she was pregnant. There ought to be a visible trail worn into the asphalt from all the walks she'd gone on back then. She inhaled deeply.

The scent of sweet grass and clover laced the air, and miles and miles of gently rolling hills stretched on forever to meet the darkening blue sky and the blazing orange of the setting sun. She continued on, her pace intense, trying to burn off some of the anger still thrumming through her.

About a mile down the road she finally began to calm down, and then it registered how good she felt now that she'd gotten everything out in the open. The tight knot of anger and sadness lodged in her chest had unwound, and she could think again.

She and Brad had been too young to fight the collective wills of their parents in any meaningful way, but she was a grown woman now. She knew herself, and she alone directed the course of her life. She stopped where she was and stared out over a ripening field of soy. If it hadn't been for Wyatt, it might have taken her years to realize how much she'd matured.

Moments they'd spent together rushed to the forefront of her mind, his tenderness, creativity, intelligence, subtle humor . . . his sexiness. Wyatt was so great with Brady, always encouraging and caring toward her little boy. Tears filled her eyes, and realization swept over her with all the force of high tide. She loved Wyatt, and it was the kind of love that grew with each revelation about his personality, his character. He was a good man, solid, dependable, and she'd hurt him.

She turned and began walking toward home. Resolve stiffened her spine. Brady would be here with her parents for the rest of next week, and she knew exactly what she wanted to do with her child-free time. She'd seduce Wyatt, and then they'd talk. Or, they'd talk first, and then she'd seduce him? Either way, she'd explain she'd made a mistake, and she really did want to date him.

Gulp. Did she have the guts to pull it off? What if he turned her down? After all, she had broken his heart once already. What would prevent her from doing so again?

Kayla woke up to the smell of bacon and coffee. She stretched and checked the cot that had been set up in her old bedroom for Brady. It was empty, which didn't surprise her. Yawning, she got up and stretched before grabbing clothes and padding down the hall toward the bathroom. Spurred by the scent of bacon, she took the quickest shower possible, dressed, brushed her teeth and tidied up in record time.

The sound of her son's chatter from the kitchen brought a smile to her face. He loved his Gammy and Pops, and it would be great for him to spend a week on the farm with them. "Good morning," she trilled, and then froze. Her mother-in-law sat at the breakfast bar next to Brady, while her mom stood in front of the stove, scrambling eggs in a large skillet.

"Good morning, Kayla. It's good to see you," Joyce said, her expression wary.

"It's good to see you too." Kayla moved to the counter, grabbed a mug from the cabinet and poured herself a much-needed cup of coffee. Maybe the caffeine would wash away the guilt from last night's outburst. Her in-laws loved Brady, and they'd always be a part of his life. It wasn't their fault she'd been ill equipped to stand up to them when she was eighteen. "Smells good in here."

"Breakfast is almost ready," her mom said, glancing at her. "I called Joyce last night. Once your dad is finished feeding the critters, we're going to have breakfast, and then he and Brady are going into town to the clinic to look in on a dog who had surgery yesterday."

"OK?" She shot her mother a questioning look.

"The three of us," her mom said, nodding toward Joyce, "are going to talk."

Yikes. Her appetite disappeared. "Great."

"It's way overdue," Joyce murmured. "There are a few things we need to clear up."

Kayla swallowed against the guilt climbing up from the pit of her stomach to clog her throat. In a matter of seconds, she'd been reduced to an uncertain eighteen-year-old again, about to face yet another intimidating lecture—four adults against two scared kids. At least this time it would just be two against one.

Sighing, she took a sip of her coffee and leaned against the counter. She wasn't that kid anymore, dammit. And this time she'd speak her mind, tell the truth and clear the air. In a respectful way of course, because that's how mature individuals did things.

The sound of the front door opening, and her dad stomping his feet on the stoop drew her out of her thoughts. "Can I do anything to help, Mom?" she asked.

"Grab plates and put them on the table." Her mom transferred the eggs to a serving dish and handed it to Joyce. Her mother-in-law got up and carried the ceramic bowl to the old oak kitchen table where Kayla had eaten her meals and done her homework her entire childhood.

Kayla went to the cabinet where the plates were kept, counted out the right amount and placed them at each place setting. The basket of cinnamon rolls already on the table brought Kayla's appetite back. She was an adult now, well able to handle an uncomfortable conversation with other adults. *Gah. I hope.*

Her mom grabbed an oven mitt and pulled out a pan laden with bacon and slid the strips onto a platter. "Let's eat."

"Come on, kiddo," she said lifting Brady off the bar stool. "Gammy made her super-delicious cinnamon rolls. We're in for a treat."

All through breakfast she worried about what the other two women at the table might throw her way during their talk. She snorted. Obviously eighteen-year-old Kayla insisted on sticking around.

"You OK?" her dad said, patting her back.

"Eggs down the wrong throat." She gave a little fake cough. "I'm fine, thanks."

He winked at her, his eyes sparkling. "Well, Brady, you ready to go check on our patient?"

"Yeah. Mommy, do you know what? Pops did *surgery* on a dog that had a . . ."—his brow scrunched—"structed bowl."

"An obstructed bowel." Her dad chuckled.

Brady bobbed his head. "He couldn't *poop*, but Pops fixed him." He climbed off his chair and carried his plate to the kitchen counter. "I'm going to be a vet like Pops when I grow up, and a comic book drawer."

"A comic book illustrator, you mean. Drawers are where we keep your Spiderman underwear." Kayla grinned and held her arms open. "Come here, you. I need a hug." Her son obliged her, and then his two grandmothers also requested hugs.

"Know what, Grandma?" he said during his hug with Joyce. "My friend Wyatt is gonna miss me this week. *He* needed a hug too, and I jumped from my chair all the way across the room, and he caught me. He lets me wear his Superman cape sometimes."

Joyce kissed his forehead. "Well, he sounds like a good friend indeed."

"He is," Kayla agreed. "Brady—"

"You don't gotta tell me." He shot her an affronted look before taking his grandfather's hand. "I'll mind Pops and keep my hands to myself."

Her dad swung him up into his arms. "We'll keep an eye on each other, right, grandson?"

Brady gave him a single, decisive nod and put his arms around his Pops's neck, smiling at her from over her dad's shoulder. Kayla's heart filled, and her eyes misted.

Honestly, having Brady made up for all the crap she'd gone through with Brad. She pulled in a long breath, grabbed the coffee and refilled everyone's cup before sitting back down.

"Your mom and I talked on the phone last night." Joyce flashed her mom a grateful look. "And I'm glad we did, Sharon. Thank you. This conversation is way overdue."

And again . . . gulp.

"Dave and I owe you a huge apology, Kayla."

"What?" She blinked. This was the last thing she'd expected to hear.

"We never should have pushed you into marrying our son." Joyce huffed out a breath. "What makes the whole thing worse is . . . we did what we did for purely selfish reasons."

"I don't understand." Kayla's heart pounded, and her brain struggled to come back online after the shock of hearing the word *apology*. Joyce was apologizing to her?

"The fact that Brady joined the army right after you married was in no way your fault. That had been a bone of contention between Brad, his father and me for years."

Kayla frowned. "Still don't understand."

"I know." Joyce's eyes glistened. "Ever since middle school, Brad insisted he wanted to go into the military like his uncle, whom he idolized. Of course his father and I were against the idea, and we argued about it frequently. We wanted him to go to college, get a good job and settle down near us. He was our only child, you see."

"H-he never said a word about any of that to me," Kayla stammered. "I mean, I knew he didn't want to get married, but . . ." Honestly, they hadn't gotten to know each other all that well in the few months they'd been seeing each other. Their relationship was more hormonal than anything else.

"Well, given the circumstances, the way we all forced the two of you together . . . As angry as he was, he wouldn't have said anything to you about that, would he?" Joyce gripped her coffee cup. "When we learned you were pregnant, Dave and I thought our prayers had finally been answered. We hoped having a wife and child would change his mind about joining the army. We prayed the situation would convince him to stay here and settle down near family. We offered to pay for his college education, hoping that, too, might be an incentive for him to stay. After all, he had you and Brady to think about."

"We all pushed you two too hard," her mom added. "For different reasons, but it was still wrong."

"Kayla, Brad's death was in no way your fault. His joining the army was an act of defiance against us. It had nothing to do with you."

"I don't agree with that last bit." She frowned. "I know for a fact he didn't want to be married to me, and he *really* didn't want to be a father. His act of defiance killed two birds with one stone, that's all." A weight lifted from her soul, and the resulting lightness almost made her dizzy. "All this time I believed you and Dave blamed me for . . . well . . . for everything, including getting pregnant."

"No. Never. It takes two to make a baby. I'm sorry we gave you that impression. Our grandson is the light of our lives. You must know that, and we couldn't be any happier to have you as a part of our family. Don't ever feel like you have to stay away from Decorah because of us. That would break our hearts." Her voice hitched. "We don't get to see Brady nearly enough as it is. We're all hoping you'll consider moving back home eventually."

And . . . more guilt and pressure added to the pile. "I promise to visit more frequently, but I really like living in the Twin Cities." Not to mention the fact that the man she loved was there, just waiting to be seduced back into dating her. "Once I'm finished with my program, and I have a job, you can always visit us, you know. I'll look for a place with a spare bedroom. There are lots of things to do in the Twin Cities."

"If you'll let us, Dave and I would love to be there for your graduation, Kayla."

"Oh." Believing the Malones saw her as the cause of their loss, she hadn't even thought about inviting them. "Brady and I would love to have you there."

"We're all so proud of the way you've pulled your life together, and you're such a great mother." Her mom reached out and put her hand over Kayla's. "Your dad and I owe you an apology as well. We should have backed off, let the two of you kids work things out for yourselves. No matter what, we support you. You can always come to us; you know that, don't you?"

She nodded, tears threatening. "I'm glad we talked."

"Yoo-hoo," a woman's voice called from the front door. "Anybody home?"

Thank you, Aunt Becky! All that needed to be said had been said, and now this emotionally charged conversation could come to an end. She had a lot to think about, but not while her emotions were so raw. "We're in the kitchen, Aunt Becky." Kayla rose from her place and started clearing the table.

"We're good?" Joyce joined her, setting a handful of silverware in the sink.

"We are." She smiled at her mother-in-law.

"We're looking forward to the gathering tomorrow night, and we're taking Brady for the day on Wednesday. We thought he'd enjoy going to the county fair."

"He'd love that, but be warned. He'll drive you ragged with the rides."

Becky swept into the kitchen. "I couldn't wait until tomorrow to take a look at those comic books. Hey, Sharon, Joyce, I haven't interrupted anything, have I?"

"No, of course not." Her mom flapped a hand in the air. "We were just having coffee and visiting."

"I need to get going." Joyce slung her purse over her shoulder. "We'll see you all tomorrow. Can I bring something, Sharon?"

"A salad or fruit would be great." Her mom grabbed the rest of the dirty dishes and brought them to the sink.

Relieved, Kayla waved good-bye as her mother-in-law left.

"I'll clean up here," her mom told her. "Go get your friend's work, and we'll all take a look. I'm dying to see his comic books too."

"You're sure?"

"I'm sure." She patted Kayla's cheek.

Kayla hurried to her room, debating whether or not to keep the last revealing episode hidden. She could always slip it in right before she gave the envelope to her aunt. Yep. She'd leave that one out for now. It would be hard enough as it was, to explain her uncanny resemblance to the Mysterious Ms. M.

Chapter Fourteen

"Thanks so much for all the information you've given me," Wyatt said over his phone to the realtor. "I'll get back to you as soon as possible."

"Don't take too long. The building is going to sell quickly. I already have several showings scheduled for next week."

"Good to know." He didn't doubt it after hearing the listing price. He ended the call and hit his sister's speed dial number. She picked up right away for a change. "Hey, Jo. I just got off the phone with the listing agent for this building. You won't believe how low it's going for."

"Tell me."

"A million and a half. The agent said the owners want a quick sale because of the building's age and condition issues. If you take the third-story apartment, and all of the residents decide to buy, that's only one hundred twenty-five thousand per unit. It would be crazy not to do this."

"I agree. Do you want me to come over and talk to your neighbors with you? I know how hard it is for you to—"

"Nope. I need to do this on my own." Wyatt needed to be bold, and Kayla would have to know he'd done this for her, because of her. He needed to show her and himself how much he'd changed these past few months. Before Kayla entered his life, he'd cut himself off from the rest of the world. She and her son had changed all that.

It was still early Saturday morning. He had time to create an informational flyer of sorts to hand out to his neighbors. He'd explain the difference between cooperatives, involving collective ownership through shares of stock in the building, and condos, which they'd each own outright.

He'd create a table with all the financial information, like the down-payment costs and the need to set up a general fund, and an LLC. Then, when his mouth went dry, at least he'd have something to hand to his neighbors, giving them all the pertinent information.

"Are you still going to fill out the lease application for the empty place, Jo?" he asked.

"I don't know if it's necessary, or even if the apartment is still being offered in light of the impending sale. I'll buy in. Can you talk to all of your neighbors before Monday?"

"If they're in town for the holiday weekend, I think I can. Call Sam and Haley for me, would you? I need to do a few things before I knock on any doors." By the time Kayla got home, he'd be able to present her with actual numbers, along with a list of who'd committed to stay and who hadn't.

"If the current residents don't buy in, we need to figure out how and if we're going to do this on our own," he continued. "Five percent down would come to twenty-five thousand each. I'd have to borrow from my retirement account." Which meant he'd also have to pay it back. Another thing to consider. "I will if we're all in this. We can at least scrape together the earnest money to make an offer. That will buy us time to talk to a mortgage broker."

"It'll be worth it, Wyatt. We'll triple the value over the next few years. I'm excited about this."

"Me too."

"Let's meet at your place Monday around lunchtime. I'll bring Indian takeout. We can talk more, and by then you'll have a better grasp on who is interested, so we'll know *our* next step."

"Good idea. I'll talk to you later." He ended the call and grabbed the notes he'd taken while talking to the realtor. Wyatt moved to the desk in his studio and turned on his computer. Steve Andrews had been very informative when it came to co-ops and condos, the money part and the pros and cons of entering into a venture like this.

Two hours later, with flyers in his sweaty hands, Wyatt climbed the stairs to the third floor. His heart hammered, blood rushed to his face, and he could hardly breathe. But dammit, if he wanted to get the girl, he had to do this. And if he didn't get the girl? Well, at least he'd proved to himself that he could push through the shyness when needed.

He pushed off his hood. Symbolic, really. Kayla had told him he didn't need to cover up, so he wouldn't. Not today, even though he doubted anyone else in the building would even notice. Kayla would have to see what he did today, forcing himself past his shyness, for what it was: a courageous feat of superhuman strength—for him, anyway—meant to win her heart. If she didn't, he'd explain it to her.

Swallowing convulsively, he knocked on the old hippie's door first.

His neighbor opened his door and blinked at him. A cloud of pot smoke wafted out of his apartment. "Another fire, man?"

"No. It's Dennis, right?" Wyatt handed him a flyer. Did this guy *ever* wear a shirt? "I'm sure you've noticed our building is for sale, and I've done some research. I'm hoping we can form an LLC and buy the place ourselves. We can own it cooperatively or as condos." His ears rang with the pounding of his pulse. Had he said everything OK?

"I dunno." Dennis scratched his thick beard, and peered at him through the smudged, thick lenses of his glasses. "Seems kinda permanent, you know? I don't do permanent, man. That's how Big Brother catches up to us."

"Really? How long have you lived here, Dennis?"

Another beard scratch, and Dennis's gaze fixed on the ceiling. He looked as if the effort to concentrate hurt his brain, as he ticked off the years with his fingers. "Eighteen years," he said, a bewildered expression playing across his features. "Whoa . . ."

"I think Big Brother would've found you by now if he were looking. Eighteen years already sounds kind of permanent to me." Wyatt pointed to the flyer Dennis held in his hand. "The pros and cons for going condo or co-op are listed there, along with the financials. At the bottom, there's a place for your name and boxes to check the option that interests you most, or if you're not interested at all. Can you think about this over this weekend, and get the form back to me by Monday before noon? If we're going to do this, we're going to have to act fast."

"Yeah, man." Dennis stood a little straighter. "I can do that."

"Good. I've put a basket by my door. Just drop the flyer in there."

"Will do. Hey, you wanna come in for a toke, dude?" Dennis gestured with his thumb toward the smoky interior of his apartment. "It's good stuff. Err . . . for medicinal purposes."

"Uh, no, but thanks. I have to talk to as many of our neighbors as possible today."

"Thanks for including me in this, man." Dennis held up the flyer. "And thanks for making sure we all got out of the building when Kayla's place caught fire. You're good people, Wyatt. I'm glad you're my neighbor. You never know about your neighbors, but we've got a pretty good group here."

"I know. That's why we should buy this place. I'd hate to see us lose what we have, and the location is great." Wyatt grinned. "Thanks, Dennis. Take a look at that and get it back to me. OK?"

"I will." Dennis offered his hand.

Wyatt shook it. "Wish me luck."

"Good luck, man." Dennis saluted him and closed his door.

Wyatt let out a long breath. His heart rate had returned to the normal range. Talking to Dennis hadn't been so hard. He could do this. He crossed the hall and knocked on the next door, his confidence bolstered.

"Cool," he muttered under his breath. The Meyers were interested. The other third-floor tenant, a single woman whose name he couldn't recall, hadn't been home, so he'd slipped the flyer under her door. Now he stood before Mariah's apartment on the second floor. He knocked. The sound of footsteps and a rapid spate of Spanish came from inside. Mariah opened her door, her phone pressed to her ear.

Her eyes widened. "Can I call you back, *Abuela*? My neighbor is at the door." Her gaze honed in on the absence of his usual hooded state as she ended the call. "Our hooded hero without his hood? What's up, Wyatt?"

His cheeks heated. "I want to talk to you about our building." He handed her a flyer.

Mariah glanced at the paper for a second. "Come in. You want coffee? I just made a fresh pot."

"Sure." He swallowed again and entered her apartment.

"Sit," she ordered, gesturing to the couch.

He took a seat, mentally practicing his pitch, and Mariah disappeared into the kitchen for coffee. She returned, carrying a small tray with two steaming mugs, a sugar bowl and a small pitcher of creamer.

She set them on the coffee table and settled into the armchair next to the couch. "So, what's this about?"

Wyatt put a few spoons of sugar into his coffee. "As I'm sure you've noticed, our building is for sale. I believe we all ought to buy it collectively, either as condos or by turning it into a cooperative. The flyer I gave you has all the specifics." He took a sip of his coffee, which was strong enough to eat through the lining of his stomach. He put the mug down and added creamer.

"I'm talking to everyone in the building. I'm sure I don't need to tell you what a great opportunity this is for all of us, what with the great location, great schools, trendy restaurants nearby and the park. With a few renovations, we could triple our investment."

"Sounds . . . *great*." She chuckled. "Like one of those time-share sales-men presentations. How many times have you given this spiel today?"

"I've had a lot of practice." He grinned. "You're number five."

"Mmm. I don't know." She pursed her lips. "There are a lot of things to love about this old place, but there are also a lot of inconve-niences. Like having to haul my laundry all the way down to the base-ment and back up again. I don't like feeding quarters into those stinky old machines, either."

"We've thought about that. My sister is a plumber, and she's inter-ested in buying the empty unit on the third floor. I brought her in to take a look on Friday night. Our dining rooms share a wall with the bathrooms. She says it would be a cinch to build a closet with washer and dryer hookups against that wall, and the dining areas are huge, so there's plenty of room. I'd do the wiring, and she'd do the plumbing, using some of the general fund mentioned on the flyer. Then, each unit owner could purchase the washer and dryer of their choice."

"Ah." She nodded. "Good idea. What other updates are you thinking?"

"A new, energy-efficient boiler system for heat. And since we don't have ductwork, we're thinking ductless air-conditioning. Each condo would have its own condenser, and two through-the-wall units to pro-vide air-conditioning and supplemental heat. My grandparents have ductless AC in their old house, and it works great."

He'd warmed to his topic, and his palms were no longer sweaty. "We're also thinking new, energy-efficient windows, concrete work in front and back and a new roof. What do you think?"

Mariah lifted the flyer from where she'd left it on the coffee table and took a look. "I have been setting aside a little nest egg to buy a home, but I was thinking more along the lines of a townhouse with a garage. I hate having to dig my car out of snowdrifts all winter long, you know?" She sighed and looked around her apartment. "I'm tempted, since the price is so good. But . . . this building is so *old*. I want brand new, like a townhouse development. I want to live in a place where I get to pick out the cabinets and flooring, a place where nobody else's dirt has ever been."

"I hear you, and here's something to consider. The apartment you're living in right now will only cost you one hundred seventy-five thousand. The actual cost per unit is one hundred twenty-five thousand, but the fifty thousand extra will give us a good start on much-needed updates. Check out what two-bedroom condos are going for in our area, Mariah. I guarantee you won't find anything comparable for under three hundred thousand. Most go for closer to four. Stay for a few years, then sell. Housing prices are going up in this neighborhood. You'll have earned enough in appreciation to put down a big chunk on your dream home."

"Wow." She sat back. "You really think so?"

"I know so. I'm in the construction business, another advantage to us as a collective. My brother and sister also want to invest. We can do a lot of the work ourselves at a great discount, and we can get materials at wholesale. Money is cheap to borrow right now. Your mortgage—with principal, interest, taxes and insurance—would come out to less than what you're currently paying in rent."

"Are you serious?"

He nodded. "I've done the math. It's on the flyer. Will you think about it and give me an answer by Monday at noon?"

"I wonder if Kayla will be home by then? Have you talked to her about this yet?"

"No, but I will as soon as she gets back."

"What's going on with you two? I can tell by the way you look at her you have it bad for the girl, and I'm guessing she's putting up a pretty good fight when it comes to her feelings for you. Am I right?"

And there went his ability to breathe—or talk, since his tongue had welded itself to the roof of his mouth. Judging by the look on Mariah's face, he was pretty sure she'd noticed how he'd reacted to her personal question. Damn, and he'd been doing so well with the overcoming-shyness thing. He almost reached for his hood but managed to control the impulse. He stood up and shrugged, going for nonchalance. "Nothing's going on," he managed to mutter. "We're friends."

"Right." She scrutinized him. "Well, it's none of my business anyway. She's my friend, you know? I'd love to see her happy, and I know how stubborn she can be. I'll take a look at the information and get back to you. You make a good argument, and I do like living here."

"Great." He grabbed the remaining flyers and strode to the door. "I have a few more doors to knock on today. See you."

"See you." She followed him. "Thanks. I appreciate all the work and the thought you've put into this."

"No problem. I'm hoping we get enough interest to keep this place."

Mariah closed her door, and Wyatt headed down the stairs to the apartments on his floor. Two of them were occupied by the elderly women who'd lived in the River Park Apartments forever, and the tenant across the hall from his was a younger guy who was hardly ever around. His car was in the lot, though, so maybe he'd have the chance to talk to him today. Things had gone well with most of the residents, which led him to believe Kayla might be open to the possibility of buying her apartment as well. If so, he'd have more time to win her heart—his ultimate goal. An expensive way to go about achieving his goal, but, oh, well.

He knocked on the door of 101, daydreaming about a future with Kayla and Brady. Mrs. Hanson's door opened a crack.

She scowled out at him. "Whatever bill of goods you're selling, I'm not interested. Don't think I haven't heard you up and down the stairs, knocking on everyone's door this morning."

OK. Tough sell. "Mrs. Hanson, our building is for sale and—"

"I know it's for sale. I may be old, but I'm not blind. I'm moving to Arizona to live with my daughter and her family. Can't wait. Hate the winters here. So whatever cockamamie plan you're hatching, count me out."

With that, she shut the door in his face. Wyatt flinched. Everyone's initial investment just went up by several thousand dollars. He slumped against the wall and glanced at the two remaining doors he needed to approach. Two sales pitches yet to give, and he'd be done for the day. His efforts had taken a lot out of him, and Mrs. Hanson had just sucked whatever wind he had left right out of his sails. He needed a break and something to eat before braving the last two encounters of the residential kind.

Still, the majority of his neighbors had been positive. He headed for his apartment, planning to make coffee he could actually drink and anticipating a little peace and quiet. "Too much talking, too many people." If he arranged things so Kayla wouldn't have to move while going to school, he'd have made her life easier, not to mention he'd achieve his goal of keeping her close. Climbing out of his comfort zone would be worth it though, and he just might manage to impress Kayla enough to make her fall madly in love with him.

"OK." Wyatt rearranged the cartons of Indian takeout on his dining room table so he could set down the paper plates and napkins. Haley, Sam and Josey had arrived for their Monday meeting. "Here's where we stand, but keep in mind Kayla and the guy who lives across the hall from me weren't home all weekend, and I haven't talked to either of them yet. All three units on the third floor are in, including the stoner, which frankly, surprises me. I guess he figured Big Brother has decided to leave him alone. All of the responders prefer the condo approach, and the Meyers in apartment 302 said they're interested in being on our first homeowners association board."

"Make that all four on the third floor, because I'm in." Josey placed the flyer he'd given her on the stack in the basket sitting on the floor beside the table. "Condos work for me. I don't get how the whole owning shares of the building thing for a co-op works, anyway."

"Me too. I prefer to own my apartment outright, so I can make the changes I want to make without discussing it with the entire building," Wyatt said, adding his checked-off form to the pile. "On the second floor, we have two tenants who are interested, one who wants to think about it some more, and Kayla, who doesn't know yet." He took a swallow of his cola and sat down. "The two seniors on the first floor aren't interested, and both have already given their notice to the current owners that they're vacating."

"That's not a bad thing," Sam said. "Haley and I want to invest. The four of us can buy and fix up the empty units and rent them out or sell them."

"Oh, wait." Josey raised her hand, like she was in a classroom. "If there are going to be first-floor units open, I'd rather take one of those. If the four of us form a partnership to buy the empty apartments, we can stick to the original price for everyone else, and Sam's suggestion makes sense. Fix them up first, rent them out, or sell them for a nice big profit."

Sam looked around the table at each of them. "Shouldn't we talk to a lawyer and put this in a contract or something?"

"We need to do that soon," Wyatt agreed. "Do you and Haley want to count as a third or as fourths of the partnership?"

"A third," Haley said. "This is Sam's deal. I'm just here to support you guys in any way I can. Divvy the costs and the profits three ways. I can talk to a lawyer friend where I work. I'm sure we can get the legal work done for next to nothing. He owes me a favor, since it's because of me and Sam that he met his latest love interest."

"Here's to our newly formed business partnership." Wyatt held up his can of soda, and they all clinked their beverages together. "Now that we've settled a few things, let's eat. I'm starving."

All during lunch, Wyatt listened for Kayla's return, his attention divided between the business at hand and practicing what he needed to say to her. By the time they'd finished eating, cleaning up and discussing changes they wanted to make to the building, it was two in the afternoon. Jobs were assigned, like connecting with a few mortgage brokers to start the ball rolling, and gathering a few existing homeowner association bylaws to get a sense of what they needed to include in theirs. "So, you'll talk to the lawyer tomorrow, right, Haley?"

"Yep. That'll be my job."

Wyatt followed everyone to his door. "I'll call the listing agent first thing tomorrow and let him know we want to make an offer. I'll get back to everyone about what will be required and set up a building-wide meeting for Tuesday evening."

"Good. See you tomorrow morning, right? You're back on the job in Woodbury, I'm guessing," Sam said.

"Yep. I'll be there." He saw them all off and closed his door. Restless energy thrummed through him—part excitement about their plans, and part anticipation of Kayla's return. He strode to his studio, intending to begin Elec Tric's newest episode. In this one, Elec Tric would snatch the Mysterious Ms. M from DD's evil clutches. The wooing of the Mysterious Ms. M back to the side of goodness and light would begin. Besides, his studio gave him the best vantage point to keep an eye and ear out for Kayla's return.

He'd been working for two hours when he heard a car pulling into the back lot. "Finally." It had to be Kayla, or someone dropping off his neighbor from across the hall. Wyatt shot up from his drawing table and hurried to the open window. His pulse raced at the sight of her. "Here goes everything," he muttered, striding through his apartment. He grabbed his keys and headed for the back lot.

Wyatt reached her just as she opened her trunk. "Hey, welcome back, Kayla. How was your trip?" The smile she sent his way stole his ability to walk and talk at the same time.

"It was great, thanks."

"Let me get that for you," he said, taking the suitcase from her hand. "Lots has happened around here since you've been gone."

"Oh? Like what?" Her brow rose.

"Do you have a few minutes to talk? Can we stop at my apartment before taking your suitcase upstairs? There's a flyer, and I—"

"A *flyer*?" She opened the back door for him. "Sounds serious. What's the flyer about?"

"Our building. Can you talk now, or—?"

"Yes. Lots happened in Iowa, too, and I need to talk to you anyway."

Uh-oh. Now what? His gut twisted. "Is everyone in your family all right? Is Brady OK?" He opened his door and ushered her inside and set her suitcase by his living room closet.

"Everyone is fine. I had an interesting talk with my mother-in-law, and I've done a lot of thinking, that's all." She sucked in an audible breath. "We need to talk."

"Great." Maybe not so great. Last time she said that, she'd informed him they couldn't date. What now? Was she about to tell him she planned to move back to Iowa once she was done with school? Tension squeezed his chest, and his palms grew moist. He had to bare his soul and come up with a Hail Mary pass of a sales pitch. "Would you like a beer or a glass of wine?"

"I'd love a glass of wine. It was a long drive." She trailed him to the kitchen. "How was your weekend?"

"Busy."

"My family loved your Elec Tric comic books, and now they're with my aunt. Just think, an agent is going to look at them this week. Becky says if Angela likes them, things will happen fast."

"Good to hear. Thanks again for your help." He focused on opening the bottle of Chardonnay he'd put in the fridge a few days ago. He grabbed a couple of wine glasses from the cabinet and poured them both a glass. "Let's go sit down, and you can tell me all about your weekend."

She took the glass he handed her. "You first. I want to hear about this flyer you mentioned."

Shoring up his nerve, he gestured toward the living room and followed her to the couch. "Well, it all started with the building being for sale. You mentioned you were going to look for a new place right away, and I realized I don't even have your phone number. I kind of . . . panicked."

Kayla took a seat, her expression puzzled. "What does not having my phone number have to do with our building? Why on earth would you panic over that?"

He rubbed the back of his neck. "See, it's like this, I—"

"Give me your phone right now and unlock the screen." She held out her hand.

He pulled it from his back pocket, entered the code and handed it over, looking on as she entered her name, number and an e-mail address into his contacts.

"There," she said, handing it back. "Problem solved, and once you call or text me, I'll have yours."

Shoving his phone back in his pocket, he shook his head. "It's not that simple. Where to begin?"

Kayla studied him. "What's going on, Wyatt? You're making me nervous."

"Mind if I pace while I talk?" He began pacing before she answered. His heart had climbed to his throat, making it difficult to breathe.

"Go ahead."

He took a gulp of his wine and set the glass on the coffee table. Then he grabbed one of the two remaining flyers from the bookshelf and handed it to her. "See, when Sam and Haley got together, my brother really mucked things up and almost lost her for good. He came to me and Josey for help to win her back, and we came up with a grand gesture for him to win Haley back."

"OK. Now I'm more confused than ever. What have Sam and Haley got to do with our building?"

"I'm getting there." He paced again. The next part was the hardest. He drew in a long breath and tried to force his heart back to where it belonged. "Our building is for sale, and you know how it is with *friends*. They move away and lose touch, and I didn't even have your number, so—"

"Oh, Wyatt. We won't lose touch. Brady and I—"

"Gotta get this out." He came to stand in front of the coffee table and forced himself to look directly into her eyes. "I went to Josey and Sam and asked them to help me come up with a grand gesture. And what we came up with is . . . I would buy this building, become your landlord and keep your rent the same. That way, you'd have no reason to leave."

"What? You're going to *buy* this building just to . . ." She flopped back against the backrest of his couch and stared at him, looking stunned. "OK, what have I missed? You don't need to buy an apartment building to keep me in your life, that's—"

"Things kind of snowballed from there pretty fast." It took all the courage he possessed, but he circled around the coffee table and sat down beside her. "I talked to the listing agent, and then I talked to all of our neighbors."

"*You* went around and talked to all of our neighbors. God, that must have been torture for you." Her expression filled with tenderness. "You did that for me?"

Nodding, he tapped the flyer on her lap. "Yes. I overcame my shyness for an entire morning. A good portion of our neighbors, me, Sam and Josey are all buying this place together, and I'm hoping like hell you'll join us. We're turning this place into condos. It's an excellent deal and a great investment."

"You've done all this just because you didn't have my telephone number?" Her gaze roamed over his face, pausing on his mouth, then rising back to his eyes.

His blood heated. "This was never about not having your phone number, Kayla. OK, here goes."

He shot up to pace again. "You know how I said I'd switched gears from wanting you to being friends only?" he muttered, his face burning now. "I lied. I did all this because my feelings for you haven't changed." He was having trouble breathing now.

"No, scratch that. My feelings for you *have* changed. They've grown deeper and stronger every single day, and I was desperate to find a way to get you see that, and to stay here with me. I figured I just needed more time to convince you to give us a shot. The plan was to spend as much time with you and Brady as I possibly could. That way, I hoped you'd realize we're perfect for each other. See, if you moved away, I'd lose my chance. This whole thing started out as my grand gesture . . . for you."

"Oh, Wyatt, I—"

"I know." His chest curled in on itself at the possibility of impending heartache. "I know. You're still grieving over the years you believe you lost, and you need time to heal from your disastrous marriage, but—"

"No. I don't."

He froze. "You don't?"

She shook her head. "That's what I wanted to talk to you about."

Her eyes met his then, and he glimpsed vulnerability in their blue depths—and longing. Desire weakened his knees and made his head spin in a dizzying rush.

"Sit with me." She patted the spot beside her on the couch.

He remembered the first time she'd patted a couch, inviting him to sit beside her—the day her kitchen had caught on fire. Even then, at some level, he'd known she was his one and only. Was she about to make him the happiest man on the planet, or was she about to break his heart for good?

Sinking down beside her, he considered reaching for her hand, but what if she rejected him. *Be bold.* Shaky, breathless, he slid his hand nearer, one centimeter, another . . . and then he did it—he reached for her hand. She took it, gripped it actually. Good sign.

He leaned back on the couch, because he couldn't hold himself together for much longer. More than anything, he wanted to wrap himself around her, ease her down on the couch underneath him and make love to her. On edge, hyped up, he cleared his throat. "So, what is it you want to talk to me about?"

Chapter Fifteen

Oh, God. Was she going to hyperventilate herself into a faint? Kayla reached for her purse. "I'd rather show you." Wyatt still cared for her. He'd been willing to buy their building to keep her close. Who did that? If there had been any doubts remaining in the recesses of her mind, they flew the coop. She loved this man more than she'd ever believed possible.

"I bought something for you," she told him, her voice quavering. "Only, compared to what you were willing to buy for me, my gift is pretty lame." She pulled out the small box of condoms she'd picked up at a truck stop and set it on the table.

"What's this?" Wyatt's brow shot up, and his face turned an interesting shade of red.

"They're condoms, Wyatt."

"I *know* they're condoms, *Kayla.*" He huffed out a breath. "But what does this mean? And you'd better tell me quick, because I'm *this* close"—he held up a hand, showing her the millimeter of space between his thumb and forefinger—"to going caveman all over you right now."

Her nerves were firing on all cylinders, every single part of her a quivering mass of take-me-now. "Can we do the caveman thing first and talk later?"

"Hell, yes." He put his arms around her, eased them both down on the couch and kissed her senseless.

Wyatt's kisses, his tongue sliding against hers, set her aflame. She slid her hands under his shirt, desperate to finally touch him. Warm, soft skin over lean muscle . . . *Wyatt.* He was her own personal aphrodisiac. Heat pooled low in her belly, causing a throbbing ache only Wyatt could ease. He trailed kisses along her jaw and down her throat.

"I was wrong," she murmured. "I *do* want to date you. I'm *crazy* about you, and I . . . ohhh, that feels sooo good—I don't need a grand gesture."

Raising himself on his forearms, he stared into her eyes. "Really?" The absolute adoration she glimpsed in his expression turned her inside out. "Really. I only need you, Wyatt. Just you." She slid her palms up his arms, reveling in the feel of his sculpted biceps, his strength. How many times had she fantasized about touching him like this?

His eyes darkened. "You have me." He tugged the hem of her T-shirt up and moved down to tickle her belly with kisses. "You're so soft." He skimmed his hands up her sides, continuing to torture her with kisses that made her muscles twitch and her insides flutter. "And you smell so damn good," he whispered. Laying his cheek against her midriff, he rubbed and nuzzled against her sensitive skin.

She gasped, his stubble sending frissons of arousal through her. Clutching handfuls of his shirt, she pulled it up. He lifted himself again and helped her take it off. Then he set himself to the task of removing her T-shirt.

His expression intense, heavy lidded, he caressed her breasts, his touch reverent. "Perfect." He kissed her along the swell above the lace of her best bra. "Can we take this off?" He ran his tongue over her skin. "Please and thank you?"

Chuckling, Kayla slid her hands underneath her back and unhooked her bra. He drew it off and tossed it to the floor.

"Oh, yeah," he groaned. He teased one nipple into a hard peak with his tongue, and then the other before burying his face between her breasts, his hands continuing to explore and tease. "I'm in heaven." He took one nipple into his mouth and suckled.

Electric currents shot from her breast straight to her core. "Wyatt."

"Hmm?" He kept his face buried between her breasts, kissing and nipping, driving her insane and impatient to feel him inside her.

"Maybe we should—"

"On it." He shot up and took off his shorts and briefs in record time.

As she'd suspected, he was gorgeous from head to toe. His erection? Magnificent, and he was all hers. To think she'd almost let fear from her past ruin things with him for good.

Wyatt reached for the box of condoms, tearing it open with so much force that cellophane and cardboard flew. He pulled out a foil packet and ripped that open too. Sheathing himself, he murmured, "Ready," and sank to his knees on the floor rug beside the couch. He tried to unbutton her shorts, and fumbled, and blew out a shaky breath.

Kayla reached to help, but he moved her hands away. "Let me do this." His expression one of absolute concentration, he tried again, and this time he got it free. His hands trembling, he worked her out of her clothes. "Kayla, I don't think I'm going to last long this first time. I'm just warning you, but the second time . . ." His eyes met hers, an endearing earnestness suffusing his beloved features. "The second time will be all about you. I promise."

Her eyes stung, a lump formed in her throat, but she managed to smile. "I'm not worried."

"I just want to look at you for a few minutes. Can I?"

She nodded, unable to answer, so caught up in the moment and the intensity of her emotions. Still on his knees beside her, he leaned close and kissed her deeply. Breaking the kiss, he straightened, his gaze roaming from her head to her toes and back up again.

"Wow." He ran his hands over her, his expression one of awe. Beginning at her collarbone, down over pebbled nipples aching for his attention, and continuing lower to her torso, his touch elicited delicious shivers along the way. When he got to her sex, he raised her knees and spread her legs. "And again . . . wow."

The sudden intake of his breath, the hooded sexy look in his eyes, shot right through her, and brought a rush of wetness to her core. Never had she felt so vulnerable or so completely open to anyone before, but this was Wyatt, and she loved him. He touched her then, sliding a finger along her slick cleft. He leaned over and kissed her belly, circling her navel with his tongue, and she arched into him.

"Can I taste you?" he asked, the wavering in his voice.

She wasn't alone in her vulnerability. "I thought you said you weren't going to last," she teased. "The *second* time was supposed to be all about me, and this time is for you."

"Oh, believe me when I tell you . . . this *is* for me." He spread his hands over her hips, his gaze riveted on her sex. "I really, really want to do this." He leaned in, took her mouth in a scorching kiss, inserting a finger into her. Bringing it out again, he circled her clitoris.

Moaning, she raised her hips, trying to bring his touch to where she needed it most. "I'm all yours."

"Kayla mine," he rasped out before kissing and stroking his way down her torso to make love to her with his mouth. He held her bottom with both hands, and licked, nipped and sucked. He flicked her clit with his tongue, and she was lost.

"Oh . . . don't . . . stop." She tangled her fingers into his hair, guiding him to where she needed him to be, holding on for dear life. Waves of sensation washed over her, the pleasurable pressure building with each flick of his tongue. Her back bowed, she came in a rush, shuddering and pulsing against him, her eyes closed tight. Once he'd wrung the last shudder of pleasure from her, she opened her eyes to find him watching her with an intensity that robbed her of the ability to breathe.

"You liked that," he said, his expression full of masculine pride. "Seeing you come is the sexiest thing I've ever experienced."

"I did like that." She shot him a wry look. "Turns out I'm the one who didn't last."

"Guess I have a few superpowers after all." His expression wolfish, he came back onto the couch to cover her.

Kayla laughed, not so much because anything about this was funny, but because she couldn't contain her happiness. She hadn't been too late, and he hadn't given up on her. Tenderness and love for her shy, funny, creative sexy man overcame her. "I want to see and touch all of you, Wyatt. You said you had other scars from your burns. Let me see them."

He frowned. "Now?"

"Please?" She stroked his shoulders and down his arms.

He blew out a breath and twisted around so she could see his left side. "They're here on my side."

She touched the scattering of scars down his rib cage. "They're not bad. Do they bother you?"

"Not at the moment. Not if they don't bother you." He propped himself on his forearms again and cradled her head between his hands. "I love your hair." He tangled his fingers in it and nuzzled her temple, and his hips rocking gently against her. "And your eyes. You have the prettiest eyes." Kissing one eyelid, then the other, he kissed his way over her face to her mouth. "And your lips. I love these lips."

Kayla wrapped her arms around him, bringing him in for a kiss, and all talking ceased. She wanted him so badly. She hadn't known sex could be like this, all consuming and intensely emotional as well as physical. It was her turn to explore, and she did. Every contour, every bit of his long, lean body. When she finally got to his member, she ran her hand over him from base to tip, and back down again to caress his testicles. He groaned and pressed himself against her palm.

"Ahhh, that feels so damn good. Kayla, I can't wait any longer."

Desire once again coiled tight within her. She opened her arms to him, and he covered her. Skin to skin from chest to toes, she exalted in the feel of his warmth and his weight against her, the way the hair on his legs and chest tickled her skin. His hands were everywhere, inciting a riot of need to a feverish pitch. "Now, Wyatt."

A growling noise rose from his chest, reverberating all the way through to the very marrow of her bones. He raised himself, and she reached between them, positioning him at her opening. Wyatt entered her, and the fullness of their joining brought a sigh to her lips. "Yes."

Swept into a tide of sensation, she met his thrusts, raising her hips to meet his. They moved together, finding their own rhythm. His movements were slow, deliberate, and his heavy breathing against her ear as he held her close was the most erotic thing she'd ever experienced.

The tension began to build again; he filled her just right, the friction perfect. He groaned, and his pace accelerated. She was close, so close. Pausing, he raised her knees, supporting himself with his arms on either side, seated himself even deeper. Thrusting into her with greater force, touching a place inside her that sent her over the edge. She fell apart, her muscles tightening around him. He threw his head back and called out her name and stilled above her.

Lowering her legs, he collapsed on top of her. "Stay with me tonight?"

"Yes," she whispered, running her hands up and down his back.

He sighed into her ear and smoothed her hair back from her sweaty brow. "Are you hungry? I make a mean sandwich. I have ham, pastrami and all kinds of cheese. I'm starving." He rose from the couch and stretched.

"Me too." She thoroughly enjoyed the view. "Shower first?"

He reached out a hand to help her up and pulled her into his arms. "Oh, yeah. Can't wait to get my hands on that sexy body of yours, all slick and soapy. You are so gorgeous, Kayla."

Her eyes misted at his praise. Yep. After the dearth of anything good that had been her sham of a marriage, Wyatt's compliments, his adoration, renewed and healed her like nothing else could. She twined her fingers with his. They walked to his bathroom together as if it were the most natural thing in the world to walk naked by his side, like he hadn't just tilted her world on its axis. Her muscles barely held her up; she'd gone that boneless with satisfaction.

"Kayla?"

"Mmm?"

"I'm crazy in love with you."

Tears filled her eyes, and she sniffed. "I love you too. I was so afraid you wouldn't give me a do-over after the way I hurt you. I was going to seduce you back into dating me, and I planned to tell you what a fool I'd been either before or after, but I hadn't decided which to do first, and then—"

"Don't cry." He drew her into his arms again and rocked her gently. "Please don't cry. I never stopped wanting you, you gotta know that. My plan was to make myself like your shadow . . . always there for you, until you finally gave in and loved me back." Now that he heard his words out loud, he worried. "That's not crazy, is it?"

"No. It's sweet, and these are happy tears," she muttered against his shoulder.

"I know, but if you keep this up, it's going to make me cry too, and then my superhero image will be all shot to hell."

She laughed through her tears and backed out of his embrace. "Never. You'll always be a superhero in my eyes."

"And a sex god?" He took her hand again, and led her to his bathroom.

"Yeah, about that. Have you been holding out on me?" She looked askance at him, frowning. "For a shy guy, you sure do know your way around a woman's body. How is that?"

"I've had lots of practice."

"What?" She blinked. "The shy thing is all an act?"

"No." Shrugging, he flashed her a sheepish grin. "I have a vivid imagination, that's all. And I've done . . . research."

"Hmm." She wasn't sure what to make of his claim. "I told you when I lost my virginity. When did you lose yours?" Why it mattered, she couldn't say, but suddenly it did.

"Kayla . . ." He got the shower ready. "Does it matter?"

"Right now it does."

"I'd rather not say." His face reddened. "Can we let this go for now, and come back to the conversation another time, like never? We have a soapy shower coming up. We can play car wash." He winked at her.

Kayla arched a brow. "When?"

"All right." His shoulders slumped. "I lost my virginity about ten minutes ago."

"No." Still skeptical, but inordinately pleased, she shook her head. "You knew what you were doing, and you did it really well. And when I say really well, I mean life-altering, mind-blowingly well."

"Thank you." He grinned. "Like I said, I've had a lot of practice . . . in my fantasies. Visualization is a thing. Athletes do it all the time to improve their performance." He held her in his arms again, this time cupping her bottom. "I know all kinds of stuff we can try out together." He waggled his eyebrows and kissed the tip of her nose. "Now, let's shower, and then I'll make you dinner. Afterward, you can put my claims to the test."

A half hour later, clean and clothed, Kayla sat at Wyatt's dining room table, the sandwich he'd made sitting in front of her. Wyatt explained what he'd done toward buying their building. She glanced at the flyer he'd placed beside her plate. Munching on a pickle spear, she read through the financial part. "You talked to everyone in our building?"

"I did. Without a hood on, I might add. I wanted to prove to myself that I could do this, and I wanted you to see it as the declaration I meant it to be—that I'd do whatever it took to convince you we're perfect for each other."

"I'm convinced, not to mention grateful and amazed. All right, I'm in, but I'd like to move from the second to the first floor, since the two seniors are leaving anyway. You and I would only be across the hall from each other then."

"I'd like that. In a couple of years, when both our condos have been updated, we can sell, and come out of the deal with a nice chunk of change to put down on a house with a yard. Brady needs a yard and a tree house. He can help me build it. Wouldn't that be a blast? We really need to get him his own fishing pole too." He glanced at her, his expression shy. "What do you think?"

"Sure. Let's do that." Her eyes misted up again. He wanted her. She hadn't believed she'd ever get to experience the kind of joy that sent her heart racing, and here was her hero, envisioning a future for the three of them. A brand new kind of happiness bloomed within her. And man, was that her heart opening up, expanding all at once? Wyatt was such a loving man, the best. She could hardly believe her luck.

Somehow, after all the crap she'd been through, she'd ended up loving and being loved by the most amazing guy in the entire universe. She had to come up with a word for this. Something the opposite of *BAM*, an expression for the good stuff happening in her life: Brady, Wyatt, school . . . their future together. Something to think about anyway, and she would, because every minute she spent with Wyatt the desire for such a word grew. "I need a thesaurus."

"Why? Are you going to take up writing?"

"No, I just want to look up something."

"I have a thesaurus in my studio, and another one on my desktop computer. You're welcome to use both."

"Thank you." She grinned. "Now, about those sex things you mentioned we could try out together . . ."

He dropped what was left of his sandwich and did that sexy, deep growling thing again.

She laughed, shot up off her chair and let him chase her to his bedroom. Her life with him would always be good. Maybe not always easy, but worth any struggle that came their way.

Late Tuesday afternoon, all their neighbors, and Josey and Sam, gathered in Wyatt's apartment. Sweat beaded on his brow, and he glanced at Kayla to steady his nerves. She nodded and smiled encouragement.

He'd texted his siblings as soon as Kayla had fallen asleep last night, informing them that "he" was now a "we." His chest swelled with a mixture of pride and love. He couldn't wait until Brady came home, so he could do fun things with his new pack.

Hippie guy Dennis sat on the ottoman, and he even wore a shirt today. The other residents were scattered around the room. The two seniors from the first floor were the only ones absent. Even Erik from across the hall had joined them. Mariah sat on the couch, with Rosie on her lap. Kayla took up the spot next to her friend.

Wyatt paused before launching into his spiel, considering how far he'd come in the past couple of months. Though he sometimes had to force himself not to pull it up, he no longer hid inside a hoodie. Let people look at his scars if they wanted to. He knew who he was and where he wanted his life to go. Besides, Kayla kept telling him how good-looking he was, and as long as she saw him as hot, that's all that mattered.

He held up his hand, calling for quiet. "OK, here's what's going to happen next," he began. "The listing agent will be here in about twenty minutes, and we're going to write up a contingent offer for our building together."

"What does the contingent part mean, man?" Dennis asked, looking puzzled and a little alarmed.

"It means the deal depends upon our securing financing. Each of us must go through the process of being approved for a mortgage, and that will take time. If we aren't all able to qualify, we'll have to write up a different offer with only those who do, or we'll lose our building to another bidder."

Wyatt leaned over and took a handful of half sheets of paper from the coffee table. "On that note, I made up a list of several local mortgage brokers." He handed them to Josey. "If you don't already have someone you want to work with, take one and pass them along."

While the list of brokers was being distributed, Wyatt mentally checked off the topics he needed to cover.

Erik, his neighbor from across the hall, held up his hand. "For those of us who just found flyers under our doors, can we talk about what we plan to do with the general fund?"

"Good question, man," Dennis added, nodding.

"Well, for starters, we need to address unsafe conditions, like the cracked and crumbling front and back concrete steps and sidewalks." He summarized the rest of what needed to be done to bring the building up to date.

Sam came to stand beside him. "Besides needed repairs, a general fund is necessary for the upkeep of common areas, water, garbage pickup, hallways, snow plowing in winter and lawn upkeep in the summer—stuff like that," Sam told the group.

"Everyone will have access to the financials at all times," Wyatt added. "Once we own the building, we'll set up a website for members."

He surveyed the group. "You'll each have a vote as to how our money is spent."

"Sounds good, man," Dennis nodded again, propping his hands on his knees and sitting up a little straighter. "It's like we're going to be a commune."

Wyatt struggled not to roll his eyes. Thankfully, the security buzzer for the front door went off. "There's the listing agent. Jo, will you let Steve in?"

Josey pushed herself off the wall she'd been leaning against and hurried down the stairs to the front door, and Wyatt added, "I'm going to have him set up here at the coffee table, so if a couple of you wouldn't mind, let's make some room."

"He can have my spot," Kayla said, rising from the couch. She came to stand beside him, and he put his arm around her waist and kissed her forehead. He needed to touch her. Somehow, she grounded him. "I can't believe we're actually doing this."

"I can't believe you're finally doing . . . that," Mariah quipped, pointing at his arm around Kayla.

"*Finally* is right." Wyatt laughed. He leaned in and whispered in Kayla's ear, "Love you."

"I love you too. After everyone leaves, there's something I'd like to try tonight," she whispered back.

"Oh?" His pulse sped up. "What's that?"

Kayla leaned close. "My turn to taste."

Heat rushed to his face and to his groin simultaneously, and his knees went a little weak. "I'm willing to give that a try."

Kayla laughed. "I love that I can make you blush."

"It's a good thing you do, since I can't control it."

Jo ushered the realtor into the living room and made introductions. Steve set a briefcase on the coffee table and pulled out a stack of official-looking documents, and the excitement in the room grew.

"You know what?" Wyatt drew Kayla closer. "Today we're making an offer on our future. That's pretty amazing. Three months ago, I never could've seen this coming."

"Me either," Kayla said wrapping her arms around him.

"You know what's even more amazing?"

"No, what?"

"You." He held his future in his arms, and that was worth more than any piece of property he could imagine.

Chapter Sixteen

Wyatt awoke Thursday morning to the sensation of having his face peppered with sweet kisses. Kayla's naked, luscious curves were snuggled against him, and he looped a leg over hers and drew her closer. He could definitely get used to wrapping himself around her each night, with her warm, soft skin next to his. Her hands roamed all over him, finally slipping between their bodies to stroke his morning wood. He could get used to that too.

Keeping his eyes closed, he smiled. "I could become a morning person for you." He shifted slightly, giving her better access. Kayla's husky laugh in his ear sent sparks of desire cascading through him.

"You mean you aren't normally a morning person?" she asked, taking his earlobe between her teeth.

He shivered and groaned. "Not even close." Caressing her full breast, he ran his thumb over her nipple. "What time is it? The alarm didn't go off, did it?"

"It's only six, but I have to get going."

He opened one eye a slit and thrust against the palm of her hand, which she was using to drive him crazy. "By 'get going,' I'm assuming you mean . . ." He thrust again, hoping she'd pick up on the hint.

Chuckling, Kayla sat up and reached for a condom from his nightstand. "Well that too, but then I need to get ready for school." She tore the foil packet open with her teeth, took it out and unrolled it slowly down his aching hard-on while caressing his testicles.

He had to be the luckiest man on the planet, because his woman woke up all hot and ready to rumble. Wyatt pulled her in for a long, heat-producing kiss and some much-needed petting. He came up for air several moments later and nuzzled her temple, working a hand down to where he knew she liked to be teased and touched. "Did you know I've had the biggest crush on you since the day you moved in?"

Kayla moaned and pressed closer, a sexy smile lighting her face. "Couldn't help noticing Ms. M appeared in your comic books around the same time I arrived."

He pinched a nipple, then licked the hardened bud, reveling in the way Kayla's breath hitched in response. "I tried so many times to talk to you. I wanted to ask you out so badly, but it took a fire to make it happen."

"Ahhh, that feels so good, Wyatt." She rolled on top of him and leaned in for a kiss. Her hair tickled his shoulders as her tongue swept into his mouth to tangle with his.

Caveman Wyatt took over, and he flipped them both so he was on top. They'd tried a lot of different positions in the past couple of days, but for now, this was still his favorite. He nudged her knees apart and plunged himself home. "Love you, Kayla."

"Love you, Wyatt."

Two hours later, Wyatt pulled into the Woodbury Hills development where he'd be working for the next few weeks. He was still high over being coupled up, and Kayla filled his every waking thought. Tonight he planned to wine and dine her. Yep. Shy guy had a date with his girlfriend. *Girlfriend.* Wonder of wonders, *he'd* gotten the girl. Hmm. She'd look great in a Wonder Woman costume.

Too bad he didn't really know how to whistle, because if he did, he'd be whistling a happy tune right now. Turns out, sex was every bit as amazing as everyone claimed. Though he suspected the quality of his and Kayla's lovemaking far surpassed that of most mere mortals, what with him being a sex god and all. Grinning, and now a little turned on, he walked into the house he and his siblings would be working on today.

"Good morning," he called cheerfully to the crew setting up for the day. Sam and Josey stood among them. He joined his brother and sister, put his toolbox on the subflooring and strapped on his tool belt.

"Morning," Josey said. "Have you heard anything from the realtor yet?"

Jo's question only heightened his buzz. He, shy Hoodie Guy, had organized the collective offer on their building, and soon they'd learn whether or not it had been accepted. "No, not yet. We should hear any day now," he said. All his joints and limbs were loose, relaxed. Sex must be good for him, because he'd never felt this good before in his life, and he couldn't keep the grin off his face.

Josey scowled. "I can't even be around you right now." She grabbed her tools and stomped off.

"What's wrong with Josey?" Confused, he watched her go. What'd I do?"

"She'll get over it." Sam grunted. "Ever since you traded in your 'I'm solo' card for that shiny new 'party of two' ID, you've worn that half-drugged, man-getting-plenty-of-sex look. I'm getting married, you have a girlfriend, and Josey is having a hard time with all the changes. Her love life is stalled out."

"Oh." He continued to stare down the hall after her. "I hadn't thought about that. We'll have to make a point of it to spend time together, just the three of us."

"Yeah, like it used to be," Sam agreed. "It's nice to see you've finally given up your security blanket."

"Huh?" His gaze swung to his brother.

"The hoodies. You aren't wearing them anymore."

"Oh. Right."

"Let's get to work." Sam strode off down the hall toward the bedrooms.

Wyatt's hand went to his scars. Every day without the hoods got easier. He unpacked the box of light fixtures for the kitchen and got busy.

By ten, he'd finished with the kitchen light fixtures and outlets and moved on to a bedroom to install a ceiling fan and light fixture combo. He'd just set up his ladder when his phone buzzed and vibrated. He pulled it out of his back pocket. "Hello."

"Hey, Wyatt. Steve Andrews here. I wanted to talk to you about your group's offer. Do you have a minute?"

"Sure." A rush of adrenaline hit his bloodstream. He was about to learn whether or not he would soon be a property owner.

"The owners are not outright rejecting the offer, but they plan to continue showing the building to see if any other bids come in while your group gets their financing together. Once the contingency is out of the way, they'd like the tenants to present a new, noncontingent offer."

"OK. Fair enough." His stomach dropped.

"This is not unusual in situations like this. Let me know the second everyone is preapproved, and we'll write up the new bid right away and overnight it to them."

"I will. Thanks for all your help, Steve. I'll let everyone else know what's going on. Call me if anything changes."

"Count on it. It's not over yet, Wyatt. Encourage everyone to act quickly on getting qualified, and don't be discouraged."

"All right." Yeah, he already was discouraged. Pushing his disappointment aside, he ended the call and brought up his e-mail. He entered the e-mail group for everyone involved in the offer and composed a quick note to bring them up to speed. Everyone except hippie Dennis, of course. Dennis didn't believe in computers, e-mails or cell phones. Something about being able to hack into his business, man, and Big Brother being out to get him and all that.

Wyatt shook his head. What a character. He hit Send, and then he went back to work. He'd tell Sam and Josey about the call over lunch. Dang. He'd hate to lose their building, but at least he'd get to keep the girl. He went back to work, certain he still wore the drugged look of a man getting plenty of loving.

Showered, shaved and dressed, Wyatt sat at his drawing board, inking in the blue of Elec Tric's superhero costume. Kayla would knock on his door soon, and he wanted to get as much done as he could before their date. In this chapter, Elec Tric had rescued the Mysterious Ms. M from Diabolical Delilah. His superhero's mission now was to persuade Ms. M back to the side of goodness and light. Once Elec Tric brought her back from the dark forces, the two would become partners in the fight against evil and tyranny.

The two partnering up would be a brand-new direction for the Elec Tric saga, and it would keep the series going for several more episodes. He'd have to come up with a few new demons and plots of mayhem and destruction. Glancing at the time, he decided to quit for now. He left his things where they were, stood up and stretched. Wyatt walked into his living room just as Kayla knocked on his door, sending his pulse racing.

His hand on the doorknob, Wyatt went into Brady's routine. "Who's there?"

"It's *me*."

"Me who?" A few moments of silence went by.

"Is this a knock-knock joke, Wyatt?" Kayla asked, her tone laced with exasperation. "Or are you expecting someone else?"

He opened the door. "I'm not expecting anyone else. I miss Brady. *He* likes to play with me," he teased, going in for a kiss before she could protest. Kayla sighed and melted against him. How could he not deepen the kiss? For that matter, how could he resist caressing her shapely bottom and pressing her against his growing erection?

Ending the kiss, he gazed into her eyes. "We could stay in, order takeout and watch a movie on cable."

"We could, but we have a reservation, and I'd really like to try that new Heirloom Kitchen & Bar down the street. I don't get many opportunities to do grown-up stuff." She played with the collar of his shirt. "As much as I miss my son, I want to take advantage of this time with just the two of us." She kissed his chin. "We made a date, and I'm holding you to it. We can order takeout and hang out anytime."

"All right." Reluctantly, he let her go. "But we have to run up to the third floor before we leave. Did you see the e-mail I sent, bringing everyone up to date on our offer?" They walked out of his apartment, and he locked the door.

"I haven't checked my e-mail today. What's going on?"

As they climbed the stairs, he shared what Steve had told him. "Dennis doesn't have an e-mail address or a cell phone, and I didn't think to get his land-line number." He reached for Kayla's hand and crossed the hall to knock on Hippie Guy's door.

Dennis came to the door right away. "Hey, you two, come on in."

"Thanks, Dennis, but we're on our way out. I just stopped by to let you know I heard back from Steve."

"Yeah? What'd he have to say, man? Did the owners accept our offer?"

"Not exactly." He explained the situation. "I'm urging everyone to get their mortgage applications completed quickly. As soon as we can lock down the financing, Steve will present a new noncontingent offer on our behalf."

Dennis scratched his beard. He looked worried. "We could *lose* this place because of that contingent thing, man. Not good. Not good at all."

"It's a possibility." Wyatt nodded.

"OK. Thanks for letting me know."

"Where are you with arranging for your mortgage, Dennis?" Kayla asked.

"I'm set. All taken care of."

"Good." Wyatt breathed a sigh of relief. Out of all of the residents involved, he'd been the most concerned about this guy's follow-through when it came to the financing. He didn't even know if Dennis had a job. "Once I hear back from everyone else, we'll move forward."

"Great. We can have our next meeting in my place if you want." Dennis squared his shoulders. "I'm on the HOA bylaws committee. The Meyers and your sister . . . they're good people."

"You're good people too, Dennis," Kayla told him. "I like having you for a neighbor."

Dennis's eyes widened. He blinked a few times and shuffled his feet. "Well, I'd better get back to . . . uh . . . you two have a good evening. Got stuff to do." He gave them a little wave and disappeared behind his closing door.

Wyatt put his arm around Kayla's shoulders and turned her toward the stairs. "I think we embarrassed him."

"He's sweet." Kayla shrugged. "Odd, but definitely a good guy."

"Do I need to be jealous, man?"

"Maybe," she teased.

"Kayla . . . *mine*," he grunted.

"Ohhhh, I love it when you turn caveman on me."

"Are you *sure* you don't want to stay in tonight?" He slanted her his very best puppy-dog eyes.

"I'm sure."

Twining his fingers with hers, he savored the moment. They were a couple and already teasing each other. "All right. Wining and dining coming right up."

She sighed, an expression of happiness lighting her features. "I've never had this before, Wyatt. Being with you, it's . . . so different. I don't have any doubts anymore. I *know* you love me, and I know I love you."

"I get what you mean, and I feel the same." He opened the front door for her and placed a hand at the small of her back as they walked down the front steps to the sidewalk. September was one of his favorite months. Already the air had a crispness to it, and the nights were cooler. "Nice evening. I'm glad we decided to walk to the restaurant."

"Me too." Kayla once again twined her fingers with his.

"Grandma Maggie called. She and Grandpa Joe really want to meet you and Brady. Would you mind going to their house for dinner next Saturday?"

"I'd love to meet them, and you'll get to meet my folks this Saturday. I told them we're dating, and they want you to join us for dinner. Are you OK with that?"

"Sure." *Gulp.* So she'd told her parents about them already. Heat rose to his face just thinking about facing her father. Her dad would take one look at him, and he'd instantly know what he'd been up to with his little girl. Meeting the parents had to be done, but he didn't want to think about it anymore tonight, or he'd work himself into a mess of nerves.

"You look really pretty tonight, Kayla." He drew her close to his side for a quick hug. She wore a long, gauzy skirt with geometric designs, a silky blouse that set off the blue of her eyes, and a denim jacket.

"Thank you. You look really nice too. I like you in button-down shirts." She ran her hand down his arm. "You're such a good-looking man."

He squeezed her hand. "How do you feel about Wonder Woman costumes?" More and more he believed he might have the wedding he'd dreamed of after all.

"That was random." Kayla laughed and bumped him with her shoulder. "I'll wear one for you, if you'll put on a superhero costume for me. We haven't tried role-playing yet. Could be fun."

Content, he smiled but didn't comment. Let her believe his question referred to role-playing in the bedroom. Once he proposed and put that ring on her finger, then he'd share his ideas for their wedding. Now that he was over the hoodies, they could go with silk-screened superhero T-shirts under sport coats for the men, and a Wonder Woman costume for the bride. Surely she'd see his vision for their special day as pure genius.

Kayla's security buzzer went off, and she hurried down the front stairs to open the door for Brady and her parents. "Come in."

"It's good to see you, Kayla." Her mother gave her a hug, and her dad carried in their overnight bag and Brady's suitcase.

She hugged her mom back as her dad continued on up the stairs. "I'm on the second floor and across the hall to your right, Dad."

"Mommy!" Brady cried, launching himself at her.

She picked him up and hugged him tight. "Boy, am I ever glad to see you." It wouldn't be long before he was too big to pick up anymore, and he wouldn't let her then anyway. "I think you've grown, kiddo." She followed her parents up the stairs.

"Yep, and d'you know what? Pops let me ride the pony, and I got to feed him and brush him too."

"He's a natural," her dad said, glancing back at her over his shoulder. "He did really well, and he was quite the helper all week."

Kayla patted her son on the back. "Sounds like you had a good time with Gammy and Pops."

"I did," Brady said wrapping his arms around her neck.

Her heart melting, she continued up the stairs and set Brady on his feet on her landing. "Come on in. Lunch is ready." She opened her door wide. "You can put those bags here by the door for now, Dad. We'll get you settled after lunch."

Kayla busied herself with putting the chicken salad and the croissants on the already-set table while her mom filled the coffee mugs and poured milk for Brady. Chips and a bowl of fruit were set out, and she'd made cookies for dessert.

Her dad took a seat. "Everything looks delicious, Kayla. You didn't have to go to all this trouble."

"I wanted to." Her parents had called on Friday, letting her know what time they planned to arrive, and she'd told them to expect lunch so they didn't have to stop somewhere to eat. Then she'd made a quick trip to the grocery store. Wyatt had helped her by putting fresh sheets on her bed and straightening up while she was busy making the chicken salad and baking chocolate-chip walnut cookies.

Just thinking about Wyatt and the way he was so willing to help made her heart flutter. He'd also downed half a dozen cookies, stealing them when he thought she wasn't looking, or pretending to want a hug, then reaching around her to snatch another. He made her laugh, and she loved that about him. She'd never felt as close to anyone as she did to Wyatt, or as cherished.

"Nice place, Kayla. I love all the woodwork," her mom said, helping Brady get settled at the table.

"Thanks. We like it. Don't we, Brady?" Her son gave a happy nod. "I believe we're going to rewrite our offer on the building on Monday. Everyone has been prequalified for their loans."

It had surprised her that she'd qualified with so little credit history, but she had, mostly because of her military widow status and the insurance money she had in the bank. Since hearing back from the mortgage broker, her excitement had grown. "Hopefully our second offer will be accepted. Keep your fingers crossed."

"We certainly will," her mom said, taking her seat.

"When are we going to meet Wyatt?" her dad asked.

"Probably not until we go out for dinner tonight. He likes to work on his comic books on Saturdays since he works the day job the rest of the week." Kayla sat down and passed the chicken salad to her mom. "So, tell me about your week."

For the next half hour, she heard all about what Brady had done with Gammy and Pops, and all about his trip to the county fair with Grandma and Grandpa Malone. Her mom helped her clean up, and they moved to the living room to visit for a while longer.

"You two have my room tonight," she told her parents. "I'll take Brady's bed, and he can either share with me or camp out on the couch."

"Camp out." Brady nodded happily, like sleeping on their old couch would be a grand adventure.

"All right. That's settled," Kayla laughed. "Brady, why don't you show Gammy and Pops to my room while I get the cookies I made for dessert. We can have them out here. Dad, Mom, do either of you want more coffee?"

"With cookies? Of course," her dad rose from his place. "Come on, buddy. Lead the way."

"I'd love to see your room too, Brady," her mom said, rising from her place. "Will you show me?"

"Sure, Gammy. I have lots of toys. You wanna see them?"

"I do."

Smiling, Kayla moved to the kitchen to fill a plate with cookies. She grabbed a handful of napkins and brought everything to the living room when someone knocked on her door. She set the cookies and napkins on the coffee table and hurried to see who it might be. Probably Mariah, since they still hadn't had much time to get caught up. Kayla had been spending all her time with Wyatt. She opened her door, and Wyatt charged into her apartment, grabbed her up in a fierce hug and spun her around. "Ahhhh!" she squealed.

"You'll never guess what just happened." His eyes bored into hers, and he wore that crooked smile she adored.

"Our offer was accepted?"

"No." He set her down and kissed her.

She broke the kiss and sucked in a breath. "What is going on, Wyatt?"

Laughing, he lifted and spun her around again, putting her down abruptly at the sound of her dad clearing his throat. Wyatt's face turned rosy.

"Wyatt, I'd like you to meet my dad and mom." She took his hand. "Tom and Sharon Wagner."

"Mr. and Mrs. Wagner," Wyatt mumbled, the red in his face deepening. He crossed the room and held out his hand. "It's a pleasure to meet you."

"Call me Tom," her dad said shaking his hand.

"And call me Sharon."

"Wyatt!" Brady bounced in place. "Did you miss me?"

"Did I ever." Wyatt scooped Brady up in his arms and growled like a bear while he hugged him. Brady giggled, and Wyatt kept him in his arms as he turned to Kayla. "I just got off the phone with Angela Bronson. She loves the Elec Tric series, and she wants me to send her everything else I have." His eyes were sparkling with excitement. "She's sending me a contract. Thanks to you, I now have an agent."

"That's great news, but having seen your work during Kayla's visit home, I'm not surprised," Kayla's dad said. "We'll celebrate at dinner tonight."

"Thank you." Wyatt put Brady down.

Her dad took Brady's hand and led him to the couch. "Did my daughter tell you her grandfather and I are collectors? We've been collecting comic books since I was a youngster. We have quite an impressive variety stretching back to right before World War II."

"She did mention it. I hope I get to see your collection sometime," Wyatt followed, grabbed a cookie and took a seat. "So, what're your favorites?" he asked. Brady climbed onto his lap, and Wyatt reached for another napkin and a cookie, handing them to her son.

"Help me with the coffee, Mom?"

"Of course." Her mom slid her arm around Kayla's waist as they walked into Kayla's tiny kitchen. "I like him, honey. What happened to cause the burn scars?"

"A barbecue accident when he was kid." She sighed. "I'm crazy about him."

Her mom chuckled and patted her arm. "That's obvious, and your dad and I couldn't be happier for you. Wyatt seems to be good with Brady."

"The best. You should see them fish together, and Wyatt reads to him all the time. Brady adores him."

"I think the adoration is mutual."

Kayla nodded. "All the way around." Being with Wyatt gave her a sense of family, like the three of them belonged together. The sadness, guilt, anger and regret she'd carried around for so long didn't weigh her down anymore. She looked forward to the future, and she owed it all to the shy Hoodie Guy now holding her son on his lap, like that was the most natural thing in the world. Kayla set mugs on a tray and her mom filled them. "If we want a cookie, we'd better get to that plate soon, because Wyatt has a sweet tooth."

Chapter Seventeen

Wyatt sat next to Kayla in the oversized, circular booth at the Longfellow Grill, and Brady flanked his other side. Kayla's parents were across from him. He pushed his empty plate away and moved his beer closer as Tom slipped cash into the bill holder.

"Thank you for dinner, Tom," Wyatt said. "Can I get the tip?"

"Nope. Got it." Mr. Wagner smiled at him. "We're celebrating your good news, remember? Sharon and I are excited about seeing your work in print. Kayla tells us you're an electrician by trade, with a family-owned company. Is that right?"

"Yes." Wyatt nodded. "Haney & Sons Construction and Handyman Service was started in the nineties by my dad, two uncles and my grandfather. I'm a partner now. My sister and brother also work there."

Pride filled him. He was solid, well able to support a wife and children. Should Kayla decide to be a stay-at-home mom for a while, they'd be fine. He doubted she would, though, not after she'd worked so hard to pull her life together, get an education and start a career. Damn, he was proud of her.

"Kayla told me you run a nonprofit that rescues unusual animals," Wyatt said. "That must be interesting."

Sharon laughed. "*Interesting* is a good word for what we do."

"Wyatt, d'you know what? Gammy and Pops have a llama, and he's *mean.*"

"Oh, no," Wyatt mock scowled. "How mean?"

"He spit in my face." Brady frowned. "It was gross."

"Lawrence the llama is an old curmudgeon, all right." Tom chuckled.

Wyatt's phone vibrated, and he pulled it from his back pocket. "It's Steve." He glanced at Kayla as he hit accept. "Hey, Steve, can you hold on a minute? I'm at a noisy restaurant, and I want to take this call somewhere where I can hear you." Potential buyers had been passing through their building all week, and he almost didn't want to hear what the realtor had to say.

"Sure. I'll hold."

Kayla slid out of the booth so he could get out. He strode to the front door and walked outside. "OK, I can hear you now. What's up?"

"A cash offer came in Friday morning, and the owners just got back to me. They've accepted the bid. I'm sorry, Wyatt."

"Yeah, me too." He raked his fingers through his hair. "Well, we gave it a try. I'll let the rest of the tenants know."

"Hey, if and when you decide to buy, give me a call. I'd love to work with you again."

"Thanks. I will." They said their good-byes and Wyatt ended the call. A cash offer? That could only mean a corporation had bought the building. Not many individuals had a million and a half lying around. Disappointment lodged itself in his gut. It would be a crying shame if the new owners razed that elegant old building, but there wasn't a thing he could do about it. They'd lost their homes. He slid his phone back in his pocket and returned to the restaurant.

Kayla slid over so he could sit on the outside. "Bad news," he said. "Our building has been sold."

"Oh," Sharon said. "That's a shame."

246

"It is, but Wyatt, now that you have an agent, things could move pretty fast with your comic book career," Kayla said, leaning against him. "You won't have a lot of extra time to renovate. Maybe it's for the best."

"Maybe." He hated to let the place go. He'd met his future wife and her son in that building. He'd overcome his shyness and reached out to his neighbors there. Hell, he'd even given up his hoodies because of everything that had happened in the past few months. Like Dennis said, they were turning into a commune. "I know you're right, but I'm not happy about losing what we have there. Dennis is going to flip out over this."

"I couldn't help but notice the granite plaque next to the front door with 1911 and the name of the building carved into it. I'm assuming that's the year the River Park Apartments was built. Might the building qualify as a historic site?" Tom asked. "If so, you could try to get it registered with the historical society. At least then the new owners won't be able to change it too drastically, or tear it down."

A spark of interest flared to life. "I hadn't thought of that."

"Good idea, Dad." Kayla reached for Wyatt's hand. "We'll look into it. In the meantime, we should get going. Brady is asleep sitting up."

"True." Wyatt glanced at Superkid slumped against his grandfather's side, his eyes closed. "He's had quite the adventure the past few days, what with spitting llamas, potbellied pigs and ponies to play with. Let's go. Thanks again for dinner." He rose from his place and offered Kayla a hand up.

Kayla's dad carried Brady out of the restaurant to his truck, and the five of them piled in. Tom pulled out of the lot and drove the short distance to the bridge spanning the Mississippi River. Sighing, Wyatt held a groggy Brady on his lap and stared out the window at the river. Forested steep hills and bluffs rose on either side, and a sandy beach stretched along the west side.

"The trees are already starting to change. In a couple of weeks, the view from this bridge will turn into an amazing blaze of color." A view he'd miss. What if he had to move farther away from his grandparents? Speaking of them, who knew how long they'd stay in their house? He could see how it might be too much for the two of them to handle. On the other hand, he couldn't see them leaving it either. If they needed help, Wyatt would organize all the grandkids to pitch in.

Kayla's dad found a parking spot half a block down from the front of their building. Brady had fallen asleep again, and Wyatt held him while Kayla opened the front door. He climbed the stairs to the first-floor landing, and a white envelope taped on his door caught his attention. Erik's door had one too. "Kayla, would you grab that?" He nodded toward the envelope. "I'll take Brady upstairs."

"Sure."

Once he got to Kayla's floor, he found yet another envelope taped to her door. The other three apartments were envelope-free. Curious, he took hers down and studied the handwriting.

Kayla joined him, and he held hers out to her. "You got one too."

"Hmm." She unlocked her door and opened it for everyone.

"Let me take Brady." Sharon took the sleeping boy from Wyatt's arms. "We'll put him to bed, and you two can see what those are all about."

"Thanks, Mom." Kayla ripped her envelope open and pulled out the card. "It's an invitation."

Wyatt had his out too. He turned it over to read the back. "A party." Dennis had invited them to his place for a gathering to be held on Sunday evening at six. Food and beverages would be provided, and children were welcome.

"I am not looking forward to breaking the bad news, but since everyone will probably be there, I might as well make the announcement then."

"I wonder if it would be better to e-mail everyone first, or would that ruin the party?"

"I don't know." Dennis had included a note at the bottom of his invitation. Wyatt was supposed to extend the invite to Josey, Sam and Haley. "Let's think about it tonight and make a decision tomorrow." He drew her close. "I'm going to miss having you in my arms tonight."

"I'm going to miss *being* in your arms tonight. How are we going to handle all this with Brady?" She peered into his eyes, concern shadowing her features.

"I say we be completely honest with him." He squeezed her bottom. "We'll tell him from now on, you and I are planning to have a lot of slumber parties."

She laughed. "Slumber parties, eh? Sounds completely honest to me."

Grinning, he tightened his hold around her and rested his chin on top of her head. "As far as I'm concerned, you and I are a permanent thing, Kayla. I'm figuring it'll take months before we have to vacate our current apartments. When we get to that point, I suggest we sit down and figure out where we are as a couple . . . as a family. Maybe we'll be ready to look for a place together." His heart hammered against his ribs, and heat surged to his face. "What do you think?"

She tightened her arms around him and sighed. "I think that sounds like an excellent plan, Wyatt."

"Whew." His breath came out in a rush, and relief turned his insides to jelly. "I don't suppose you want to sneak downstairs to my place later. Your parents will be here to look after Brady."

"Not tonight, but join us for breakfast here tomorrow morning at eight?"

"OK." He smiled and leaned in for a good-night kiss. "It was worth a try."

◆　◆　◆

"So, we're in agreement," Wyatt said, glancing around his living room at Kayla, Sam, Josey and Haley. Brady was at Mariah's, playing with Rosie, and she agreed to bring him to the party with the two of them later. He and Kayla had decided not to tell Mariah the building had been sold until they told everyone.

"I'll pull Dennis aside, tell him what's up, and let him decide whether or not we should give everybody the bad news during the party, or wait until tomorrow and send an e-mail."

"Agreed." Josey nodded. "It's fair, and that way we don't ruin his big night."

"I think it's kind of touching that he's doing this," Haley said. "It seems like the fire and the building going up for sale has brought all of you closer. It's a shame somebody swooped in and bought the place out from under you."

"It is," Kayla said, her tone forlorn.

"Well, it's two minutes to six." Sam glanced at his phone. "Should we head up?"

Wyatt heaved a huge sigh. "Yeah, I guess. Dennis is going to be bummed."

The five of them trudged up to the third floor, not saying a word on the way. Dread and nervousness churned Wyatt's stomach into a froth. He'd finally gotten comfortable with his neighbors, and now everything would come to an end.

Kayla knocked on the door, and Wyatt stood behind her. A stranger opened the door, a wide smile on her round face. In fact, everything about her was round—short and round, and her hair was a mass of blond and gray ringlets. She wore a long dress and Birkenstock sandals, another throw back from the late sixties, early seventies, like Dennis.

"Hi, I'm Sandy, Dennis's old lady. Come on in." She threw the door wide. "Dennis is fussing over the way I arranged the food on the table." She laughed. "He's a fusser."

Dennis had an old lady? Wyatt's brow rose. How come he'd never seen her before? He caught Kayla's eye, and one side of her mouth turned up.

"Hi, I'm Kayla from the second floor, and this is Wyatt." She pointed to him as they started through the door. "Wyatt lives on the first floor, and this is his sister, Josey, his brother, Sam, and this is Haley, Sam's fiancée."

"Nice to meet you, but don't be surprised if I have to ask what your names are a time or two." Sandy laughed. "I have trouble holding on to names."

Wyatt glanced around Dennis's apartment, finding Erik and the Meyers sitting on the sectional couch. "Hey," he greeted them with a nod.

Dennis came around the corner into the living room, and even from where he stood, Wyatt could tell the guy was wired up with excitement. Lord, he really didn't want to have that pull-aside conversation with him. Good thing they were among the first to arrive.

"Hey, man." Dennis hurried over. "Glad you could make it. Make yourselves at home, and go grab a beer or a glass of wine." He shook everybody's hand. "Everything is set up in the dining room."

"Hey, Dennis, can I have a word with you before the rest of our neighbors show up?"

"Not now, man. Later." Dennis turned to Kayla. "I have juice boxes for the kids. Is that all right?"

"It's perfect. Thanks, Dennis. Is there anything I can do to help?"

"Nah. Me and Sandy got it covered." He gestured toward the dining room. "Go get something to eat and drink." And then he was off to answer another knock on the door.

"He's a little keyed up," Josey whispered. "Might be tough to catch him until after everyone is here."

Wyatt nodded. Dennis's dining room table was loaded with platters of deli meats, a variety of cheeses, pickles, olives, different kinds of buns and condiments, chips and salads. Two aluminum tubs had been set on the kitchen counter. Filled with ice, one held bottles and cans of beer, and the other held opened bottles of wine. A huge bakery cake with blue roses and white icing sat on top of the stove. "He's gone all out."

"Wow." Sam grabbed a plate. "I'll say."

Sandy entered the dining room then. "Dennis is happy, and he wants to share his happiness with all of you." She came to stand beside Wyatt. "I've heard a lot about you. Denny thinks very highly of you, and he's a man who doesn't let people into his circle easily."

Wyatt heaved another sigh and wiped his sweaty palms over his jeans. He didn't know for sure what Dennis was so happy about, but he hoped it wasn't because he thought they were forming a commune. "How long have you and he been together?"

"Oh, it's been about fifteen years now," she shrugged. "But I've known him since we were kids. We grew up in the same neighborhood."

"Wyatt!" Brady called.

"Hey, Superkid." He glanced up to find Mariah and Rosie right behind Brady. The apartment was filling up fast, and Dennis flitted from one neighbor to the next, beaming at everyone. Brady's hand in his, Wyatt moved to stand next to Kayla. "I don't suppose you'd be willing to tell Dennis the news."

She frowned. "Not really, but if you really can't . . ."

"I can. I just don't *want* to." Maybe he and his neighbors could find a different building to buy. A little extreme, maybe?

"Mommy, can I have something to eat?" Brady tugged at the hem of Kayla's shirt.

"Of course you can." She flashed Wyatt a sympathetic look. "Would you pour me a glass of white wine while I fix a plate for Brady? Then I need to find somewhere for him to sit."

"Sure."

Wyatt fixed Kayla's glass of wine and took a can of beer from the tub. He was too nervous to eat, but maybe he'd be able to summon the will to have that talk with Dennis after a beer or two. "Oh, wow," he said, handing Kayla her wine. "Even the two old ladies from the first floor are here. What do you suppose Dennis is celebrating?"

"Maybe it's his birthday."

Brady's eyes widened. "Is there cake?"

Wyatt tousled his hair. "There is. Do you want to see?"

"Yeah."

He set down his beer, lifted Brady into his arms and took him over to the cake, where it sat in its box on top of the stove. "Here it is."

"Wow."

Wyatt chuckled. "*Wow* is right. I love cake."

"Me too." Brady grinned.

Just then a clinking sound came from the living room, and then Dennis's voice filled the apartment. "Hey, everybody. I have something I want to say. Come on into the living room."

Wyatt's gaze flew to Kayla, who stood with Brady's plate in her hand. Shrugging, she tipped her head in the direction of the living room, and he joined her at the threshold between the dining room and the living room. Curiosity overrode his nervousness, and his attention was riveted on the wiry man taking center stage. Dennis caught his eye and grinned.

"OK." Dennis drew in a long breath and looked around the room. "First, thank you all for coming. I haven't had a party since . . ." He canted his head, his eyes on the ceiling, seeming to think about it. "Well, it's been a long time, man." He scratched his beard. Sandy came to stand by him, and you could see the guy visibly relax with her beside him.

He could relate. Wyatt glanced at Kayla. She had the same effect on him. Brady curling against Wyatt's chest—probably thinking about cake—also anchored him.

"Well, anyway," Dennis continued. "Things started to change around here when Kayla's kitchen caught on fire, and our hooded hero chased us all out of the building."

Everyone in the room turned Wyatt's way. His face burned, and . . . yeah, there went his heart. *Oh, great.* What he wouldn't give right now for one of those hoodies, so he could pull himself into his shell like a turtle. Kayla put her arm around his waist, and he blew out a breath.

"And then our hooded hero rewired our entire building, man, and we don't blow fuses on a daily basis anymore." Dennis held up his bottle of beer as if toasting him, and a round of laughter and applause filled the space.

"Oh, God," he mumbled, his gaze flying to the door and possible escape. Kayla tightened her hold around him. Did she know he was a flight risk?

"To top it all off, once our building went up for sale, who do you think organized us into a cohesive group to buy our homes collectively?"

Aw, shit. He hadn't had the conversation with Dennis he needed to have. Nobody in the room knew their deal had fallen through. Now his heart had lodged itself in his throat. "Dennis, wait. I have to—"

"In a minute, man." Dennis shook his head and shifted. "When Wyatt came to my apartment to tell me the owners wanted to keep the building on the market because our offer was contingent, I got worried. Real worried." He drew in a long breath, looked at Sandy for a second, and then announced, "So, I bought the building."

"What?" Wyatt's brow shot up, and gaped.

Dennis grinned. "I bought the building, and as soon as I close, we're going to proceed exactly as we planned. Everybody can buy their condo from me at the already agreed-upon price, and we'll make all the improvements you suggested." He stroked his beard. "Only, I want to add an elevator to the plan."

Stunned, all Wyatt could do was fixate on Dennis's last sentence. "An elevator? Where would we put it?"

"There used to be an elevator here," Dennis said. "Haven't you ever noticed the extra space between Mrs. Hanson's apartment and the stairwell? It hadn't worked for years, and rather than get it fixed, the owners walled it up." Dennis moved to a set of bookshelves against the wall and pulled out a leather photo album.

"That's true," Mrs. Hanson added. "It was an elegant old elevator with a polished brass gate, and it's a damn shame it's been walled up."

"Here, look at this," Dennis said, opening the album. He held it out for Wyatt to see, and soon everyone crowded around to peer at the old black-and-white photo of a little boy and his mother standing in front of an elevator.

Excitement thrummed through Wyatt's veins. "Wow, do you suppose it's still there behind the wall?"

"I know it is," Mrs. Hanson announced. "I lived here when the owners had it walled up."

"Look at that marble floor," Sam said, his voice tinged with awe. "I wonder what shape it's in under the funky old carpet. We can put in new era-appropriate light fixtures here, take up the carpet. It'll be really something."

Wyatt glanced at Dennis. "Who are the woman and child in the picture?"

"That's my great-grandmother and my grandfather, man. My family lived here back in the twenties. When I found out, I kept an eye on the place until an apartment became available. I thought it would be cool to live in the same building they had for a while. Nothing permanent, though, just for a while. The rest is history." He lowered the album. "I didn't like that whole contingent business, man. Like you said, I passed into permanent here quite a while ago."

"Dennis . . . where did you . . . how . . .?" Wyatt stammered.

"Denny is brilliant," Sandy cut in. "He has a master's degree in mechanical engineering from MIT. He's sold a number of patents over the years and earned a mint."

"Sandy is brilliant too." Dennis draped his arm around her shoulders. "I made enough to set up a trust, and she taught me all about investing. I don't spend much, and the money keeps growing." He shrugged, like money was no big deal. "I'm not out anything, since most of you are going to buy the apartments anyway. Is everyone still in?"

"Hell, yes," Wyatt said. Then he laughed. "An elevator. Who knew? I can't wait to get that uncovered."

Now that the big announcement had been made, their neighbors approached, shaking Dennis's hand, chatting excitedly about what they wanted to do to improve their soon-to-be condos. Then they'd drift off, forming groups to talk or to get food and beverages. Kayla took Brady from his arms, and she and Mariah found a place where the two kids could sit and eat. Wyatt followed Dennis to the bookshelf, where he put his album away.

"Dennis . . ." A lump had formed in Wyatt's throat. "I want to thank you. This place means the world to me, and I've gotten way more out of the past few months than I put in. Believe me."

"No problem, man. I'm happy. You're happy. It's all good." Dennis shrugged. "This old building means a lot to me too. Family history, you know? Can't wait to see what Haney & Sons does with the renovations, but you're going to have to write up quotes and stuff for each job. Gotta keep it on the up-and-up. I plan to run for the HOA board of directors."

"Of course." Wyatt's gaze drifted to Kayla and Brady, and the lump in his throat grew. "Here is where I got the girl, the love of my life and a family of my own," he said, mostly to himself, because . . . old Hippie Guy had already wandered off.

Wyatt laughed, shook his head and set out for the table to fix himself a plate, so he could join Kayla and Brady. Just then, a new idea for his Elec Tric series popped into his head, and he couldn't wait to write it all down.

Since rescuing the Mysterious Ms. M away from the dark side, the two of them had finally become lovers. They'd also formed a partnership to keep the evil threatening the unsuspecting, unseeing public at bay.

Surely there were other poor victims Diabolical Delilah had forced into servitude, individuals like Elec Tric and Ms. M, who had special powers. Tric and Ms. M could rescue them, form a commune of super-heroes working together for the good of all.

Ideas for new Elec Tric comic books buzzing around in his head, Wyatt took his plate of food and wended his way through the crowded apartment to sit with Kayla and Brady, the newest members of his pack. Sam, Haley and Josey joined them, and Wyatt's chest swelled. He was one lucky superhero, that's for damn sure.

Acknowledgments

A big thank-you to all the folks at Montlake Romance and their group of editors, who never fail to make my work shine, and to my fabulous agent, Nalini Akolekar! I also want to thank my critique partners and dear friends, Tamara Hughes and Wyndemere Coffey, for their unwavering support and sharp eyes! Finally, I want to thank my readers. If you'll keep reading, I'll keep writing!

I love to hear from readers, and I can be reached through my website: www.barbaralongley.com

You can also find me on Facebook: www.facebook.com/blongleywriter

On Twitter: @barbaralongley

And at my Amazon Author Page: www.amazon.com/author/barbaralongley

About the Author

Award-winning author Barbara Longley moved frequently throughout her childhood, but she quickly learned to entertain herself with stories. As an adult, she's lived in a commune in the Appalachians, taught on a Native American reservation, and traveled extensively from coast to coast. After her children were born, she decided to make the state of Minnesota her permanent home. Barbara holds a master's degree in special education and taught for many years. Today she devotes herself to writing contemporary, mythical, and paranormal stories. Her titles include *Heart of the Druid Laird*, the Love from the Heartland series (*Far from Perfect*, *The Difference a Day Makes*, *A Change of Heart*, and *The Twisted Road to You*), and the Novels of Loch Moigh (*True to the Highlander*, *The Highlander's Bargain*, *The Highlander's Folly*, and *The Highlander's Vow*). *Whatever You Need* is the second novel in The Haneys series.